Valentine's Day at the Graff

Valentine's Day at the Graff

A Holiday at the Graff Romance

Sinclair Jayne

Valentine's Day at the Graff
Copyright© 2018 Sinclair Jayne
Tule Publishing First Printing, January 2018

The Tule Publishing Group, LLC

ALL RIGHTS RESERVED

No part of this book may be used or reproduced in any manner whatsoever without written permission except in the case of brief quotations embodied in critical articles and reviews.

This is a work of fiction. Names, characters, places, and incidents are products of the author's imagination or are used fictitiously. Any resemblance to actual events, locales, organizations, or persons, living or dead, is entirely coincidental.

ISBN: 978-1-948342-33-9

Prologue

MIRANDA EVANS PUT the final flourish on the letter *s*, and stepped back to absorb the full effect of her freehand lettering in burnished copper—*Found Objects.*

Mine.

The name of her own boutique in the sumptuously restored historic Graff Hotel in her hometown: Marietta, Montana.

"Best hometown in the world," she stated and hugged herself. Her life was changing, and some of those changes made her sad, but others gleamed with promise.

"Looks good, girl." Shane Knight, one of the bartenders for the hotel's small horseshoe-shaped bar swatted her butt with a bar towel as she hurried by, long messy blonde braid bouncing down her back as she headed into the Graff bar for the beginning of her shift. Already several tables were occupied—likely why Shane hustled. Her mile-long, denim-clad legs practically blurred. "Come get a drink to celebrate your sign. One step closer to opening."

"I'll come by a little later," Miranda promised like she had yesterday and the day before although she hadn't kept her promises because she'd gotten caught up in remodeling her store's space.

"Now's always better," Shane called out as she bore down on a second table. She shook her finger playfully at Miranda. "All work and no play…" She let the phrase dangle. "Am I right?" Shane asked the two businesswomen in suits who were clearly having a meeting although indulging in an early happy hour.

Miranda smiled. Since Found Objects was her shop, decorating and organizing it hardly seemed like work. She walked back into the small, slightly awkward space that had been carved out of a storage room and part of the hall that led to the back parking lot. She lit up seeing the thin, elderly woman with blue eyes that still sparkled, with a puff of white hair like a dandelion.

"Gran." Miranda rushed forward to hug her grandmother who had helped to make all this possible. "I didn't know you were coming in today. Look at you, all dressed up."

She was thrilled to see her grandmother out of the small apartment she'd recently moved into at an assisted living facility in town to be close to her husband of over sixty years. Miranda's grandfather now needed memory care. Miranda and her grandmother had finally made the tough decision a few months ago that they were unable to sufficiently care for him.

"I'm meeting a few friends in the bar." Her grandmother's eyes twinkled. "We're tired of afternoon popcorn and drip coffee. We're going rogue."

Miranda laughed, her heart lighter seeing a glimpse of her spunky gran who'd dimmed during the past few, hard years. "Good for you."

"You should try it."

Miranda smiled. "Gran, I am going to make my boutique so beautiful and original that you'll be so proud." She looked around her store. "So my rogue days will have to wait."

Her grandmother patted her hand.

"You are the kindest, most generous and loving person. You've always made me proud, Miranda Panda."

Miranda felt tears prick her eyes. Her grandparents had always been there for her. Always believed in her and accepted her. Even turning her early obsession with pandas into a cute nickname that stuck and reminded her of happy times—baking and knitting with her grandmother and spending weekends and after school helping take care of the cutting horses her grandfather bred until his health started failing too badly.

"But I don't want you to put off fun anymore. You're young and need to enjoy it. You've given so much to me and your grandad and to so many others. I want you to build your business and renew some friendships and find a man who makes you sparkle."

"Gran," Miranda interrupted, blinking back tears and feeling a rush of affection so fierce that she nearly staggered.

"I want you to find the happiness that was mine for so long." Her grandmother seemed to force her rush of emotion under control. "You of all people deserve to be deeply loved."

"Gran." Miranda dashed away the tears.

Having a relationship like her grandad and gran had had was a beautiful dream, and as hard as it had been to admit that her grandfather needed more care, now she would have the chance at more of a life outside the defunct ranch that her grandmother had recently sold.

"This is not a time for tears." Her gran smiled tremulously, her eyes bright. "I expect an invitation to your grand opening. I'll bring my posse and your grandad and hopefully be your first official sale. Oh, there are my friends. I should join them, but first, I wanted to bring you something to remind you of home."

Miranda caught her breath. Her grandmother had brought a pale green decorated Chinese-style ceramic pot with a striking white orchid flower.

"It's beautiful," she breathed, recognizing the pot instantly.

"That lovely gal, Risa Davidson of Sweet Pea Flowers, ordered the orchid for me and repotted it in my cherished pot. Your grandfather bought it for me as a housewarming present when he finished our ranch house."

"Sixty years ago," Miranda said.

"Valentine's Day," her grandmother added, blinking back a tear.

Miranda squeezed her grandmother's frail hands, and already her agile imagination started dreaming of ways she could make this Valentine's Day special for her grandparents. It might be their last together. Her stomach clenched in dread.

"Gran, thank you," she said softly, feeling the words were totally inadequate to express how much the cherished pot meant to her. She'd moved in with her grandparents junior year of high school when her parents moved from Marietta to Seattle and her grandfather had had his first health scare. She didn't regret the time with them for a second even though her family accused her of wasting her life.

Never.

Thirty minutes later Miranda entered the bar wanting to greet her grandmother's friends and to get Shane's opinion on her store's sign she'd hand painted after researching old-fashioned font styles in Marietta during the late eighteen hundreds when copper was briefly king. She caught Shane in a no doubt brief lull. Several tables had couples at them, most drinking hot drinks. Miranda loved winter. She loved wearing sweaters, especially the ones she knit at night when she was watching TV with her grandparents and had a moment to herself when no one needed her and she could be idle.

"Hey," Shane called out. "Storefront lettering looks amazing. Popped my eyes right out."

Miranda laughed at the exaggeration.

"Want me to make you a cinnamon candy kiss mocha?"

Miranda looked quickly around and stepped closer to the bar. "That doesn't have alcohol in it does it?" she whispered.

Shane laughed. "What are we, spies? And this is a bar so the alcohol is not a secret, but no, I was planning to test the virgin version on you."

Miranda found herself flushing a deep red. She felt hot and itchy all over and she couldn't quite meet Shane's gaze. Was it that obvious? Even though she liked Shane, she felt a stab of humiliation even as she told herself that it wasn't that big of a deal. Sex wasn't everything, and it wasn't like she had no experience exactly. She just hadn't had a lot of opportunities. And that would change once she got her business up and humming. Hopefully. But still there was so much more in life than sex.

A lot!

"Yes, please—that sounds lovely," she said primly, curious about the drink. No wonder Shane could throw the V word around with ease. She'd probably not lost hers but had flung it off in her teens like a cape.

Miranda couldn't imagine any man saying no to Shane Knight.

Shane stood at the large copper-colored Italian espresso machine expertly pulling shots and steaming milk. Miranda hovered, feeling tempted by the swooshing sound of the steaming milk and then the heavenly dulled roar of whipped cream.

Shane Knight was a goddess at the bar whether it was espresso or cocktails. Miranda's eyes lit up appreciatively when Shane shaved a cinnamon stick on top of the whipped cream and then sprinkled a few cinnamon candy hearts on top. She plunged a dark chocolate straw into the drink and then pushed it encouragingly toward Miranda.

"What do you think?"

Miranda had only been working on opening her small space a little over a week, but this was the third time Shane had tried a signature espresso drink on her. Miranda had tried to pay for the drinks, but Shane had shrugged the money off. Miranda felt guilty about feeling relieved. Now that she was paying rent—something she should have been doing a decade ago, her mother and sisters reminded her during her dutiful phone calls—and she no longer had the small but steady income from her former job at the clothing boutique Copper Mountain Chic, she was adjusting to her new economic normal. She wanted to prove to her grandparents that the money they'd given her after selling their beloved ranch to move into the care center was not wasted.

"It's sinful," Miranda sighed as the flavors exploded and danced in her mouth.

Shane smiled. "I hope so."

Shane saved her creative cocktail concoction test runs for off-duty Graff staff and customers. One night, Miranda vowed, perhaps the opening night of Found Objects, she would celebrate with a couple of sips of a cocktail. Or champagne. She loved flavored sparkling water. She bet champagne would be even better.

Miranda sipped through the straw more deeply and nearly melted on the spot.

"Wow," she breathed trying to come up with the right words. "Just wow."

"Good to know. It's one of four Valentine-themed coffee drinks I'm putting on the bar menu for February."

Shane grinned and turned away, repeated the process only in smaller espresso cups, and she added a dash of clear liquor—gin or maybe vodka Miranda speculated—before placing her samples on a distressed metal antique tray and making a swing through the half full bar, chatting and smiling as she handed out her drinks.

Valentine's Day, Miranda thought dreamily. So romantic and beautiful, a time to reaffirm love and do something special for people in your life. Make cards and drop them off to friends so they knew you were thinking of them. Make a special dinner for her grandparents or call a girlfriend and make several batches of cookies and deliver them to the kids at the after-school program at Harry's House. This year she was going to…

"Don't even come near me with that drink." One of the women sitting in the bar with a laptop and nursing a chardonnay with her co-worker made the sign of the cross as Shane approached. "Valentine's is a day of disappointment, disaster and despair."

Miranda startled out of her daydream.

"It's the commercialization of our pain, mocking us," the other woman said. "February 14th should be banned from the calendar."

"From the American psyche," someone else called out.

"Burned, hung, poisoned and drawn and quartered," one of Miranda's new neighbors chimed in.

"And then beheaded and put on a spike at the gates of the town."

Miranda stared at the people in the bar in dismay. She knew more than a few of them. Her grandmother and her friends had been talking softly, each of them drinking one of Shane's specialty coffees, likely sans alcohol. Miranda felt like she had to pick her jaw up off the floor.

"Marietta doesn't have gates," she said faintly.

"An opportunity to fleece men and suck them dry!" a

man practically shouted in a deep baritone even as he took the last sample from Shane's tray and held it up in a mock toast.

It seemed popular to heap scorn on a day that should be held in tender esteem.

Not me.

"Well, that was fun," Shane mocked breezily. Her samples gone. Her smile intact. "Can't say I blame them."

"You too?" Miranda could barely gulp back her gasp of dismay.

Shane shrugged. "It's no longer an active hate, just more of a bored ignoring, but since I'm in the business of being hospitable…" she smiled and winked "…specialty drinks, hearts and flowers and cutesy cocktail napkins it is, in about…" she broke off and looked at the large, beautiful watch that always reminded Miranda of a starlit sky "…four days."

"You of all people should have many fond memories of Valentine's Day—getting cards from friends, romantic dinners and candles and dashing through the rain while a man drapes his jacket over your shoulders as you run to a theater for a concert. And if you don't have a date, you can bake specialty cupcakes and bring them to work, distribute candy kisses to the shops on Main Street and customers." Miranda's fertile mind fired up more possibilities.

Now it was Shane's turn to stare. "That's a movie Valentine's Day. Not real. No one enjoys the day except little kids and dumb new couples stupidly in love. Everyone else hates it." Shane nodded toward the bar of people happily finishing her signature Valentine spiked espresso sample or toasting their empty espresso cups high in the air.

Miranda wondered if there were a Scrooge for Valentine's Day and if so what his name was. She definitely required a word or two with him.

Or her.

Miranda looked again at the small crowd in the bar, a few still mocking Valentine's Day. And romance. The women seemed as disappointed, verging on bitter as the men.

"Really," she said hands on hips, her brown eyes narrowed in challenge. "Really. You don't like Valentine's Day. We'll just see about that, Shane Knight and Valentine haters alike."

Chapter One

Lady Gaga belted about a million reasons to stay. Whitman Telford pulled up in the circular drive of the Graff Hotel, which had been a sad ruin when he'd lived in town. He hit the power button of the satellite radio of the rented Acura MDX that still smelled new. Silence. He couldn't give Lady G, himself or anyone he'd ever met one good reason to stay in cold-as-hell Marietta at the end of January, but he could definitely think of a million reasons why he wanted to drive away. And he hadn't even stepped out of the absurd gas-guzzling SUV he'd been forced to rent due to the Montana winter he was about to experience.

Again.

Damn.

Even a promised "month only," followed by a hearty handshake was a month too long.

A smiling valet hurried down the sweeping staircase to his door. He looked painfully young and happy. Shouldn't he be in school? It was a Monday afternoon. Whitman didn't remember high school getting out so early, but then he'd played soccer and basketball and had run track—anything to keep from going home. Whitman read his name tag. Joseph. Maybe school was out for the day. Or perhaps he'd just graduated. Or got his GED so he could work full time and help his family with the bills—always the bills. Remembered despair knocked on Whitman's memory, but like always, he kept the door firmly shut.

Whitman opened the door, keys in one hand. The top of the door in the other because once he let go, it was official. He would be in Marietta for at least one long, cold, dark, boring month. Filling in as an orthopedic surgeon at Marietta Regional Hospital instead of starting his fellowship at University Hospital in Santa Monica. Blocks from the beach. Instead he was here. Small town entombed in snow, Montana, being supervised by an orthopedic specialist with not much more experience than he had. Not that Whitman would need the help. That's what burned. He'd wanted the fellowship so he could be at the peak of his game. Have his pick of jobs after. Control of his life. Respect. Acceptance. He'd honed his discipline since he was twelve to get to where he was except yesterday looked a hell of a lot better than today.

"You must be Doctor Telford," Joseph said cheerily rubbing his leather-gloved hands together and stomping a little as if to shake off the cold. Whitman had thought he was done with all gloves except surgical ones. "I can park your car after I help you with your luggage." Joseph smiled brightly.

"I can get my own luggage." Whitman pulled out a garment bag, a suitcase, and his laptop case. He hadn't brought a lot.

A Month.

Most of his clothes and all of his furniture had already

been sent to the apartment he'd rented in Santa Monica anticipating his February first start. And now they would sit boxed up waiting for his March arrival.

Joseph smoothed his hands down his wool navy vest that poked between the western-style, fleece-lined duster that was clearly part of the western-themed, historic uniform and a nod to the devastating deep freeze of the season. He was clearly uncomfortable with Whitman carrying the luggage.

"I'll show you in," he said sounding a bit miserable as if Whitman's bad mood was a virus he'd caught, but Whitman didn't relent—as if giving up the two bags and Coach leather satchel would somehow mean that he would relax a little, enjoy a part of his stay. Then Joseph drew himself up to his full height that still barely met Whitman's broad shoulders and held out his hand.

Whitman reluctantly handed over the car keys.

Is he even old enough to drive?

"Thank you," and even he heard the stiffness in his voice "I'll check in on my own."

"Dr. Telford. Welcome to Marietta."

Whitman could barely manage a nod.

"And welcome to the Graff."

The words sent a shot of doom to his gut.

IT WAS REALLY more of a staff than a stick, Miranda thought, running the broken branch through her hands. And if she could find or make a base for it, the staff would become drumroll please…her Tree of Kindness. Miranda hadn't worked out all the details of her Valentine's…hmm…she didn't even have a name for it yet, but she wanted February to be the month of kindness and giving. She wanted to involve more than couples so that everyone—children, adults and older residents; singles and couples—would have a chance to celebrate the day of love far more broadly than romantic love. Love for their friends, family and community.

Since the trashing of Valentine's Day earlier, Miranda had become imbued with grim purpose. She would make Valentine's Day in Marietta a day of celebration. The entire month would become an ode to generosity of spirit where people had open hearts. Performed random acts of spontaneous kindness that they didn't just post on social media for a pat on the back.

She scowled thinking of the bitterness in the bar earlier. Not on her watch.

Her mind spun with plans that she knew she'd have to finalize and clear with the Graff management because she wanted to have an open house in her store, and since it was small, she was hoping that some of it could spill out into the bar, the one part of the hotel she could see from her tucked-away boutique. And then she'd have to check with local businesses if they would post her flyer—which she'd have to make. And Dylan at the radio station, would he give her a plug on air? Maybe interview her? Her stomach lurched with nerves even as her mind conjured the bold colors and the words to explain her concept.

She climbed up a six-foot ladder she'd borrowed from

maintenance so that she could hang her red twinkle lights on the top of the wide, worn, western-style doorframe that had been custom-made for her before the Graff had ordered the glass for the front of the store. It made the entrance look more thematically western and historic.

Miranda hummed as she twisted little hooks into the reclaimed wood framing the entrance that a former high school classmate had brought from a job site and cut to fit. And then Colt had drilled the frame in and hung the glass door with the twisted copper handle that his sister-in-law had made for her for free. Just one of the many reasons why she loved Marietta and wanted to make Valentine's Day and her boutique special.

Miranda decided to make the small, nearly hidden hooks permanent so that she could always have twinkling lights silver and gold for Christmas and the New Year, red for Valentine's, Green for Saint Patrick's Day and spring and then…

"I need to buy shaving cream, please."

"Oh!"

Miranda was so startled by the voice below that she dropped the handful of hooks that rained down on a face so familiar from her girlhood fantasies that for a millisecond she thought she'd conjured him from the adolescent recesses of her overactive imagination like a fantasy Valentine date. Her grip loosened on the ladder and then she started to tip. Never athletic, but physically active especially the past few years when she'd helped take care of so many of her grandparents' needs and their ranch while still working a part-time job, Miranda jumped so she had a chance of landing on her feet.

Only she didn't.

She jumped straight into the arms of the most beautiful boy ever to breathe Montana air. The arms of the boy who'd featured at the top of her hottest, smartest, most brooding, most gorgeous eyes, best hair, most everything list from high school. Except now, twelve years later, the boy was a man. She jumped from mostly buried fantasies into the reality of the arms of Witt Telford.

HE'D BEEN BRACED to catch her but hadn't anticipated that she'd jump, adding momentum. Still, years of athletics supplemented by regular gym attendance kept him rooted. Plus, she seemed to weigh less than the hay bales he'd been forced to toss around from age twelve until he escaped to college far from Montana's snowbound winters. The woman pressed against his chest, with astonishing closeness and warmth, which both shocked him and slapped him hard with the reality that he couldn't remember the last time he'd held a woman. He immediately let her go.

Only she didn't.

Her arms looped around his neck. Her small breasts pressed against his chest, and her scent—something tropical and fresh like eucalyptus that reminded him of the Southern California beaches—teased his senses, and he had to fight not to inhale deeply.

He wasn't quite sure what to do. Her eyes were caramel brown and sparkled with life and humor. And her lips curved up in a crooked smile that unnerved him with its warmth like he knew her and they were in the middle of a scene but he didn't know the play or the lines. Her hair was the weirdest color—it was no one color—like it couldn't decide if it wanted to be blonde or very light brown. And it hung thick and straight to her shoulders like a bob that had grown out badly and long ago.

"Well, how's that for a welcome home, Witt," she said using the abbreviation that had started his first day he'd moved bewildered, too shocked to yet grieve, to Marietta and began middle school the very next day. "It's good to see you," she said, her eyes searching his face. "I didn't hear you were coming for a visit."

His stomach bottomed out. She sounded like she knew him. Damn. In this town, she probably did.

"Thank you." Even he heard that his voice sounded doubtful. What was he thanking her for? Typical. Give him the tools of his trade, and his OR, and he was in his zone. Confident. Cool under pressure. Knowing exactly what to do. What to say. How to lead.

Out of the OR: unmitigated social disaster. Probably why he kept mostly to himself and his mouth shut.

"Riley didn't say you were coming home when I saw her over the holidays."

His sister didn't know.

None of them knew.

"Oh." One of her hands, small and pale, lightly freckled,

rested on his forearm. "I get it." She moved her hand away, and he stared at the empty space where the cuff of his tailored white Oxford button-down peeked out from beneath his dark gray cashmere sweater. She gave his forearm a little squeeze, and the contact while not expected wasn't unpleasant. But she didn't know him. Not really. Why was she being so open and friendly? He couldn't shake the feeling she thought he was someone else.

He looked at her and was startled when she pressed a slim finger against her pursed bow-shaped lips that were a little puffy like she had an allergic reaction or collagen although in Marietta he doubted it. "It's a secret. Shhh."

He wasn't quite sure how to respond and so he did what he often did when in doubt. Said nothing.

"Am I right?"

She seemed so cheerful. Confident. Sure of her place in the world. He hated to let her down, which was, he knew, more than stupid. She might have known his half-sister in high school perhaps. She did look young. Twenty-two or twenty-three at most. No wonder he didn't remember her. Nothing at all was familiar about her. Except her voice, a little.

"Witt? Do they know you are here?"

Damn. It was going to start again. The awkwardness. Being pulled in half, even though his mother was long past the ability to physically pull anything. He hadn't fit in Marietta eighteen years ago. He hadn't wanted to. And he still didn't. But he was here for a month, an eternity. He could hardly expect his "homecoming" to stay under wraps.

Not contacting his biological dad, stepmother or half siblings would be near impossible and worse if he didn't than if he did. But he never knew what to say. He always felt like the outlier. The spurious point on the graft of their lives. The awkward embarrassment.

"It will be a surprise," he finally managed through stiff lips.

And then she was down at his feet. Like she was bowing to him. What the...hooks, he remembered with a startled flush. The gold metal hooks were scattered around his feet, and she picked them up while he stood there like the dumbest, most arrogant prig on the planet.

"Let me help you," he said, bending down just as she stood up.

"Ow," she nearly yipped as the top of his jaw collided with the crown of her head. "Rumors are true. That romance-novel-worthy heroic jaw is made of iron." She rubbed the top of her head and her eyes sparkled at him.

He felt...he didn't know what he felt. Out of place. Uncomfortable. Was she teasing him? What rumors? Did she know him? He decided to ditch the shaving cream and just get to the hospital. He'd be more comfortable there. He was familiar with Marietta Regional Hospital from when he'd job shadowed and volunteered as a teen. He'd just go check into the hospital to see if his credentials had cleared and meet with Dr. Wyatt Gallagher. He did remember the Gallaghers from high school. They had always been top students, ambitious and as charming as he had been stiff and determined.

"Ahhhh," he failed to answer her, but wasn't sure there'd been a question in her bursts of speech.

"You don't remember me do you, Witt?"

Chapter Two

IT SHOULDN'T HURT. It really shouldn't. He'd been in AP classes. College prep all the way. More her older siblings' caliber of a student. And he'd been an athlete—soccer, basketball and track. And she'd been none of those things. But still they'd attended Marietta High School together for four years. And middle school before that. And their graduating class had not been huge. And he hadn't noticed her enough to remember her or even know that he should.

But she'd noticed him.

She'd remembered him.

Usually stuff like this she could blow off. Laugh at. Forget. But her nonchalance, her sunny-side up seemed stuck behind a cloud. Twelve years had passed since she'd had her last glimpse of him striding across the high school stage, diploma in hand, eyes looking far away. He looked taller, fitter, face more carved and angular and cologne-ad ready— aloof expression in place as if the photographer had already started shooting. And his posture just screamed 'get me out of here.' Or maybe it was true what the other kids had said about him in school. He'd just thought he was better than any of them.

Something in Miranda just couldn't quite believe that

assessment. She hadn't then. She'd defended him hotly, coveting and explaining away his brooding, aloof personality fiercely. In her mind, he'd been a non-blood-sucking Edward Cullen, horribly alone and misunderstood. And standing here in her store, closer to him than she'd ever been. And him more handsome and more removed and in her mind more awkward than ever, she still believed she was right.

He was lonely and shy.

It seemed impossible if you just accounted for his physical beauty—face and tall, athletic body, coupled with the fact she knew he'd finished medical school and residency so he was officially a doctor, it seemed like he'd be striding around feeling like he was all that. But she got the feeling he didn't feel like he fit in his skin.

Her heart ached.

"High school." He dug up the two words as if they were a foreign language.

His tone made it worse.

So Miranda did what she did best. Made it better. She waved her hand and laughed it off, and she let her eyes look around her store—the stacked recycled wood shelves Colt Wilder had helped her to make after he'd seen her scavenging some scraps from an old barn east of town that he'd been rebuilding with a crew. Then she looked up at the vintage chandelier she'd cleaned and repaired and had had an electrician rewire—anywhere but at him.

"That was a long time ago," she said. "A lifetime."

She knew he'd gone back east to college, Davidson College in North Carolina. Then Duke Medical School. She'd stayed in Marietta by choice even as her family scattered far away conquering their dreams and building empires.

"Miranda Evans," she said.

"What?" He looked startled. Uncertain. Almost icy cool.

Give it up.

"What brand?" she asked perkily, years of retail easing her way through this embarrassing moment for them both.

She'd be lying if she said she wasn't disappointed. Not that she'd expected anything, but still. It did make her feel a little smaller, and her store a little emptier. He stared at her. Gosh he was gorgeous. A million miles away. Tall, angular and sophisticated in a way she wasn't used to seeing. And his hair was perfect. Thick and springy and ink black. It waved back from his face as if sculpted and frozen in time in a photo. And it probably was. Even gravity didn't defy Whitman Telford.

Edward Cullen my ass, she thought cheekily. He made Rob Pattinson average and Edward Cullen a warm breeze instead of stone. She bit her lip to hold back a smile.

She wondered if he ever got aggravated and ran those long fingers through his hair when he was searching for a cure to some mysterious ailment, although he was an orthopedic surgeon so probably not too many diseases tormented his professional milieu. Infections though. She used to work early mornings at the Java Café and a lot of the doctors and nurses would come in early for coffee before their shifts started so she heard a lot of medical terminology as she'd caught snippets of conversation in between steaming various milks.

"I beg your pardon?"

No one spoke like that in town. Miranda imagined a king or prince maybe. This time the smile dancing on her lips was genuine.

"Shaving cream."

HE WAS AN awkward idiot who managed to make a hash of a simple purchase. Imagine if he'd needed to purchase condoms and the salesperson had been one of his retired teachers or a preacher's wife. And why was he thinking about condoms? He couldn't have been more of a douche not remembering a girl from high school who'd so clearly remembered him. Why? He didn't know. He'd kept his head down, face planted into books and his computer on a single-minded soul quest to get off his biological father's struggling ranch where he hadn't wanted to be in the first place and into college so he could get his life back on track. Prove his mother's parents wrong. Make his mom proud even though she was dead. He'd been determined to not "turn out like the cowboy." He'd make his own name for himself in the medical field. Live the life he was meant to. The life his mother had set him up for before she'd died so young and randomly.

Not here.

Not with them.

He squirted the gel on his brush and worked the lather into his face. He loved a clean shave and couldn't believe that even in his haste packing he'd left behind his specialty brand of shaving cream. That was what the Internet was for he thought as he began to scrape the blade in a practiced pattern across his jawline.

He shouldn't care about...Miranda. That was her name. He didn't care, he reminded himself although he could still see her dark caramel eyes rounding. Fluttering and blinking. Hear her sucked-in breath. The telltale flush across her cheekbones. The step back she'd taken. He didn't care. He shouldn't care. He wouldn't care. He was in Marietta for a month, or two tops.

And then she'd packaged up some Russian olive jelly for his "mother."

"Stepmother," he'd quickly and automatically corrected, and then he'd wanted to kick himself for sounding defensive and obvious. Clearly TMI for Miranda, who'd been packaging up the jelly as well as a lavender sachet or something along those lines that his stepmother, Sarah, could chill for thirty minutes and then put on her forehead or the back of her neck to help soothe her headaches.

Lord, small towns. Some girl from high school remembered his stepmother, Sarah, got migraines.

And now he was back here as socially lame as he'd been when he'd left. He'd not been this ridiculous in school. Definitely not.

When he'd told Miranda he didn't yet have plans to see his stepmother, her look of astonishment would have been funny if he'd been someone else—someone who laughed easily and delighted in the absurd. Neither of which he did.

And then he'd dug himself deeper by staying in the store instead of hurrying out.

"It is a surprise, Witt. They will be so happy to see you. I can make up a gift basket for you to bring. I'm not really open yet and haven't organized all my vendors but this is my store, and I'm going to be officially open in a few days so plenty of time to shop for Valentine's Day." She'd smiled and winked like he had a sweetheart stashed in his pocket. And then her voice had gushed like she was a town tour guide. "And I'm going to carry only locally made products and feature local Montana artists along with all the other products that hotel guests will need: sundries, snacks, drinks, magazines. I'm going to carry a few books too by Montana authors."

Her enthusiasm made him feel exhausted. Overwhelmed. And somehow he'd agreed to a gift basket.

"No rush," was all he'd managed to choke out before a feigned look at his watch had him striding back out through the door to the quiet sanctuary of his room. Had he even paid for the shaving cream? And the…he'd looked down at the book she'd tucked under his arm—a book about Marietta hauntings.

Really. Someone had written and self-published a book about possible haunted sites and experiences with spirits from the beyond in Marietta? He tossed the book across the room into a chair.

He'd never read a ghost story in his life and wasn't about to start at age thirty.

Although, he thought grimly rinsing off his razor, this

town did haunt him.

Déjà vu.

※

"Surprised as hell to see you here." Dr. Wyatt Gallagher shook his hand with force and then pulled him into some sort of man hug that involved an arm that felt like a steel cable, a chest bump like a sport and beer should be involved, and then a slap on his shoulder that was hard enough to rock him.

Wyatt laughed as if he knew he'd startled him and made him uncomfortable.

"Opportunity for a do-over," Wyatt said. "You're a long way out of high school. Your folks must be ecstatic to have you back."

No one had been ecstatic to have him anywhere except perhaps a patient with an open fracture.

"Step," he started to say and then grit his teeth.

He respected Wyatt. Even though he was young, he was already renowned as a talented, diligent surgeon highly skilled with traumatic orthopedic injuries that were not uncommon on the rodeo circuits and in ranching. He had also just watched him operate on a young ranch hand who had nearly been crushed by a bull when trying to move it. Whitman had been impressed with Dr. Gallagher's skills, calm, speed and way of directing the operating team. He'd also been a little shocked at the efficiency of the hospital and the advanced technology he'd seen during all stages of the emergency.

He had just checked in to meet Wyatt, whom he hadn't seen in years, when the call had come. By the time the cowboy had been brought in, everyone was ready in the ER, the surgical team was assembled, the emergency room doctor was communicating with the paramedics. Whitman hadn't imagined a small hospital team could work as smoothly and efficiently as in Houston.

And then during surgery, Wyatt had had country music softly playing that he'd sung along with, which had made Whitman want to grind his teeth and slam his Bose noise-canceling headphones on his ears, but of course he couldn't. Still Wyatt had operated with a skill and precision and confidence that had made Whitman reluctantly admit his time here, at least professionally, would not be wasted—although his ears felt like they were bleeding.

He'd seen the extensive damage to the cowboy's hip, pelvis, left femur and lower ribs. Wyatt referred to the X-rays, now and again, but hadn't seemed to hesitate or question himself once. No one else had questioned him either. Whitman, who'd just spent four years in a highly coveted residency spot and before that four years in a high-pressured medical school, had been floored by the lack of ego and tenseness in the OR. Frankly, he'd never seen anything quite like it.

"Thanks for letting me view the surgery," he said.

"Not a problem. Likely we'll be assisting each other in the coming months," Wyatt said, and Whitman thought about correcting him—a month—that's what he'd agreed to although the CEO of the hospital's parent company had waved his hand a little indicating that it might be a little more time than a month. But not months. He kept his mouth closed just as he'd done about the music choice in the OR. He knew, absolutely knew it was the lead surgeon's choice of play list and if anyone bitched, the music was turned up louder.

He didn't want to kick up a fuss so that his month became two or three unless he had to.

"Good to see you back in town." Wyatt's voice brought Witt back to the present. "Can't say I wasn't shocked to get a surgeon of your caliber here as part of a fellowship. Too bad you're not looking to stay permanent," Wyatt said, his smile easy, but his eyes were sharp with curiosity. "Early spring and summer's when the fun for me really begins when ranch life kicks into high gear with the rodeo and bronc and bull and horse trainings and practices, but I don't have to tell you that. You grew up ranch all the way."

It was all Whitman could do to not recoil, but his spine did snap a little straighter, and he sucked in a breath. He was not ranch. Even when he'd been exiled to Paradise Springs Ranch at age twelve, to endure six years in exile, he had not been ranch. He could feel Wyatt's gaze honing. Whitman had left his father's ranch far, far behind in the rearview mirror and his conscious mind. He didn't want Wyatt or anyone else reminding him about it.

"Thank you again," he said formally. "I'll check in with administration to ensure all my credentials have cleared so I can start tomorrow."

Wyatt rocked back on his heels a little. "You just arrived earlier today. Don't you want to settle in? Reacquaint yourself with the town? Relax a bit with your family? When's the last time you were home?"

"I prefer to work," Whitman said not answering any of Wyatt's "friendly" questions. They wouldn't be friends. They were colleagues. Wyatt was his supervisor. "Don't want to miss any of my training. Besides you're short a surgeon."

"Good enough," Wyatt said after a long beat of silence when there was nothing but the hum of the vending machine and ambient noise of a busy hospital that both men were so familiar with they probably automatically tuned most of it out. "My fiancée will be thrilled that I might make it home to see her a few times before the wedding, and I can tell her the honeymoon is definitely back on. Owe you for that. Good to have you here, Dr. Cowboy." Wyatt shoulder checked him hard. "I'll go down to admin with you. They like me there."

Everyone probably liked Wyatt, Whitman thought trying to quash his envy. He had that easy charm and comfort that had always eluded Whitman. Not that he wanted it. But still, he knew his social skills were lacking. Every review mentioned his lack of easy warmth, and he'd compensated by out-studying, out-working, out-performing everyone in his way to the top. As a doctor, skill, knowledge and confidence were king. And those cultivated and practiced traits had never once failed him.

He declined Wyatt's offer of a drink at Grey's. And also a dinner invitation to meet his fiancée and brothers and their wives at the ranch with a vague 'another time,' uttered by Wyatt not him. He avoided walking down Main Street though preferring to walk along the back side of the hospital to the back side of the Graff. Wyatt had been astonished to learn that he intended to stay at the Graff. He'd offered to put Whitman up or find him an apartment. Whitman had deflected and said the Graff suited for now.

"You're not going to sneak out in the middle of the night are you?" Wyatt had demanded after they'd both ensured his paperwork and initial emergency credentialing had all cleared through the board.

"Certainly not," Whitman said, shocked to have his work ethic questioned. No one had queried his academic or professional commitment ever. He might not want to be stuck in a rural hospital, especially not in the town where he'd endured his teen years, but he would never shirk a job assignment and his personal preferences would play no part in his professional performance.

"I was joking, Witt." Wyatt laughed.

Whitman hesitated and then forced himself to speak. "Actually I go by Whitman now," he said, not sure why he felt like wincing inside. He'd always gone by Whitman only no one had used it, certainly not his biological father who'd tried the word out and then said it sounded like a box of chocolates. Or a college, which Whitman had later found out it was—in Eastern Washington.

"That's probably not going to work here," Wyatt said easily. "Not much ceremony, pomp or circumstance in Marietta, and that's how I roll. But whatever. Give it a try.

See you tomorrow, Doctor."

Whitman retrieved his long navy overcoat from the doctor's locker room and braced himself for the cold. After four years in Houston with the average daytime winter temperature hovering in the mid-sixties, the frigid Montana winter that would likely stretch into April, was really going to suck. One more reason he wasn't likely to stay at the ranch—if they'd even have him.

He exited the hospital out of a side door and the hulking outline of the Graff was visible a short walk away across the railroad tracks. He jammed his hands deep into his navy trench-style overcoat and walked quickly down Railway Avenue hoping that the back entrance to the Graff was open so he wouldn't have to constantly face the cheerful faces of Bob or Cathi at the front desk every time he walked in and out of the lobby. Early this afternoon, he'd still been stewing about being back in the town he'd worked so hard to escape. Then there'd been the front desk clerk, Bob, who'd checked him in so cheerfully as if he truly were happy to have him as a guest and had then provided him with a list of restaurant suggestions, activities and places to visit. There was only so much perky he could take, and he'd hit his max in the first thirty seconds.

He was in luck. The back door was propped open. A sound of a bitten-off cry, followed by a scrape against metal, and then a soft thud and clang had him whirling to meet the threat.

That wasn't. Even as his heart slammed ridiculously hard and adrenaline coursed through his body, he tried to remind himself he was no longer at one of the tougher inner-city hospitals in Houston.

The girl from today.

Woman.

Miranda.

Huge eyes, butt planted in the snow, a stepladder tipped over beside her, its legs jammed into her side.

"Are you hurt?" He squatted beside her. "Did you hit your head? May I see?"

"It's you," she breathed.

He stilled. Not sure how to take that. She sounded surprised. No, not that. More like amazed. Awed.

But like most social situations—although this barely qualified—he was likely reading it wrong.

"Your head, Miranda. Are you injured?"

"You remembered," she said. Her breath was warm against his slightly exposed wrist as he attempted to tilt her head slightly forward away from the edge of the dumpster. She winced.

"I'll take that as a yes," he said softly.

"My name. You remembered this time."

"You told me early this afternoon so that's hardly an academic feat of memory," he said, sliding his hand into the breast pocket of his wool blazer and fishing out his retinoscope. He shone it first in her right eye and then her left.

"Witt, did you just make a joke?" she whispered.

"Unlikely."

She laughed. The sound was light and sweet like wind chimes and again he saw her mouth split into the lopsided grin he'd noticed earlier today. Something niggled at his memory, but he ignored it. Her loopy smile made him feel a little strange inside. Warmer, like the wind chill had loosened its grip.

"Follow my finger," he said turning off the light.

She did, her gaze intent, but focused on his face, not his finger. "You're shaking."

"The adrenaline," he dismissed. "My finger," he repeated.

"Your face is way more interesting. And why do you have so much adrenaline? I fell, not you."

He stopped moving his finger and stared at her. A memory crowded in of his first year of residency in Houston. All hands on deck in the ER from a gang shooting with a lot of vics. Him in the ambulance bay with an ER doc helping get the patients into trauma and the loud crash of metal as a car screeched to a stop, hitting a dumpster before several shooters poured out of the car, shooting like they were in a heist movie and him flinging himself over the two patients, grabbing the ER doc and making a lunge for the young medic. He'd been a little too late. She'd been hit, but had survived. He'd managed to put pressure on her wound while the cops and hospital security did their jobs.

He'd been jumpy around loud noises since. And he hated that three years later, he still couldn't control his racing heart and adrenaline surge when startled by loud bangs.

"I didn't get hit that hard, Witt. I'm okay." She assured him, but he wasn't convinced. Her gaze was a little…goofy. Good thing he'd gone for bones because he was positive 'goofy expression' was not in any neurology text, and he wasn't quite sure why his brain had come up with that term. But her pupils were the same size and responded appropriately to the light, although her conversational asides were making him mentally dizzy.

"Why adrenaline?"

"You startled me." He gave up ignoring her comments. "But I'm not sure if you're neurologically uncompromised. You're not making total sense," he said softly. "I can bring my car around and drive you to the hospital emergency. We can get you a CAT scan."

"I'm fine." She batted his finger away. "It's just the distraction of you. I always thought you were the most beautiful boy in high school and now I bet women throw themselves in your path on a daily basis. You're likely used to stumbling over them. Good thing you rocked the hurdles in high school. You were so fast and smooth. Like a gazelle. Do you have to hurdle over star-struck women on your way to work or to get a coffee?"

He dropped his retinoscope in the snow and stared. Miranda picked it up and handed it to him. One corner of her mouth quirked up.

"Don't freak. I didn't fall because I'm taking up stalking you as a hobby. I'm fine. Besides, I heard you were an orthopedist specializing in sports injuries. Shouldn't you be looking at my bones?"

"Did you injure your coccyx?" he asked cautious now, suddenly realizing they were alone at the back of the hotel in the dark and he wasn't sure if she were concussed or coming on to him or hoped he would come on to her… He couldn't think of another reason and even those were ludicrous. For years his studies had demanded all his attention and then his intense work schedule during residency had made anything except working out and volunteering at one of the free children's clinics nearly impossible.

"Is that my tailbone?"

"Yes."

Her eyes dropped to his mouth and then jerked up again. "Yes, it hurts, but I'm fine," she said. "Just a little bruised and embarrassed, and…um…pretzeled." She glanced down at her sprawled-out legs tangled in the legs of the bright yellow step stool. Even in the dark it looked garish.

"A hand?" He held out his hand. She looked at it and then at him, clearly a question in her eyes, and then she smiled. "I knew I was right."

"About?" He took her hand and then slid his other under her arm and wrapped it a little around her waist. "Steady," he said and then stood, taking her with him and keeping his grip light, but definitely present.

She sighed. "Everything."

"You would be the first."

"I think that's another joke, Witt. Progress."

"Don't go jumping to conclusions now," he said and righted the step stool. "What were you doing out here with this?" It seemed the height of stupid with the snow and ice and evening closing in.

"Trying to get the fake Christmas tree out of the dumpster. I don't know who threw it in here, but I spotted it when

I brought some boxes out to the recycling."

His glove was smeared with blood. Her head was definitely injured.

"Miranda, do you have a first aid kit in your store?"

She looked at his glove. "Oh. That's mine? My bad. Sorry. I have a leather cleaner. I can clean that for you."

She was worried about his glove, not her head?

"Let's get you inside and in better light."

"I'm fine," she said. Her cheeks, in the wash of light from the open door went from white to bright pink. "First I want to grab that tree."

"We're long past Christmas," he said herding her toward the door. "When was your last tetanus shot?"

"I saw a show on the Science Channel about the bacterium Clostridium tetani and the tetanus booster shot being given every ten years is just a random guess. Doctors used to tell people to have it every year. But now some speculate you can go thirty years without a booster. Did you know that?"

"I might have heard something about that." He kicked the door to the Graff shut behind them.

Chapter Three

"YOU'RE NOT GOING to need stitches, Miranda," Witt said after gently probing her scalp and then carefully flushing the wound with fluid and patting an antiseptic wipe on her scalp.

She held herself very still. He was touching her, and it felt so wonderful. He smelled amazing. Not at all like how she imagined someone who worked in a hospital would smell—cold, scary, sterile, chemical, but instead Witt smelled fresh like the mountains—pine and cedar. She wanted to lean in and inhale him, absorb his warmth and maleness, and she was afraid she'd give in to the impulse, which she knew would be really, really weird, especially for someone so reserved. In her mind she knew she could rationalize it—she was lonely, she hadn't been on a lot of dates, and even with trying to get her store completely opened before February 1st, she had too much time to think now that she was no longer helping her beloved grandparents to stay in their own home. She hated living alone in the single bedroom apartment converted from a garage on Bramble Lane. She hated being alone.

And Witt had been her biggest fantasy since forever.

And he was here. Talking to her. Touching her. Taking

care of her. She knew it wasn't personal. She didn't get that lost in her fantasies. He hadn't even remembered her from high school although she'd tried to put herself in his path at every opportunity back then.

Stalker.

She'd probably been lucky he hadn't noticed her and had her arrested for harassment. With his brain and ambition, they hadn't been in a lot of classes together. But she had joined the chess club just so she could watch him, tanned arms folded on the table, concentration absolute, his dark hair so thick and full of body waving back from his face, and falling too long over his collar. And then she'd joined the debate team just to listen to him speak.

He rifled through her first aid kit, frowning a little.

"This isn't bad," he said. "But you may want to consider an upgrade."

"Okay," she said, realizing that she'd probably agree to anything he suggested. Miranda knew technically he was considered way out of her league—probably a whole different game—but still, she could look. And smell. Gosh he smelled as gorgeous as he looked. And his hands were beautiful. Large, square, tapered fingers, a little rough, which surprised her as she had suspected doctors would keep their hands pretty protected.

"What did you think of the hospital?" she asked, desperate to be more than a patient.

Immediately his face shut down; the professional interest as he had examined her scalp was gone like a light turned off.

"It's fine."

He turned his attention to a leather satchel that she thought perhaps contained some medical supplies as well as his computer.

Miranda huffed out the breath she'd been holding and relaxed her posture into a slump. Her head did throb. And her…what had he called it—a coccyx? That sounded like Russian soldiers to her, the historical kind marching in the snow fighting Napoleon's army or maybe the dancing ones or the ones who somersaulted off galloping horses. Her coccyx felt like someone was hitting her with a hammer. Pain radiated up her spine and down her right leg. It had been hard to sit still while he'd examined her head, but she could hardly have him look at her butt—at least not in a professional context.

She bit her lip, feeling herself flush all over. What would it be like to be naked with Witt—have him touch her without gloves from her first aid kit? Have him stroke her skin with those beautiful, healing hands, let her touch him? Goose bumps popped up all over her body, and she throbbed a little low in her body. Miranda hugged herself tight, savoring the feeling, the attraction. She was alive and attracted to a man who was going to be here for a little while at least. She hadn't gotten up the nerve to ask Bob how long Dr. Telford would be staying.

And it wasn't like they'd be dating, but since she'd moved in to help her grandparents, her opportunities with men had been rather limited.

Dr. Telford.

Mentally she tasted the words. Happy that he'd met at

least one of his lofty goals growing up. That made two of them, she thought proudly thinking of her little shop that would soon open.

She stood up, gasping a little at the pain that radiated and burned and snarled in her tailbone. Her head throbbed and her elbow now throbbed. So stupid to have fallen. She had taken the time to brush away most of the snow with a stiff-bristled broom she'd borrowed from housekeeping.

"What are you doing?" Witt was back at her side.

Dr. Telford. She needed to keep reminding herself that that they weren't friends, even though his dark blue eyes, framed by midnight brows that seemed to perpetually scowl, and his chiseled jaw and cheekbones made her forget. And he was tall to her short. And slim with broad shoulders. His long overcoat swung behind him as he tried to reseat her on a wooden box with a round hole cut out so it doubled as a drum. A young musician in town made them in his off time and his girlfriend painted Montana landscapes or wildlife on them. The stool tripled as a side table or a drum. Miranda loved them and had taken three on consignment.

"I want to go get the artificial tree out of the dumpster before who knows what will be dumped out there from the kitchen tonight."

He gently pushed her down again. His hand felt like a brand and she closed her eyes to remember the warmth, the feel.

"Headache?"

"No. It just throbs where I hit the side of the dumpster." She opened her eyes to drink him in while she had this marvelous opportunity.

Wow she lived a lame life if it took taking an ungraceful tumble to get the attention of a beautiful, masculine man.

"I believe that's the definition of a headache."

Did his mouth twitch, just a tiny bit? Witt had been a loner in school. A very accomplished, very athletic and very quiet loner. Girls had been crazy about him: spying, wondering, making up all sorts of heated fantasies about what was going on in his dark head, perpetually averted gaze and Heathcliff combined with Edward Cullen worthy brood. He'd been fantastic and he'd been nobody's.

She wondered if he had a girlfriend now that he'd achieved his professional goals.

What kind of woman would be able to get into that complicated, locked-up head of his? Who would be able to breathe warmth into him and steal his coveted heart?

"Actually my tailbone hurts more," she said. "But that's not exactly an exam that can happen in a gift store." She grinned. "Except maybe in a naughty movie."

A flush slashed his Copper Mountain granite ledge cheekbones, and Miranda felt like doing a happy dance. He was noticing her as a person, not just a clumsy potential patient.

"I can take you to the hospital," he said gravely. "I have a rented car."

And just like that her triumph faded. "No! I mean no thank you, Witt." She softened her voice, dulled the panic. "I don't have insurance. I can't go to the hospital."

"That is very foolish not to have insurance," Witt said.

It was. And of course he'd point that out as a doctor and as a ***responsible*** and ***successful*** man all in bold. Miranda sighed.

"I know," she said softly and laid her hand on his arm. "I know. I can't afford it right now though. I'm an independent business operating at the Graff, not an employee, and I'm just getting started. I'm not even officially open."

Not that she'd had insurance before when she'd worked retail. She'd mostly been part time at Marietta Western Wear, then the Java Café and then later at Copper Mountain Chic as she tried to pick up a class or two at the community college. Once she'd hit age twenty-six she'd lost coverage through her parents and now she just crossed her fingers and hoped, but she wasn't going to tell Witt that. He was like her brother and sisters—driven, focused on professional goals and the future, never the here and now. And seemingly also like them, not focused on family either. She'd taken care of her grandparents alone. When she'd worried as her grandfather's conditioned worsened and her grandmother's health started declining, she'd tried to talk to her mother and siblings but had been brushed aside with an impatient "get them set up at the assisted living place in town. They're too old to live on their own."

"Thank you for taking care of me, Witt," she said softly. "I know you're busy and have many demands on your time, but I'm fine. Really fine."

And then his gaze met hers. It really was just like in the books. Falling into his eyes that really were the deepest blue. Like night swimming. Girls in her school had talked about his eyes. Whispered about them, but she'd never had an excuse to stare and—until today—he hadn't really looked at her. In fact, he'd looked everywhere but at her. And by the dumpster, it had been too dark to see him and she'd been blinded by his silly light anyway.

"There's nothing to be done with a bruised, possibly fractured coccyx," he said, leaning back on his heels and frowning. "Just time and rest and not climbing in to dumpsters."

"Or hanging from chandeliers?" she teased.

He did smile then. It was brief. Maybe in her imagination.

"Definitely not for a month or so."

"I'll do my best to refrain," she said sitting up virtuously and crossing her heart dramatically with her finger.

"It's probably not fractured," he said standing up at the same time she did. Her mouth came to his sternum. She didn't know why she thought that was sexy. She wished just for a second that he was hers. That she could kiss him right on his heartbeat. Put her palm on his cheek so she could remember later what he felt like.

Thank God he's not a mind reader.

He'd send her to a different type of hospital.

"Thank you, Witt." She defaulted from fantasy and went to socially appropriate. "The hospital is really excited to have you. I heard a few of the staff talking about you this evening when I went to the Java Café for a caffeine fix." He'd repacked his medical kit and returned it to his satchel. Then he repacked hers but paused as she spoke. But didn't acknowledge what she'd said as he returned her kit to the large butcher block with shelves and three drawers that she was going to use for her office and gift wrapping supplies and payment area.

"Good night." He nodded curtly.

"Good night," she called out even as he strode out, coat swinging like he was Benedict Cumberbatch in a Sherlock Holmes episode.

WHITMAN WALKED DOWN the hall toward the grand staircase that led to the second floor. He was on the third, but he avoided elevators and took the stairs whenever possible. He walked by the small bar and thought about getting a nightcap that he could take to his room. Then he wondered about dinner. Should he order room service or eat in the pub-style restaurant behind the bar? A tall blonde with a messy braid was dressed all in black and mixing cocktails with a flourish as several couples sat at the bar watching her.

Too public. He'd look too alone. Someone would feel sorry for him and want to talk. Room service.

But as he lightly ran up the stairs, a vision of Miranda floated into his brain. Her pale face. Warm, curious eyes. The determined set of her mouth when she'd told him she was fine even though she probably hurt like hell. He was being stupid. She wouldn't go back for the tree. Or she'd get someone to help her. Her boyfriend or husband maybe. But she hadn't worn a ring. He was trained to notice details.

He muttered a curse and headed back down the stairs and back through the hall. A quick look in her shop revealed no Miranda. She'd also plugged in the twinkle lights he'd seen around the door and strung up lining the ceiling. It gave the small space a warm glow. He pushed open the door.

Just as he suspected. She was climbing up the stepladder again. He vaulted the rail and dropped down. She didn't even turn around to see who was coming up behind her.

"You have no sense of self-preservation," he accused.

"And you seem to be auditioning for a white knight role," she said. "And while it would likely suit, I don't think you want the fan base that comes with it."

"Half the time you don't speak English," he muttered. He lifted her off the step stool and folded it up with purpose.

"Witt, I need the tree," she said. "It's for a Valentine's promotion that will help the town to see Valentine's in a new, less negative light."

"A broken, artificial Christmas tree?" He was no neurologist but she wasn't making any sense. His voice bled skepticism.

"Yes. I'm going to paint it. And repurpose it, and I'm not a tall dark and handsome lead in a movie so I need the step stool." She held out her hand like she expected him to give it to her.

He tried to process what she said. "Do you always speak so randomly? I'm having second thoughts about the CAT scan you say you don't want because you can't afford it. You can," he said. "It's the law. Hospitals have to accept all patients and stabilize them. They can put you on a payment plan or perhaps you would qualify for…"

Something flashed across her face almost like anger. "I pay my way," she said interrupting him calmly, her hand still out for the step stool.

Aggravated now, he tucked the stool under his arm and lifted out the fake Christmas tree one-handed. It was a sorry sight. Bent, twisted, limbs drooping, some missing. Probably covered in the filth of age and exposure.

Seriously?

"Thank you," she said and her crooked smile showed all her small, white, perfectly aligned teeth. "I don't suppose you'd be a hero for another thirty seconds and carry it into my store?"

He didn't have an answer for that, and wasn't really sure why he was out here in the freezing cold probably getting his coat dirty with who knew what.

"This could be a health code violation," he said as he picked his steps carefully back toward the short flight of cement stairs that led to the back door. What had possessed him to hurdle the rail like he was back on the track team? This wasn't Houston. There was snow on the ground, likely ice. He could have fallen and needed his own CAT scan. Fat help he'd be to Wyatt and the short-staffed orthopedic department then.

"I'll take that risk," Miranda said sweetly behind him.

And for some reason, that made Witt want to smile. But he kept his expression stone. He didn't want to engage. Didn't want people asking him about his day, his feelings, his "family," his future because it sure as hell wasn't here.

WITT WAS FINISHING up his informal orientation with the medical director when he got paged to the ER. Eight-year-old patient. Potential open fracture coming in. Witt thanked the director and took the stairs down to the emergency, already giving radiology a heads-up. He hit the ER just as he heard the ambulance siren.

Witt checked in with his team and met the paramedics as they were wheeling the patient in.

"That's one way to get out of school," he said smiling down at the young boy.

"Name?" he asked softly to the paramedics.

"Parker Wilder. Third grade."

"Parents on the way?"

"Dad on a job site, no cell service. Mom's in school in Pullman. Two aunts on their way and uncle driving to the job site to get Dad."

"Soccer or basketball?" he asked the boy, who was desperately trying not to cry.

"Soccer," he said, voice tight.

"Showing off for a girl, huh?"

The screwed-up disgusted expression Parker answered with made Witt laugh.

"Dad will be here soon. In the meantime you can hang with me."

"Will I get a cast?"

Witt looked at the angle of the arm and the open wound that was dirty.

"Definitely."

"I want camouflage."

"Good stylistic choice," Witt said, assessing the boy's color and asking a few more questions of the paramedic. "Can you wiggle your fingers for me?"

He asked a few more questions interspersing them with questions about soccer.

"Hey want to see a cool machine? It's down the hall. Way cooler than the one in the ER." Witt walked beside his patient toward radiology, even as he asked the nurse to contact him when Parker's father or other family members arrived. "Hey, buddy, when did you eat lunch?"

"I have recess first before lunch. I'm starved," Parker announced.

"That bites," Witt said. "But makes my life easier." He grinned at Parker's skeptical expression. "What was for breakfast?"

"Blueberry pancakes with chocolate."

"Lucky."

"Not really," Parker kept trying to look at his arm, which had been stabilized and covered. "My mom is going to freak. And my coach will be pissed if I can't play when the season starts in March."

"Six weeks you'll be good as new."

He left Parker in radiology and texted Wyatt for a consult in case the growth plate was involved.

It was. He and Wyatt looked at the X-ray. Wyatt whistled. "He couldn't have broken that worse if he'd tried."

"Skidded on the gym floor running for a ball and fell and

his arm got caught under the bleachers so he kept moving, but his arm didn't."

"Should we fly him out to a pediatric orthopedic specialist?" Wyatt asked.

"Open fracture, gym floor under bleachers was filthy, and he's showing signs of nerve impairment. Hasn't eaten since breakfast. I operated on a lot of pediatric cases in Houston."

"Let's rock and roll," said Wyatt. "I'll be done with my case and join you in your room before you're likely ready to operate."

>>><<<

WHITMAN EXITED THE hospital several hours later. It had been beyond a satisfying day. He'd done rounds with Wyatt early in the morning, consulted on several cases and settled into the small suite of offices in the hospital that the orthopedic surgeons used. He'd also handled two emergency cases. The first—Parker Wilder's—could have been flown out to a larger hospital, but Whitman had felt completely confident to do the surgery, and when he laid the options out before Parker's dad, Colt Wilder, a former high school classmate, Colt hadn't hesitated, choosing to keep Parker local where he had family, and when the risk of infection and potential permanent nerve damage would be mitigated by operating more quickly.

The second case—car accident on highway 89 heading toward Livingston with two victims—had been challenging, but the outcomes had been excellent.

Whitman felt good. Useful. The cases had been interesting. His OR team had readily accepted him and followed his lead even though he knew each surgeon always required slight adjustments on the part of the surgical nurses and scrub techs. No one had questioned his confidence and decision to keep Parker local and operate. And the families had been beyond grateful, far more than he was used to in Houston.

It had been weird to see Colt again. Colt had been his academic rival for valedictorian and had been even quieter and less social than he had. And just as antsy to leave Marietta behind. Witt had heard Colt had joined the Army. He hadn't even walked at graduation, leaving Witt to make his speech alone. He'd been even more shocked to learn that Colt was living on the ranch he'd once hated. And that he had a kid.

Wyatt had shrugged off Whitman's dismay. "Colt came back last year, fell in love, finished his enlistment and boom left the Rangers and got a wife and kid within months. Also discovered he had brothers and a mom and that he'd had been adopted. Changed his last name from Ewing to Wilder to match theirs and now they are one big-ass close family. Marietta has a way of messing with your plans. Watch yourself."

Wyatt had laughed like getting stuck back in Marietta was funny.

Whitman huffed out a breath and headed down Main Street to pick up a to-go meal from the Main Street Diner that he had called in before leaving the hospital.

Colt's thanks and parting words still rang in his ear as if Wyatt's casual teasing hadn't been enough. "That's how it starts," Colt had said when Witt had explained what he was doing back in town and that his "job" at the hospital was *very* temporary. His golden gaze had been intense and disconcertingly amused. Witt had felt chilled to the bone as if Colt were uttering a prophecy, which was just fanciful and stupid. "Doing a favor for someone. I came back to help Coach D and next thing I know I'm being auctioned off like a steer. Less than a year later I'm married and adopting her kid. Best thing that ever happened to me."

Witt had felt everything in him recoil and Colt had laughed. "So watch your back, Doc."

Witt didn't know if he'd answered. Probably muttered congratulations. But *that* wouldn't happen to him.

"Not staying," he said aloud as if he needed any reminders. As he opened up the diner's door, and the familiar, long-time waitress Flo hurried up to greet him, his takeout meal already packaged up to go even as she had a welcoming smile on her face.

"Sure you don't want to eat here, Dr. Telford? Sounds so good to say that, Witt. I still remember when you first came to town all tall and skinny and so serious. I know your folks are so proud of you. They must be excited to have you home."

He'd already paid with a credit card on the phone and hadn't wanted to get dragged into reminiscences with Flo, who'd been at the diner since forever. He muttered something noncommittal and made his escape. Keeping a low profile was proving impossible. He took his meal of minestrone soup, steamed vegetables, meatloaf and mashed potatoes and a mystery dessert that Flo had added as a freebee with a smile as she declared "it's to die for."

"To die for," meant he'd have to run an extra mile or add an extra circuit with the weights at the hotel's gym.

By tomorrow, if not already, his "family," would hear that he was back in town. Probably a lot of people would let them know. And it really should have been him to make the call. Guilt settled around his shoulders even though he told himself over and over that he'd done his best just as they probably had. They just hadn't been a good fit, and Witt had felt like a burden, a mistake even though his biological father had never once complained, and his stepmother had been the antithesis of wicked.

His cell phone burned a hole in his pocket. He should call. After his dinner. Or tomorrow.

The back door closed at eight p.m., and Whitman slipped inside with eight minutes to spare. The bag felt hot in his hand, but the thought of calling his biological dad or his mom made him lose his appetite. He knew he was being unreasonable, but the longer he went without communicating with them, the harder it got. They hadn't come to his medical school graduation, but he hadn't invited them enthusiastically, and his youngest half-brother been injured in a rodeo accident so his stepmother and sister had gone to him, and his father had had to stay back at the ranch. Whitman had been a little relieved. North Carolina would have been a long and expensive flight, and he had been worried that his biological dad would have shown up in his worn Wranglers, boots and Stetson, thinking nothing of it. Not what other parents wore to medical school graduations.

"Miranda?" Whitman had intended to walk straight to his room and eat there, but to do so, he had to step over a pair of very slim legs in bright red tights with white hearts and sparkly black cowboy boots with red hearts embroidered on them.

"Oh, hey Witt." She looked up and smiled. Her face lit up and her warm caramel eyes glowed. Witt felt a bit taken aback and looked behind him to see if someone else had come into the store behind him. "Wow you really worked a long day today." She paused in what she was doing—drilling holes into a long highly sanded and polished branch.

"I could say the same of you," he said, trying to ignore that she was wearing a fairly short denim skirt with snaps going up the front and her legs stuck out partially blocking the hallway. She had already been in her store this morning, painting one wall bright red "for Valentine's Day," she'd called out to him as he'd left slightly before six a.m. this morning.

"Sorry I'm a bit in the way. Trying to get ready for my grand opening in a couple of days as well as Valentine's Day. You saw the wall before it was finished this morning. I've added a little sparkle. What do you think?"

He wasn't sure what to think—the lurid red wall that looked glossy and had a sheen that hurt his eyes a little.

This morning, he'd just nodded a greeting and hustled out the door intent on getting to the coffee shop when it opened to avoid line, gossip and questions. Now it seemed rude to just march off although he was hungry.

"That's some red." He winced at the obviousness.

Miranda laughed. She started to scramble to her feet. Her eyes scrunched and her breath hitched and she sat back down.

"Still hurts?"

Her creamy complexion paled further than her lightly freckled, snowy cheeks usually looked. "Master of the understatement on both counts," she said then she smiled, even though her eyes still registered pain. "I'm making a lot of progress. I want to be open by February 1st."

He looked around at the area that held the typical hotel shop fare—sundries, basic medicines, newspapers, magazines, snacks and drinks. That was complete and organized. The rest of the store was mostly empty.

"Congratulations," he said surprised to find himself a little curious as to what she had planned for the rest of the small, misshapen space. It looked like it had been randomly carved out of another room, but Miranda looked happy and undaunted by the work ahead. He admired that. He'd yet to see someone in to help her. She must have family here. Why else would a young woman stay in such a small town far away from a metropolitan area? "You going to close up soon?"

She shook her head making her almost colorless brownish-blondish hair swing back and forth around her face like a curtain. "I want to finish this first because this is the most important piece of my Valentine Plan."

He took in the polished branch that looked a bit like a staff a wizard might point at some hapless creature in a fantasy movie. The dismembered branches of the fake Christmas tree lay scattered around her. He wasn't sure what a tree had to do with Valentine's Day, and he wasn't about to ask.

Miranda held her hand out. He stared at it.

"Let's try this again," she said. "Perhaps you could resurrect your white knight hero character from last night long enough to give me a tug up."

He was absurdly clueless at times. Miranda grinned at him, and he felt a little warmer instead of awkward, like he was in on the joke. He pulled her up. Then he saw the pillow on the floor with a large ice pack.

"Still really sore?" he asked, thinking about how much it must have hurt to paint several coats on that wall today and then do whatever else she'd done to make it shimmer.

"I'll deal. I took some Aleve. What do you think, pink or red?" She held out some of the scraggly branches from the rescued artificial tree.

"No opinion." He barely repressed a shudder. Trees should remain green, and discarded ones should remain in dumpsters.

"Don't be a typical guy," she pleaded.

He held his hands out in a 'I am what I am' move. The smell of his dinner made the empty space seem a little more homey.

"Oh hey, is that the meatloaf from Main Street Diner I smell? Good for you finding that on your second night. It was recently sold to Gabriella Marcos and she's changed up the menu somewhat, but not the meatloaf. I think it has its own Twitter account. The town would revolt if she ever took it off the rotation."

Whitman didn't know what made him do it. The invitation was out before he'd even thought about it.

"Are you hungry? Why don't you join me?"

Then he froze. Why had he said that? He wanted to be alone. Wanted to stay uninvolved.

Miranda's eyes were huge, and her mouth formed an O. The invitation hovered between them like it had wings, and he considered giving her the whole bag and then saying that he'd just been paged back to the hospital because her shock made it seem like a date. And it was not a date. Absolutely not. She'd get that right? Not that she'd want to date him if he'd asked. It was just convenient. Friends. They'd gone to high school together. Not a date.

His mind went a million miles an hour.

"Wow. Watching you think is like watching one of those war video games—cacophony of your neurons clashing with the visual stimuli of your face bombarded by an exploding cluster of expressions." She grinned her crooked grin while his mind struggled to keep up. "Don't play poker, although I bet you'd be a marvelous card counter."

Huh?

Was that a yes or a no? He didn't dare ask. Who knew what would come out of her mouth next?

Then her stomach growled, breaking the silence that he seemed unable to do.

"That would be great. Thanks. I'm starved. I forgot to eat today."

"Okay. Good." Then he stood there. Not sure what to do next. He would not take her back to his room. Too intimate, and he didn't want her to think he was hitting on her. Taking the food into the bar would be too public, and rude since the food was from another establishment. Whitman wasn't sure what he was doing. Sharing a meal. Avoiding another quiet, empty night? He'd had thousands of them. Making up for his sullen and withdrawn teen years? Who knew? It had been an impulse. And he was so rarely given to impulse he couldn't think what to do next.

"Going to let it get cold?" She smiled at him. "Put it on top of this wine barrel. It will work as a table even though the glass top for it hasn't come in yet. I'm going to use this as a display table. But it is for sale. The artist is an older gentleman who used to work for a vineyard in Sonoma, but he retired here to be close to his son and his daughter-in-law and their three kids. So sweet when families stick together."

Was that a dig at him?

Witt took the food out of the bag. But no, Miranda didn't seem to be judging. Instead she walked out to the bar and the bartender—the same woman from last night—handed Miranda plates and silverware and napkins. She said something to Miranda that made her look back at him.

Great.

Anyone seeing them would think they were having a

date. And this was anything but a date. He should have kept his mouth shut. He was here for a month. Not dating. But rumors would fly. His family would hear. The staff at the hospital would hear that he had a date. The questions. The looks. The awkward denials that no one would believe.

He sucked in a breath. He was being presumptuous and paranoid. Miranda probably had a boyfriend, who should be here having dinner with her and helping her with her store since she was injured. Or her family since she thought close families were sweet.

"You've made us civilized," he said. He'd imagined eating out of the boxes alone in his room, and he wasn't convinced that that's what he shouldn't have done.

"Sharing a meal is one of the most sacred things we do as humans," Miranda said, startling him.

"Ummmm," was all he could manage with his twelve plus years of higher education.

Miranda smiled at him. "Do you want me to dish out?"

"Sure," he said, trying to stifle the urge to flee. "I'll go get us some water." He nearly sprinted to the bar for a reprieve. It was just a takeout dinner, he reminded himself. Not a date. Miranda had a whole life in Marietta that didn't involve him. She was opening her business. She didn't want to get involved with him any more than he wanted to get involved with her. He was going to be gone soon. She was deeply rooted. He wasn't leading her on.

He knew he was over-reacting, but after his recent experience at the end of his residency when what he'd thought of as a casual friends-with-benefits on again off again with a colleague had turned to an embarrassing and very public "breakup," Whitman was feeling especially cautious.

He waited for the bartender to be free and when she glided over, with a professional smile and a "what can I get for you and Miranda?" Whitman had to cork his groan. He knew the power of curiosity running through the veins of small towns. Damn. He should have kept his mouth shut like he usually did.

"Water."

She quirked her brow.

"We're just…ah…we went to high school together." And that just sounded like a dumb excuse. Why did he feel the need to justify a glass of water and a meal with Miranda?

"Enjoy," she said handing him two glasses of water. "I'm Shane Knight. Enjoy your dinner and time in Marietta, Dr. Telford."

The anonymity of Los Angeles called like a siren. Whitman carried the glasses of water back to the gift shop.

"Thank you," Miranda said. "I splurged and am trying one of the scented candles from a local woman who distills down different essential oils and blends them with soy wax. This one is pine. Can you smell it? What do you think?" She waved her hand over the dancing flame as he sat down. The golden glow lit her high, wide cheekbones and shadowed the lower part of her face. She looked a little like a…pixie or a fairy maybe. He didn't know. He'd never been into fantasy, but since she was so petite and her face was a bit of an odd shape like a heart and her chin was pointy and her mouth a bit too big and crooked when she smiled she looked a little otherworldly or magical somehow. Her eyes were wide set and always glowed, making her seem so vibrant and alive in the frozen white of winter.

"Can you smell the pine? Is it pleasant? Should I also carry candles from a different vendor? I want to carry as many local products as I can but am very limited by my space so must be choosey. Be honest."

"I have no opinion," he said more coolly than he intended, but what did she expect him to do, hang over the candle and inhale?

"Of course you do," Miranda said, and pushed the candle toward him. "Sniff."

Witt inhaled dutifully. The scent reminded him of hiking in the woods—something he didn't get to do that often unless he had a weekend free. Then he would drive to the woods and run a trail or hike a longer one, maybe even camp overnight. The quiet always energized him. He hadn't often been to the woods since leaving North Carolina.

Woods weren't too convenient in Santa Monica, but the runs on the beach would compensate.

"It reminds me of hiking," he said when he realized she was still staring at him waiting for his verdict.

"You love to hike too," Miranda breathed like that was the best news ever. She looked especially shiny tonight. The candle or had she been attacked by glitter?

Witt jerked a nod not wanting to get caught up in getting an offer to hike with her in this God-forsaken tundra. Small talk was something he'd never mastered nor had he wanted to. Goals were what mattered, his mother had drilled into him. "You need to set clear goals and the steps to achieve them. Your biological father never had any. He was all good times. No feasible goals."

His mother's goals and achievements had been cut very short. And when he'd finally met his father at age twelve, his father had seemed more about living in the moment—long days of ranch work and then evenings playing with his kids and chatting about the day with Sarah. Not planning for the future. Not a lot of focus on professional achievements as far as Witt had been able to tell.

The table was set. The food plated like they were at a restaurant. The soup was split into two bowls, and they even had a small side salad. He looked at it in inquiry noticing the heirloom mini tomatoes, sugar snap peas, cranberries, dates, blue cheese and candied pecans.

"Good thing I forgot to eat lunch, huh? I love to make salads, and bought a small fridge for the shop so I wouldn't be tempted to eat hotel food every day. That would be disastrously expensive and probably bad for my waistline."

He knew not to comment on weight or to look like he was looking. He'd been around enough women to know at least that much. But from what he had seen, Miranda was petite, almost elfin in her slim, supple body.

"Thank you, Miranda. This is very lovely," he said meaning it.

There were no chairs so they stood.

The setting reminded him a little of a wine bar he'd been to in San Diego when he'd been interviewing for a residency.

"Do you like jazz?" she asked.

"Why jazz?" He looked up. "Don't figure me for a Drake fan?"

"I can put Drake on. Or The Weeknd? Bruno Mars? Taylor Swift?"

"Are you seriously asking or teasing?"

She grinned. "Both."

"How about your space, your choice?"

"I like that," Miranda said, and called out to Siri to play some Esperanza Spalding.

"A toast." Miranda lifted up her water glass. "To new adventures."

Whitman swallowed hard. He felt like a fraud. She was so earnest. Sweet really. Making the best of each moment, whereas he was internally grumbling because he was back to where he started, delayed in achieving a return to California and a fellowship at a huge teaching hospital. Marietta was a dreaded pit stop, but she was living her life here. Making her own plans to stay and thrive. His heart lurched a little when he thought about the failure rate of small businesses. Clearly Miranda worked hard, but did she have capital? A business plan? A degree in marketing or… Not your business, he told himself sternly.

"What?" she asked. "Why are you looking at me like that?"

"To new adventures," he repeated not willing to say what he was really thinking. Other than a diagnosis and a course of medical action, when had he really?

They clinked water glasses but as they put them down on the wine barrel table, Shane arrived with two goblets of deep burgundy wine.

"I saw the candle and couldn't resist," Shane said. Then she clinked the glasses together lightly in a toast and winked at Miranda as she handed one to her and then one to him. "To catching up with old friends. Bon appétit and, Miranda, it's on the house so don't even think about turning it down. You either." She shook a finger at him and then sauntered back to the bar, the thick rubber-waffled soles of her combat boots quiet on the wood.

"That was unexpected."

"Not if you know Shane, and I don't really, not yet." Miranda took a little sip of the wine. "But I'd like to. She's friendly but real. And I sense she has a lot underneath. I can tell she's had an interesting life. And it's lovely that she can also give people their own space."

Witt took a sip and nearly choked thinking of the irony of Miranda wanting her own space.

"Isn't it good?" she asked.

It was delicious, and probably should not have been comped. He'd need to order something at the bar and give her a huge tip.

"You tell me."

"I don't know." Miranda looked at him a little wistfully. "My parents have a wine cellar with over three thousand bottles. My brother has his own winery in Southern Oregon. They say I don't know anything about wine because I haven't taken the time to study it and master the traits of the different varietals and different wineries, but I…never mind. It is what it is, and it was my choice and the right one."

Whitman stared at her, not quite sure how to take that. He had started collecting wine. Not a lot, but he'd rented space for his wine in a storage facility in Houston and it was being shipped to another wine storage facility in Santa Monica next month.

"Do you like it?" she persisted.

"Do *you* like it?"

⇛⇚

THE WAY HE said *'you'* made her feel warm inside and a little light-headed.

Stop it.

But her heart still fluttered.

"I'm not sure how to taste it," she confessed, unable to be anything but honest. She was who she was, and she had tried to please her parents, her family, and failed, but she hadn't apologized about who she was and what she wanted, and she still wouldn't.

"Not sure I follow."

Witt held the wine, stem between his fingers, his palm cupping the bottom part of the bowl of the glass.

"I know there's a procedure to tasting," Miranda said. "Do you know how? Can you show me?"

He paused. "Sure." He cocked his head and looked at her, and Miranda felt a little dart of something hit her low in her tummy, then radiate out. "But it's not necessary, Miranda. You can just drink wine you enjoy. You don't have to prove anything to anyone."

"I know. I just…" She paused, searching for the right words. "I like to learn new things, and I was thinking that with my boutique I could maybe feature some different local breweries or Montana wineries or even some distilleries and maybe pair up with the bar or…I don't know." She smiled, a little nervous with his scrutiny. She wasn't used to people, especially men, looking at her so closely. Or listening to her plans and her dreams. Her family had rolled their eyes with her 'enthusiasms' they had called them. She'd called her mother and sister to tell them about her store, but they hadn't shown interest or responded to any of the pictures she'd sent of her progress except general wishes of good luck heavily laden with "well-meaning" advice geared to help her avoid doom.

Miranda had shrugged them off just as she had her entire life, but she did wish she had a closer relationship with her parents and siblings. She felt like her parents had done such an excellent job raising her three siblings but when she came around nearly ten years later, her parents were too tuckered out to make a full-court press raising her.

But she felt like Witt was really listening, and it made her want to choose her words carefully, so that she deserved his attention.

"I haven't worked it all out, but there are a couple of locals—Laird Wilder is one—who are starting to distill their own whiskey and gin, and several others who are brewing microbrews. I want to feature local products in my store. I know Montana's cold for wine, but there are some wineries in the state. I could feature a different winery each month and have gift baskets featuring the wine and wine-related products."

Witt looked around her store. She knew it didn't look like much yet. There was still so much to do, but in her mind, she already had the hand-painted shelves from recycled wood mounted on the walls that she'd already stained, and a few she'd painted, the display tables with gift baskets, jewelry, and Montana-themed specialty items. And then there was her Valentine Giving Tree.

"Will you teach me to taste wine, Witt? And to talk about it?"

"Will you call me Whitman?"

"Why do you prefer that?"

"It's my name."

"You just seem like a Witt in my mind. You always did. Tall, dark, handsome, smart, making quick decisions, striding down a hallway, always in a rush. Thinking. Solving problems. Whitman seems like a scrawny guy in tennis whites who doesn't even play. Sorry." She took in his rounded eyes. "I talk too much. Waaaaay too much."

And they were silent. He was sharing his dinner and she'd offended him about his name.

"Whitman," she said trying it out. "If you could have a super power what would it be?"

"Your conversation makes me dizzy."

Not the first time she'd been told that. Her family had always shushed her. She'd been a motor mouth in school. At least no one had ever once called her boring. She couldn't even say it was an acquired taste.

"It's a skill."

He was quiet while she waited for the comeback.

"Wine tasting." He seemed to rouse himself.

"Maybe we should eat first. I don't have a microwave here."

"You should taste the wine before you eat anything," he said and then squared his shoulders like he'd come to a decision. "I'll teach you fast, like I'm striding down a hall on the way to a meeting and about to make a crucial decision."

She laughed, totally charmed. "That's the spirit," she murmured.

"I like to cup the wine like this…" he palmed the glass, letting the stem dangle between his hands "…to warm the wine a little if it's been cellared, which this has."

Miranda palmed the glass. He looked way cooler because he had such large, capable hands. She stared at them.

"And then people like to swirl the wine to oxygenate it a bit to get a better flavor of the bouquet."

He put the wine down on the table and deftly gave it a couple of quick twirls that had the wine dancing in his glass in a beautiful burgundy swirl.

"Then you put your nose close to the bowl of the glass and inhale."

She followed suit. Everything assaulted her at once, and she had to resist the urge to pull away and rub her nose.

"Do you scent anything?"

"Like a particular fruit or slate or tobacco? My mom was always going on about tobacco," Miranda rolled her eyes. "My dad would talk about graphite. Did you ever lick a pencil or slate on someone's patio?"

"Ummmm, no." Witt paused and then seemed to rally with an effort. "Well, do you smell anything that reminds you of anything like cherries or something sweeter, lighter like peach or strawberry or wet earth, barnyard?"

"Manure." Miranda laughed and wrinkled her nose. "I haven't had enough of that in my life living with my grandparents for the past twelve years, and I bet you had your fill of that when you were a teen."

"That I did," Witt murmured, and Miranda was sure she saw a hint of a smile grace his lips. She felt so proud like she'd won a geography bee or something equally impressive.

"Try again." Witt leaned forward and swirled his glass. "I think she gave us different wines. Your color is not as deep and it's in a pinot glass. I can smell the barnyard from here."

"Lucky me."

He tilted her glass toward him and inhaled. "And strawberry. Try." He swirled it with a flick of his wrist and Miranda dutifully inhaled, holding on to his wrist lightly to steady the wine. She looked up at him. In the candlelight his face was so mysteriously beautiful, sculpted, but his eyes were warm and intent like he really cared what she thought, and she wished, oh how she wished she had something really interesting to say to him, something that would make him notice her, remember her this time.

"I think it smells like a flower, but I don't know what kind."

"That's fine. Floral. Start with that. Now taste."

"Just sip? My brother always has to give a long dissertation on what we are going to taste, and of course I never taste half of it."

"But do you enjoy the wine he has you sample?"

Miranda scowled. "Not usually, but I don't know if it's the wine's fault."

A brief smile lit his face. "It's true company makes a difference." He swirled his wine and then sipped it, swished it around his mouth. "I'd say I have a zinfandel, and yours is a pinot noir."

"I always loved how that sounded," Miranda said dreamily. "Pinot noir. Noir is almost an onomatopoeia, and I love that Shane's trying to get the best of you, but you prevailed." Miranda held out her glass to him. "Taste."

He hesitated, and Miranda felt her face heat. She was being forward. But when would she get this chance again? It was like one of her favorite romance books come to life. She was not heroine material, but if she acted like it, maybe she could have at least her own scene with the hero if not her whole book and the happy ever after.

He placed his hand over hers. It felt so warm, and she had to fight not to shiver as darts of heat zinged around her body in a drunk happy dance that was way over the top compared to what was actually happening. Still. He tilted the glass to his lips. What would it be like to kiss him? What would it be like to think she even had a chance?

"Definitely a pinot. I think a Harper Voit Antiquum. I've had it twice before. My favorite pinot noir out of the Willamette Valley hands down. I bought a case when I was interviewing at OHSU for a surgical residency position."

"What do you like about it?"

"It's a perfectly crafted blend of ripe and blue fruit and tinged with chocolate, sea salt and a hint of caramel on the finish and the middle of the wine carries more than a hint of spice to taunt my tongue, and the wine has a long, gorgeous finish. When I drink it, I feel like I'm on the porch of a cabin in the woods with the wind rustling the leaves, streaks of light through the trees, a few bird calls and there's a hint of warmth in the air, a harbinger of summer to come."

Miranda felt like she was going to melt in a puddle. Witt was a poet. She wondered how he'd describe a woman he'd fallen in love with. No. Too depressing. She wouldn't think about that.

"And my brother thinks he's the expert on wine," she said pulling her thoughts back to the here and now.

"Are you going to think about it or drink it?" he asked.

Witt was already eating his meatloaf, each bite precise, not mixed with the mash potatoes or sautéed veggies like the way she ate. Probably summed up their differences better than anything else could, if you didn't count the million hours of college study he'd done compared to her community school dabbling.

"You never stick to anything. Nothing ever sticks," her mother had complained for as long as Miranda could remember—ballet, no, soccer, no, Girl Scouts, no, flute, no. It just went on and on until her parents had thrown up their hands and left her alone. Miranda, an empty bulletin board.

"Did you always want to be a doctor, Witt, I mean Whitman?" she asked. "Never a cowboy?"

"Never a cowboy." His voice was dark and hard.

"Your dad's a cowboy," Miranda said cheerfully, her voice a bit tinged with awe. "He was one of the best saddleless bucking bronc riders there ever was on the Montana rodeo circuit. I remember as a kid watching him ride. And he used to…"

"I always wanted to be a surgeon," Witt said. "I like to fix things. Not break them."

Chapter Four

ROUTINE.

That's what he needed, a routine. Keep his mind centered. Focused. His body healthy. Instead of the dreamed miles running along California oceanfront and weekend sprints on trails in the San Gabriel Mountains, he was logging fast miles on the hotel's treadmill and elliptical machines. Then he lifted some weights to keep his bones and muscles strong.

He wasn't nervous about his first official day at Marietta's hospital. He was more unsettled about last night. Sharing dinner with Miranda in her boutique. What the hell? What impulse had driven him to open his mouth? He'd felt almost like he was under a spell wanting to leave even as he wanted to stay. He'd felt almost like he was somebody else—not quite fitting in his skin the same way. She was so warm and friendly. So open. Saying anything that popped into her head. So different from anyone he'd ever met.

He hadn't known what to do with himself. He'd felt on the verge of…what? Something. All night.

He'd wanted to scarf down his dinner like he'd been in high school again, gulping dinner after practice and bolting upstairs to do his homework. But Miranda had savored each bite. She'd seemed to have so many stories about people in Marietta including the new owner of the diner, Gabriella Marcos. But she'd also been so interested in him—why he became an orthopedic surgeon instead of another kind of doctor, why he'd chosen the residency in Houston instead of Portland, how he'd gotten interested in wine, what he liked about running.

He hadn't talked so much in one evening ever. Sure he'd dated casually in college and residency, but not a lot. He'd been focused on his goals. He hadn't wanted to get close to anyone and had been content to let the few women he had dated do most of the talking. But Miranda had made short answers impossible. She'd built on his answers and asked more questions. She'd made him think. And laugh. Her stories and questions had been earnest or funny and her warm gaze had glowed in the candlelight. He felt like she'd really been listening, absorbing everything he said until he had seeped into her bones, or if he were more fanciful like his stepmother, her soul. Or his.

And her eyes. They did something to him. They were so warm and deep and dark at times it was like night swimming, fully immersed, free, safe.

Safe. Where the hell had that word come from? Whitman straightened up from his last lunge and squat sequence and put the fifteen-pound medicine ball back on the rack and quickly wiped it down. He checked his watch. Eighty-five minutes exactly. Five minutes to stretch to cool down. Routine. This would be his for the next month. He'd shower, grab an egg white breakfast sandwich and coffee, and hit the hospital well before his rounds with Wyatt started.

He bent into his first runner's stretch when the gym door opened and a huge man came in with what looked like a large cylindrical punching bag like the kind boxers used. Hard, massive body. Hard face. Gold eyes skimmed Whitman as he paused in his stretch.

"Colt?" The name popped out of his mouth even as he'd been regretting how much conversation he'd engaged in last night. He should be worded out for the next six months, but no, apparently he wasn't.

"Witt." Colt shifted the bag like it was a sack of groceries even though it looked like it should weigh something that would likely even have him groaning though he always hit the gym or went running at least five to six days a week.

He shook Witt's hand. Damn. Colt had been fit in high school. He'd been a football player and humiliatingly fast on the track as well, far out-fasting any school record Whitman had hoped to set, but Colt had been more rangy, wiry. Now he was solid muscle. And taller.

"How's Parker?"

"Pleased with his cast. He has signatures from fourteen girls and counting."

And then they just stood there. Facing each other. Strangers who felt like they shouldn't be.

"Still surprised to see you back in town." They spoke at the same time. Then stopped. Stared. Witt shifted, looked at the large boxing bag. Then back at Colt. Witt should have been able to laugh at their awkward silence. Miranda would have known what to say. Colt had been his academic rival. In all of his AP and honors classes. The only one who could best him on a test, and it had made him worker harder, study longer because Colt had made everything look so easy.

"You joined the Army." Witt finally spoke as it seemed Colt was still as quiet as he'd been in high school. Whitman had been stunned to hear that news years ago. Colt hadn't seemed soldier material. Whitman had figured he'd go to college. Become an engineer or something. "You out now? Working here?"

"No. Thought I was out. But I'm a training instructor one week every couple of months at an Army training facility in Texas. Also doing some construction work with Big Z's and a pole barn builder and also have a side project keeping me busy."

Witt nodded. That sounded good. But random and didn't fit with the image of what he'd thought Colt would do. Not that he'd known Colt other than as another silent teenager who'd kicked his ass on the track and threatened to kick it on every paper and test. Of all the people to leave Marietta, Whitman would have thought Colt would have been least likely to come back, but then, he would have said the same about himself.

Colt pulled a step stool out of a closet and a drill out of a tool belt slung low on his hips and fished a large metal hook out of his pocket and stuck it between his teeth as he climbed up the few steps to reach a beam in the ceiling.

"Need help?"

"I'm good."

"You back here for good?" Whitman asked, resuming his

stretches.

Colt drilled in the hook then re-holstered the drill with ease that made Whitman think Colt was used to using power tools and was probably considered good with his hands. He immediately thought *what a waste of a mind*—in his grandmother's voice—but then realized, he too used power tools and rebuilt and repaired things. Just got paid more. And had had to study a hell of a lot more to do it.

"Looks like." Colt lifted the bag and attached the three chains to the hook. He judged the height of the bag. Climbed back up and raised it two links. "My wife's studying to be a large-animal vet. Finishes last three years at Washington State. Might move with."

Colt was the one person Whitman had met who spoke more economically than he did, except for last night. Pullman, Washington, was probably as isolated as Marietta but it was a college town.

"She'd likely have her pick of towns," Whitman said. "Blow out of here once and for all."

Colt didn't answer. Might have shrugged but the movement was fluid and subtle. He pulled a pair of boxing gloves out of a backpack he had slung over one shoulder.

"Give it a try." He jerked his head toward the pristine and massive bag and held out a pair of bright blue boxing gloves. Wasn't phrased as a question. His expression gave nothing away, but Whitman felt the dare to his bones, just like he'd felt it all those years ago when a teacher would hand out a test or a project and he'd look at Colt the exact minute he'd look at him. That same coppery intense stare that had read him and his ambition and his fear like a book.

"No." Whitman took a step back. "I can't do that. You know I'm a surgeon."

Colt's head jerked a little as if he were agreeing, but his glittering gold eyes unnerved him a little as if thinking he was a wimp. Whitman straightened from his stretch casually and stomped down the need to rip the gloves dangling in Colt's large hands and wail on the bag. What would that be like, to give in to impulse? To let something inside him loose? To show off a little?

Dangerous.

He had a career and a plan and sticking around Marietta doing odd jobs or whatever Colt was doing with his life was so far out of his career lane, he couldn't see the white lines defining it.

"That's why I brought gloves." Colt's face was expressionless. "Or you can kick it. Good for getting out aggression and other…" His voice, soft and low, broke off leaving the rest unsaid, and Whitman felt like Colt was accusing him of something as he shrugged his massive shoulders negligently. "Unless you operate with your toes."

Definitely a challenge.

"You sell exercise equipment as well?" The second he said it, the second he heard his tone, he wanted to kick himself, not the bag. Now he was his grandmother, mother and grandfather all rolled into one mean, ugly and unsociable package.

"No. Donating it to the hotel gym along with gloves if any guests want to slay any personal demons." Colt fished smaller hooks out of his mouth and drilled them into the walls where he hung a few different sizes of pairs of boxing gloves.

Whitman felt compelled to say something, but what? He'd never been good at the social part and hadn't really tried. His life had been about pursuing excellence. Achieving his goals. Challenging his mind to dig deeper, solve unsolvable problems. He hadn't turned his focus to making friends. He figured he'd do that once he was settled in a top hospital and building his career. And why was he bothering this morning anyway? He likely wouldn't see Colt again unless he was bringing his son back to get his fracture checked out. They hadn't been friends. He wasn't going to be in Marietta long enough to make friends.

Colt finished just as Whitman finished his stretches. Not really wanting to walk out with him, he refilled his water bottle as Colt cleaned up the drywall shavings.

"See you," Whitman said stiffly, pulling on the handle of the door, and when Colt looked up from his crouch on the floor, his hands palming a few speckles of white, Whitman wished again he'd kept his mouth shut. Colt rose up and brushed the shavings into the trash.

"Maybe. You're still a self-righteous dick, Witt, but then…" what might have passed as a shadow of a smile touched his hard mouth "…some days so am I."

FIFTEEN MINUTES LATER, Witt had showered, dressed and,

shrugging into his wool overcoat, he took the stairs two at a time down to the lobby as he called in his mobile order to the Java Café. He paused in the lobby, not sure which exit would be more anonymous. The back way out—more convenient to the hospital—now felt like a hazard, but surely Miranda wouldn't be in her shop at…he looked at his watch…six a.m.

Bob at the front desk waved and smiled at him. Whitman, feeling obvious and foolish, nodded back then turned on his heel and strode down the wide hallway. He would not look to the left at Miranda's shop. He would not look at the painstakingly careful copper-colored lettering proclaiming the small space 'Found Objects.' Instead he pulled out his phone, but light caught his eye as well as movement, and Whitman couldn't help the sideways glance through the wall of glass. Miranda was sticking—piece by piece—lurid pink branches from that cursed tree last night into that large, thick, polished branch she'd been drilling holes in last night.

His stomach lurched almost as if it needed Pepto-Bismol and his eyes hurt with all that flash of color. How did she not go blind from all that pink? Just as he forced himself to keep moving and not to get caught rubbernecking as if watching an accident, Miranda looked up. Her smile was quick and huge, her eyes sparkled, and holding one of the scraggly pink branches she waved at him.

Witt kept walking.

This town.

Like a David Lynch movie. First Colt with the bag and Miranda with whatever the pink abomination was. And though he couldn't see her, the small crooked tilt to her lips that were moving, made him think she'd been singing. He slapped open the door needing air. A lot of air.

Less than ten minutes later he was slogging through snow flurries, his egg, spinach and tomato breakfast panini wrapped in tinfoil and tucked deep in his pocket while he palmed his ginormous coffee and hurried to the hospital. From now on he was going to make his own breakfast and coffee in his room. As soon as he could shed his gloves he'd do an Amazon Prime spree. Walking in Montana winter morning was dumb. No idea why he thought it would clear his head. Instead his brain felt frozen. Obviously he still had California on his mind.

"Who wouldn't?" he demanded under his breath as he pulled out his name tag and swiped in at the hospital staff door.

"Whitman." The voice was quick, a little desperate and even after so many years away, familiar.

He paused, door open. He had an impulse to run. Let the door shut behind him. Like he was twelve all over again and wishing himself far, far, far away.

"Sarah." He let the door go. Felt the click in his gut as he turned toward his stepmother. Excuses as to why he hadn't called appeared in his consciousness, but he discarded them. He should have called. He hadn't. And there wasn't a viable excuse. He couldn't explain it, and didn't try. And he didn't know what was expected of him. It was awful having all the right answers in one area of his life, but none in the area that seemed so important to everyone else.

Stick to medicine. Stick to science.

She hurried across the icy employee parking lot. She was bundled for the weather. Her face looked pale, tense.

"Sarah." He felt a thump of concern. "What's wrong?"

As if twelve years hadn't passed with just birthday and Christmas cards and stilted, reluctant, and guilt-ridden phone calls. He did better with strangers, although Sarah had tried to welcome him—this awkward, quiet, grieving kid who hadn't been hers and didn't want to try to fit in. He'd rebuffed almost all of her efforts.

"Ahhhh." She stopped short and swallowed. She wore a blue knit cap that made the blue of her eyes vivid against her pale skin. Her blonde hair was in a thick side braid nearly to her waist. She'd been a rodeo queen and still, in her mid-forties, Sarah Telford was a very beautiful woman. But scared. And tense.

Whitman walked down the few steps toward her. His practiced doctor eye noted her extreme pallor, dark circles like bruises under her eyes that were slightly red and puffy, and the way her gloved hands moved restlessly at her sides. He might have selfishly wished to delay this reunion, but she'd come to him, and it hadn't been to warmly invite him to stay with them out at the ranch.

"What is it? What's wrong?"

Was that even his voice? It broke a little. Sounded under water.

"Your father, Taryn," she added, and Whitman winced even as he felt as if his heart stuttered and then sped up. He reached back for the railing for the stairs that led to the medical staff door. The brief flash of him hurtling the railing, rushing to work even though he didn't start for an hour, shamed him. He mentally shook himself. He was a doctor. He was accustomed to bad news. Gave it often.

Grow a pair. He wasn't twelve anymore facing his father for the first time. Bewildered. Alone. Stunned by grief. Furious. His life and his emotions unrecognizable.

Not dead. Someone would have told him. But no, everyone just kept asking if he was staying out at the ranch and wasn't that wonderful for his family.

His family.

"Sarah." He took another step toward her, and without thinking he put his hands on her shoulders. Tears swam in her eyes and then she threw her hands around his neck and burst into tears. Not the silent type. Noisy, wounded animal tears. He wrapped her in his arms, and could feel deep trembling. Her or him?

He remembered crying like that. Not after a police officer had arrived at his school to tell him his mother had been hit by a speeding cyclist and knocked down causing brain trauma. But weeks later. Alone. In the double bed of the small bedroom Sarah had tried to decorate for him even though he'd refused to tell her anything he liked including colors.

"I just…I feel so guilty…but I think it's the…best for now."

She made no sense.

"Tell me," he said, feeling his heart race, but he kept his voice doctor calm.

"What's wrong? What are you doing to her?" Whitman looked over Sarah's shoulder, even as she gulped her tears to a stop and dashed her hands over her face again and again. A girl stood there. Tall. Thin as a pole. Black hair dead straight under her white beret. Eyes squinted in suspicion. Whitman had no idea of her age, but she looked about ten. She glared at him. Whitman felt sideswiped. True he didn't do great at keeping in touch but surely they would have let him know if they'd had another kid.

"It's okay, Petal. This is your cousin, Witt. The one who…" She broke off with a wince. "Wait in the car sweetie, then we'll go for a hot chocolate before I take you to school."

She crossed her arms. "No."

But no to which part of the suggestion, Whitman had no idea.

"Tween girls," Sarah whispered softly. "I don't…I'm not sure…" She looked at him helplessly. Whitman was reminded of a case his first year of residency—a top high school athlete, a horrible injury, the boy and his parents and his coach all looking at him for answers, and he hadn't had the ones any of them wanted.

The tension in his gut that had transferred to his shoulders crept up his neck. Sarah was an only child. He knew that because she'd wanted a lot of children. She'd told him that when he'd unwillingly come to live with them. She'd smiled like she really meant it. And now it looked like she might have another stray. He knew his biological dad had another brother. But he'd rarely come around and when he had, his biological father would take his brother out to the barn, and then his "uncle" would leave not too much later looking smug. Whitman had always had the idea that he wasn't welcome.

"Sarah, it's cold out here. Let's go inside to the hospital lobby. You can tell me there and..." He gestured toward the girl who was still doing a pretty good cross between a scowl and a glare. He felt jacked with tension because Sarah had a story to tell and not a quick one because the stress rolled off her in waves. It hit him like a body blow. The words she'd managed to squeeze out, 'your father,' still echoed.

"Sorry. No time. I have to catch a flight. Denver. Last seat left. I have to go."

The choppy sentences were like slaps and heightened his alarm.

"Come again?"

"Sorry, Witt. I am. Your father's in Denver. He, ah...he was injured at a stock auction and air flighted to Denver, but they found a...um..." She dug a piece of paper out of her pocket and handed it to him.

"Abdominal aneurysm," he read.

Was that his voice so calm? So clinical? Who was he? What the hell was wrong with him?

"It's unrelated to his injury, and the doctor...ah...I can't remember her name. It's on the paper. She said the injury probably saved his life, but they are operating today, and I want to be there."

"Of course," he said woodenly. Too many things hitting him at once. He didn't even bother to sort them. He preferred not to do feelings. But he did note she looked guilty.

And that did not compute.

"Of course you have to go," he reiterated. "Do you want me to call the surgeon?" And he realized how stupid that sounded. Was he going to worm some secret procedure out of him as a professional courtesy? "Do you want me to go with you?" How would he manage that? Today was his first official start day. Denver couldn't be on his agenda. But it was a family emergency. And he imagined Wyatt, who had siblings, would tell him to go. He'd probably drive him to the airport if he could get away. But she'd said she had the last seat.

"I can talk to Wyatt. See if I can…"

"No. You know your dad doesn't like fuss." Her lips curved a little in a half smile even as they trembled, and her eyes shone, but the worry clouded in again. "I could have lost him," she whispered turning her face up to look at him.

Whitman took an involuntary step back when faced with her intense fear and grief, but overlaying all of that was an intense love that staggered him. Sarah loved his father. Loved him still after twenty-six or twenty-seven years of marriage and a hard life of being a rancher's wife and raising four kids, one who hadn't even been hers.

He sucked in a breath. He'd always seen Sarah through the angry, hurt eyes of a grieving and resentful child and adolescent. Now he was an adult, and he could see how difficult he'd made it for her. For his biological father. Purposely.

Witt felt ice cold to the tips of his toes and with his sheepskin-lined gloves that were supposed to protect his hands well below freezing, he felt numb. He hated Montana. He hated winter. He hated being blindsided by emotions and memories he didn't know what to do with. And now this. His father, the cowboy, injured and facing a massive operation.

"I need you to…" She looked behind her at the girl, arms still crossed, face still smushed in a scowl, as she kicked at the iced layer beneath the dusting of fresh powder. She smiled sadly and bit her lip. "Take care of Petal while I'm gone. I'm hoping after the surgery Riley can come back and help you. She met Riley once."

She continued to talk, but Whitman couldn't hear anything over the phrase 'take care of…' looped over and over again.

"You look a bit done in." Sarah, touched his arm. "I am sorry, Witt. I know it's a lot but Reese only dropped her off last weekend. He's off the grid. Said her mom…you know…" Sarah's voice dropped to a whisper, but no, Whitman didn't know.

"She's missed so much school. She's had no consistency. And now this." Sarah's voice broke. "I'm sorry. So sorry, but I don't know what to do? I don't know how bad Taryn is. What will happen? How long I'll be in Denver."

She gulped in a breath and her gloved hands clutched his forearms through his coat.

"I need to get to Taryn, and tomorrow's flight's booked full as well, and she needs school. Needs to make friends. We're applying for custody. She needs normal. She needs normal so badly, and I just can't right now. I can't."

Her words kept coming in that soft little rush of confession, her agony and sorrow beat around them like wings, but Whitman felt his jaw drop. How could Sarah think he could provide anything remotely related to normal? He opened his mouth to tell her something like he knew nothing about kids except their orthopedic needs. He was living out of a suitcase in a hotel suite. He was a doctor working long hours and Petal…what kind of name was that? But Petal didn't know him. He wasn't anyone's answer to a family problem.

"Sarah?"

"I know, Witt." She laid her gloved hand on his chest and smoothed down him a couple of times. "It seems like a lot to ask, but we are family. And family is family, even when they are apart." She touched her heart and then his sternum where he could feel his heart still galloping—his dad injured. What? How bad? Aneurysm. How large? Being responsible for a child he didn't know. For how long?

"She needs family, and I need to be with Taryn. Boone is flying out. Rohan's on a deployment. I can't reach him. Riley's flying to Denver tonight."

It was all arranged. Except for him. No one thought he should be there or want to be there. He was still on the outside. But that's what he'd always wanted. He kept himself there. But he didn't know what to do with his hands. His feet. He wanted to go for a run. Keep running. Wasn't sure what to do with everything banging around inside of him.

"We'll call you after the surgery. He'll need two. One for the aneurysm…" she hesitated over the word "…and another to put some pins in his femur."

"I want to see the X-ray," Witt said without thinking.

"Of course." Sarah nodded. "I'd like that. Taryn will want you to. He's so proud of you. His first born."

Witt winced.

"I'm not sure about the recovery time," Sarah shook her head as if to shake her musing out of there for good. "Our foreman can manage the ranch. He's called his son who buckled in the Montana Pro Rodeo finals to help during his break so we are covered at the ranch." She bit her lip. "We should only be gone a week, maybe two depending on how quickly Taryn can get mobile. He's stubborn so likely faster than he should." She held up her gloved hands. "Fingers crossed," she whispered.

"Sarah, I can come with you," he said, hating the idea of it, even as he knew he had to.

"No. No. You have your life here. He'll be pleased you're back and working local. I know he hoped for it, though he never would admit it. Stubborn like you. Wanting you to have choices since you didn't as a child."

Jesus, Sarah knew how to poke him with a stick without even trying.

He opened his mouth to correct her. Everyone seemed to misunderstand the situation, what a temporary placement—a stop gap was. He wasn't staying. "It will probably get him out of the hospital bed that much faster."

Whitman closed his mouth.

"Her name is Petal. She's in fourth grade. She's wicked smart like you were. She has walls too like you did."

Do.

Sarah smiled as if that had been a good thing.

"But I…" He broke off as Sarah's blue eyes met his.

He'd been a jerk as a kid. He realized that now. Oh, he'd had his reasons, his excuses. Righteously valid at the time, but looking at his preteen and teen self from the stage of thirty, he'd been a sullen, resentful, and ungrateful jerk.

Whitman stood in the hospital staff parking lot and felt like the icy wind blowing off Copper Mountain was sheering through his soul. He looked down at his loafers. Even his footwear looked pretentious and out of place. Wrong. Out of place like he'd always been in Marietta. And he was supposed to take care of a kid.

"I know it seems like a lot to ask," Sarah said nervously. "But Petal needs to be in school. She needs some stability. I don't know how it will go with Taryn, I don't know…" Her voice broke off, and Witt felt like he'd been pushed off a cliff.

Sarah had never asked anything of him except that he do basic chores around the house and the ranch as the "oldest brother." She'd given him equal rank with his two younger brothers and sister, and had never treated him differently than her biological children, and he'd given her nothing but stony silence, internal criticism and monosyllabic answers as he buried his head in book after book.

"Okay," he heard himself say and continued to feel like he was in free fall.

Chapter Five

"I CAN'T HAVE a latte? What kind of rule is that? Hot chocolate is for kids."

No to the latte was only the second thing he'd said—after nervously introducing himself, or more accurately letting Sarah do it and him muttering 'hi' accompanied by a no doubt lame smile—and Petal was in full-blown scornful and very public mutiny at the Java Café.

"You can't be serious about hot chocolate. That's what I was going to get. Hey Witt." Miranda nudged him from behind in line, and he staggered a bit. For such a little thing she had some power. "Who's your friend?"

Miranda had already peeled off her gloves and she stuck out all ten fingers and waved them. "I'm Miranda. Do you know the dragon handshake?"

"No?" Petal's tone had changed slightly to add curiosity wafting through her deep skepticism.

"Love it." Miranda grinned. "My first convert. Okay. First our wing tilt." Hands on her hips, elbows out she shifted her weight left and right. Petal slowly followed suit. "Then the good morning or evening cross greet." Miranda stuck her arms out to the sides and then swung them in front of her fingers splayed and crossed one and wiggled her fingers against Petal's when she copied and then the other. "Now my favorite part. The 'today is going to be a fabulous day' twirl." Linked fingers Petal and Miranda turned in a circle. "Now we greet the sky and 'make it so,' oops." Miranda grinned when the back of her hand brushed Whitman's mouth and nose as she flung her waving hands up in the air. "And if it's a special greeting like meeting a new dragon, then I do the happy to meet you dance with my arms up." Miranda did what looked a little like a truncated Irish jig.

"You don't really do that," Petal said, putting her arms back down to her sides.

"I just did."

Petal scrunched her face, not quite sure what to make of Miranda, and Whitman couldn't fault her there. But Petal didn't seem as outraged, which was good because he had to get her to the school so he could get back to work. As it was, he'd be cutting it tight so he was going to text Wyatt and give him a heads-up although it killed him to have to do so. Whitman took study and work seriously. Very seriously. To be late meant there was an unavoidable crisis, and even though his biological father's injury and aneurysm and surgery definitely qualified, it still burned his conscience. He felt like he was failing Wyatt and the hospital. Showing weakness. A casual disregard for patients and a lacking work ethic.

"You do know there weren't really dragons, don't you?" Petal's scorn was back. "I saw a mock-doc online on the possibility a couple of years ago. They even covered the part about the minerals they'd need to ingest to make fire and how with heat or less heat they could kill or change the sex of the developing embryos, but still highly unlikely."

Petal had a 'that's that' tone to her voice that made Whitman want to laugh as much as it made him cringe. She sounded rude, which he should probably say something about, but she also reminded him of how he'd felt when he'd arrived in a new living situation when he'd been just a few years older than Petal and had been unwillingly dumped on his "family"—a group of people who had a history whereas he had none.

"You might have to tell the dragons in my shop that they are not real."

"Dragons? Like toys?"

"Shhh! Don't let them hear you say that. Art, but I think...I feel that if I do something special, a little ritual for each one that..." Miranda broke off dramatically and whispered something in Petal's ear.

Her face lit up. "Like the Dragon Greeting?"

"Yes. But something beautiful and tangible to add to the dragons to show everyone how special they are." Miranda's look was far off. "Unique." She looked at Petal speculatively just as their turn came to order at the Java Café's espresso counter. "Maybe you can help me think of something. You and I can make a soul quest if Witt agrees."

"What's a...?"

"My treat." Miranda cut in front of him and waved away his wallet. She ordered after checking with him and Petal and he took out his wallet anyway because he'd given his undrunk and very hot Americano and breakfast sandwich to Sarah after she had again declined to let him at least drive her to the airport. Miranda waved off his wallet again and grinned cheekily at him.

He'd have to find a way to repay her. She couldn't make much money with her store barely open and having worked mostly part-time retail since high school judging from the stream-of-conscious conversation she'd released yesterday and last night. Not that he made a lot during residency, but it was an income, and his undergraduate scholarship and mother's legacy had allowed him to attend medical school without incurring massive debt.

"A soul quest," Miranda said when she handed Petal her hot chocolate after ordering her own and tapping her cup with Petal's and then his. "Is when we ask ourselves an important question, think about it, confer, and then wait for the answer. So," Miranda said as they all got their order. "What's next on the agenda, Doctor?"

LOST. WITT LOOKED lost. And so did Petal. Miranda had no idea what was up, but her heart squeezed with the need to make it better for everyone. The young girl looked like a turtle lugging a backpack larger than herself. She also had a suitcase that she wheeled behind her.

"Are you taking a trip?" Miranda asked chirpily.

Petal shrugged. "This is my life," she said indicating the suitcase.

Miranda's heart plummeted. Witt, about to sip his coffee, froze. Miranda, always on the imaginative side could imagine so many scenarios that could fit Petal's situation, but not one of them was good. As much as she'd been the oddball in her family, she'd always had a home and security and care. And with her grandparents she'd had unconditional love and she'd been needed. Important.

Witt was taking a deep gulp of coffee, likely stalling. Miranda looked at Petal and then at Witt. She didn't have the story, but he must need to get to Marietta Regional Hospital. And Petal might have school, unless she was on vacation or…any question that formed on her tongue made her feel nosy. She didn't want him to think she was trying to follow in the footsteps of Carol Bingley—local busybody.

"Can you show me your dragons?" Petal's voice was small and hopeful but littered with doubt as Miranda spun lots of cheerful things to say in the face of Witt's silence.

"I'd love to," Miranda said shooting a look at Witt, who glanced at his watch. "If that works with your schedule?"

She was really flying blind here. Who was Petal? Why was she here? Because she hadn't been with him yesterday and they seemed wary of each other. Black hair dead straight and silky. Tall for her age. Awkward and thin. Pale. None of Witt's healthy lightly muscular glow. Where did she come from? Judging from the backpack and the rolling bag, she'd recently been thrust upon him.

Impossible. Totally unWittlike. He was too focused and determined to have an oops of that magnitude. And if he had gotten a woman pregnant in college, he would have married her, or at least kept in touch with his child. And Miranda couldn't imagine a woman born who would ever give up all that earnest, mouthwatering yum. If she had a chance with him, she'd wrap herself so tightly around his heart, she'd put a boa constrictor out of business.

"My shop is just over there." She pointed to the Graff Hotel. "There's a bit of a secret back entrance. Your…Witt discovered the secret entrance easily, but not too many other people know about it. My shop is just down a hallway, a little hidden away, but I'm putting up lots of lights—red for Valentine's Day this month because day after tomorrow is the big day."

"What big day?" Petal asked falling into step with Miranda as they traversed the snowy blocks back toward the Graff. The sidewalks weren't as clear on Front Avenue as they were on Main, and Miranda made a note to do something about that. Witt followed behind them. A silent, coffee-drinking shadow.

"Grand opening of my shop, and yes it will be ready, well mostly ready. I am receiving more stock from local merchants today, and Colt—a friend of mine—is bringing me a few more pieces of reclaimed lumber from one of his job sites to make shelves. And…" Miranda made her voice dramatic "…I have a secret and stealthy plan that I am implementing around town today. Maybe right around the end of school time." She looked at Petal as she said this, because the child looked so fascinated and no one had ever looked fascinated by anything she had planned or said. "But it will be hard to do on my own."

"Do you need help?" Petal asked quickly.

"I do, but…" She turned around to look at Witt, who clearly hadn't been looking at her because he collided into her. Miranda fell backward with a squeak of dismay, already wincing in fear of jarring her still very painful tailbone again.

Only she didn't. Witt caught her around her waist and pulled her back upright so she was nearly flush with his chest. For a moment it was hard to breathe because even though they were both bundled up, the contact shot a thrill through her entire body. She looked up at his face. Wow, oh wow, he was so casually and carefully and effortlessly handsome even though he always looked so deadly serious.

"You're pretty quick on your feet," she said feeling a little like she was drowning in the blue of his eyes.

She was probably looking stupid. Googly-eyed. And he'd worry she was crushing. Well, she was crushing. Had been crushing since he'd arrived all dark and brooding and keeping himself apart since middle school. But she knew better than to do more than wish and hope and dream. No, Witt was her secret crush and she'd leave it that way. If she didn't, he'd start avoiding her so she took her own step back—away from all that tempting masculine warmth. And her chest felt hot and ached in protest, as if she'd ripped herself away, and was now bleeding. Melodramatic and immature. Miranda knew that. So Miranda did what she did best. Pasted on a smile. And said something. Anything to break the tension and want and wishful thinking that crawled through her body and her brain.

"And neither of us dropped our coffee. To the dragons."

WHITMAN DROPPED OFF Petal's suitcase in his room and quickly re-hung his suits and shirts in his garment bag and repacked his suitcase and took the stairs down fast. He had no idea what time the elementary school started, but he knew it was walkable from here. He still had no idea how this was going to work, but he would need to get Petal a room key, and maybe they'd need a larger suite. He saw Bob at the front desk engaged in an animated discussion with another front desk clerk, Cathi. He dreaded talking to them, explaining, knowing behind their friendly personas they were probably thinking or judging or wondering. It was human nature. Something else to love about big cities and megalopolises. Anonymity.

He squared his shoulders and stuffed back his natural shyness. Forced himself to the front desk and made his request for a suite with two bedrooms with en-suite bathrooms. It also had a sleeper sofa although why Bob felt the need to add that information, Whitman couldn't guess. He wasn't going to make the habit of collecting unknown cousins.

Now all he had to do was get Petal to school and himself to the hospital. It still seemed surreal—all of it. A rural hospital. Marietta. A cousin—an unexpected and inconvenient arrival just as he had been. His stomach felt weird, twisted, no longer hungry.

Whitman held Petal's key in his hand and hoped she was the responsible sort as she'd have to let herself in the room and order room service when she was hungry. He'd stayed on his own when he was far younger, but maybe things were different with children today. Sarah had mentioned after-school care and activities at some place called Harry's House.

Then there was the school. Would she have homework in fourth grade? Was she responsible enough to do it? All the kids he saw now were on their phones. Did she have a cell? What time was school out? Could he trust her to get back to the hotel on her own? Marietta was small, but not impossible to get lost in for a kid unfamiliar with the town. And would he be at fault? Of course he would! His stepmom had left him in charge. Of a child. How the hell was he supposed to work when he'd be worried about her? He didn't know her. She could be doing anything—playing by the iced-over river and the ice would crack, and she wouldn't realize the danger. Or she could be pouting, not realize the danger the cold could present. Or she might steal something from an art store and run away into the street and…

Each image just got more horrifying. He knew nothing about her—where she was from, her experiences, behavior. The questions and concerns snowballed and Whitman was nearly running across the lobby by the time he arrived back at Miranda's store.

"It's Sculpty clay." Miranda had something in the palm of her hand that she and Petal had their heads bent over. "I like it because it's so flexible and colorful and it really sticks together and then when I bake it, it gets pretty hard without losing the vibrancy."

Petal stared transfixed. "Can I touch it?"

"Sure." Miranda handed over the creature.

"Look, Witt." Petal walked over, holding something blue in the palm of her hand. "Miranda really does have dragons here. She makes them. And they even have hearts and wings."

The heart looked like a small glass heart-shaped bead with swirling colors and the wings were stiff ribbon. It was a blue dragon, about three inches long and curled up a little, wedge-shaped head resting on block feet. Petal stroked the dragon's head and down its spiny back.

"Miranda is going to sell them in her store. She's an artist."

"Oh, no I'm not an artist," Miranda said quickly. "I am going to carry the work of local artists and other Montana artists."

Both Petal and he looked at Miranda, and he nearly laughed because the oval beveled mirror behind Miranda's sleek ash-brown bobbed head reflected their nearly identical expressions—thick dark brows slanted down, dark blue eyes skeptical and their mouths twisted down. Damn genetics were hard to ignore. And he felt like his heart skipped a beat. Petal was his biological uncle's pawned-off daughter. Just like his father had pawned him off, only to get him thrust back into his life again. No viable alternatives. Whitman knew little of his uncle except he hadn't made it in the rodeo circuit like his older brother, and he'd been dishonorably discharged from the military. Reese Telford had, to Whitman's knowledge, never found a job he could keep.

Poor girl.

Not her fault but the long legacy of her parents' failures trailed after her.

"I make the dragons for fun." Miranda cheerfully broke into his gloomy thoughts. "I drop them off at the kids' ward in the hospital. I'm not selling them. I just thought…what?" She trailed off—maybe because he and Petal were giving her the same look again.

"You made these. You're an artist," Whitman told her, his voice indicating the possibility that she was a few IQ points short of normal. "And you could also sell them. Kids come to the Graff. Lots of families." He'd learned that from Bob who'd insisted he could bring a roll-out bed for Petal instead of a sleeper sofa or upgrading to a two-bedroom suite. Still, craving space and privacy, Whitman had chosen the two-bedroom suite.

"You could make families of dragons, little baby ones too, and then make a little habitat for them and write a little story for each one." Petal's eyes shone and her pale, thin face lit up.

"You're hired," Miranda said.

WHITMAN BUTTONED UP his overcoat and stepped out of the hospital.

"Sub-zero," Wyatt said next to him. "Makes you feel alive."

"Makes me feel like my balls are going to freeze off."

"There's that." Wyatt laughed and tilted his head back

and actually stuck out his tongue to catch a snowflake. "Maybe you should have Miranda help you with that."

"Miranda," Whitman echoed in disbelief. He'd been looking across the road and railroad tracks at the Graff Hotel practically a stone's throw away. He'd been thinking that he definitely couldn't beat the commute and that call would be ridiculously convenient if it weren't so damn cold. Now he turned to Wyatt determined to shut any speculation down. He was not in Marietta to hook up with anyone, especially not a sweet, unsophisticated woman like Miranda who held her heart out in her hand practically daring a man to take it and smash it.

He couldn't live with himself if he did that to her. He chose career-obsessed women like himself who just wanted to burn off some sexual energy a few times before digging back into the books or the hours at work or climb a few more rungs on the ladder.

"What's wrong with Miranda?"

"Nothing."

"Saw you two in the Java Café this morning and you had a kid and were talking up a storm."

"Miranda was talking." Whitman stirred a little, uncomfortable with the idea that anyone was noticing him talking to Miranda and starting a rumor based on that. And he didn't want to explain about Petal yet. "I was listening."

"She's like that. Chatty. Involved in the community. She took care of her grandparents for years. Lived with them. Her older brothers are arrogant pricks," Wyatt said cheerfully. "And her older sister was an ice queen. She could deep freeze a volcano. None of them stayed local. One's in Seattle with a huge software company that he just sold for billions or whatever. The other's a partner in a huge law firm in California but owns some boutique winery or whatever, and the sister is a professor at an Ivy, I think. I pity the grad students who have to cozy up to her. Brrrrr. I think they took all the ambition and left all the nice to Miranda."

"Don't want a sales pitch." Whitman felt the need to interrupt Wyatt who could talk nearly as much as Miranda at times.

"Not my product to sell," Wyatt said easily. "Just saying."

"Don't," Whitman said, but Wyatt just grinned.

"Nothing's between us. I'm staying at the Graff. Miranda's opening a shop there so she shouts out a hello as I go past. That's it."

"Yeah." Wyatt looked skeptical. Then he smiled again. Damn he was cheerful. "That's how it starts. Next thing you know. Flat on your ass. Goofy expression. Doing stupid things."

"Unlikely," Whitman said coldly. He preferred tall, athletic, sophisticated, ambitious and highly educated women who wanted short-term. "Thanks for the assist today in surgery."

Wyatt made a rude noise. "I witnessed a thing of beauty but didn't lift a finger."

That wasn't exactly true but still Whitman smiled. He'd had another good day. Three surgeries. One very complicated from a traffic accident. The ER staff had considered Life

Flighting the patient out, but Whitman and Wyatt had felt they and the team could handle the case. He and Wyatt had made a good team, and Witt had been impressed with the surgical staff. He'd also loved how he'd been able to do a surgery that in a larger hospital would have gone to a specialist—like he would be someday. It felt good to stretch and build his skills.

"We're small, but we're top shelf," Wyatt said proudly.

Whitman had already conceded that his time here wouldn't be wasted, and a smaller hospital with less hierarchy and posturing would allow him to take cases that he wouldn't normally get to be lead surgeon on.

"Kinda like Miranda," Wyatt added.

Whitman shocked himself by flipping Wyatt off. He would never have done that anywhere else, especially as Wyatt was his supervisor. Marietta was rubbing off on him and not in a good way, but Wyatt just laughed.

"Calling it like I see it." Wyatt jammed his hands in his pockets and walked toward his car. Then he stopped and turned around. "Want to grab a beer at Grey's?"

It had appeal. He would love to discuss the cases today. Petal had walked over to the Graff after school to do something with Miranda. He'd never grabbed a lifeline so quickly when Miranda had offered Petal a place to come and "help" her get the store ready for its grand opening tomorrow. He'd said he'd be finished with work around six tonight, but it was just past four. He knew the value of networking. He hated doing it, but he did what was necessary. Wyatt would make it easy, and knowing Wyatt's family, it was likely his physician brothers and others would join them. He could practice for when he hit the big leagues next month.

"Yeah." He changed his mind. "I have time for a quick drink."

"I'll walk with you," Wyatt said. "And text my brothers to join us if their cases are finished. Getting done before it's dark is rare. I still see a bit of blue sky."

Barely. Whitman noticed the sky for the first time today. A few snowflakes were falling, but lazily, like they couldn't quite work up the energy to care. And slivers of orange and purple of the sunset slit through the dark gray to the west. He called Sarah and checked in. His father was still groggy from the anesthetic. Whitman had already talked to the surgeon. His half-sister Riley had arrived and insisted on getting on the phone and talking a mile a minute, but it was her sign-off request that threw him for a loop.

"Send pictures of you and Petal doing fun things."

He mumbled something but felt a little outraged. Fun. He was in Marietta to work. Not have fun. He should put Petal on a plane as his half-sister's enthusiastic response clearly meant Petal would have a friend. But days at a hospital bedside wouldn't be "fun" either. What would be fun for a nine-year-old girl? Besides, enthusiasm aside, his half-sister was finishing up college, and in a band that toured during the summers. She wouldn't be there for Petal. God, that name. He still couldn't wrap his head around it. Who named their kid that? He didn't even want to think about it.

"All's good?" Wyatt, gloveless, rubbed his hands together and blew on them as they walked toward Grey's Saloon, one of the oldest—if not the oldest—buildings in town. A saloon. Wild West. Brothel history. Figures.

Nothing was good, Whitman thought, but he supposed by Wyatt's standards—today's patients had done well. The new temporary surgeon was pulling his weight. Whitman's biological dad had survived the surgery for the aneurysm and was scheduled for another surgery in a couple of days to put a plate in his femur so it looked like Whitman wouldn't have to miss any work, and Wyatt's brothers had said hell yeah to the beer—it was good.

"I ALWAYS WANTED to fly." Petal ran down Main Street arms outstretched, the blue clay dragon curled around one finger. She jumped up and whooped. The stiff, blue-and-silver bow on the dragon's back fluttered a little with the speed. She jumped up reaching for the sky. Again and again.

Miranda pulled a slightly beat-up red wagon—one more thing to refurbish—watched her and smiled. Imagination. It was so precious. Petal slowed at the corner and then turned and ran back to Miranda, jumping up and down again as she ran, her black hair streaming behind her in the gray, golden light of the impending sunset like a cape. Joy lightened Miranda's heart and eased her tiredness and throbbing tailbone. She'd been working sixteen-hour days, sometimes longer getting her shop ready to open. Plus at least twice a day, she ran over to the care center to visit with her grandmother. Miranda still grieved that she and her grandmother had had to make that choice for her grandparents to leave their home. She missed the ranch and the dwindling livestock that she had started selling off. It had been her home for fourteen years. Her small apartment felt foreign.

Tears pricked her eyes. She felt so alone now even though she still saw them both every day. But there would come a day her grandfather wouldn't recognize her at all. It was starting to happen. The blank stare. Turning inward. No longer responding to her forcefully cheery comments and stories about her day. Even reminding him of things they'd done together didn't elicit the same engagement. He smiled vaguely, but Miranda felt he wasn't really listening.

Her grief was a heavy backpack weighing her down. She kept focusing on the positives—a fresh start, building a business of her own, having more social opportunities—but the feeling of failing her grandparents, of giving up when maybe she could have managed a little bit longer still hung heavy around her.

But she couldn't think like that. She had to keep her spirits up for her grandmother and for herself.

"Thank you for all the help today." Miranda dragged her thoughts to the present.

Petal took the handle of the red wagon and pulled it behind her at a much more sedate pace alongside Miranda. Even with the worn wood sides, the wagon was packed with products from a variety of local merchants and artisans. Her favorites were the recycled T-shirt skirts and scarves made by a young single mom, who had started a sewing club once a week at Harry's House, an after-school space for kids.

The house had opened last August, and already it was wildly popular with kids as it offered a variety of classes for kids of various ages and also a place to get help with homework. Teens could hang out or get high school service hours by helping, and many members of the community offered their expertise teaching different skills. Miranda had taken Petal there not only to pick up the recycled T-shirt art and quilts made by one of the regular volunteers, but also to show her a place she could make friends and play after school.

Petal had gone quiet at Harry's House, clearly not wanting to stay. Miranda knew it would help Witt if he had reliable after-school care for Petal, and it would be good for Petal to socialize more as she seemed intimidated by other children. But if she were honest, Miranda really enjoyed Petal's company. She felt selfish and guilty, but she'd loved walking over to the school, waiting outside with the moms and seeing Petal's face light up when she'd been slowly walking out the door, dragging her backpack as if too tired to take one step more.

"You came," Petal had said, astonished.

And the hint of a smile had nearly undone Miranda. She'd felt such a sense of purpose. And connection. Someone had waited for her. Wanted her to show up. She was needed again.

"Witt should be off work in a couple of hours," Miranda said. Petal had explained her relationship to Witt during their afternoon together. Miranda pushed aside the gloomy thoughts. Petal should be playing after school with friends, and she would when she settled in. Miranda would build her own new life. It would take time, but she could and would do it. "So let's head back to my shop and... Oh, speak of the devil," she said as Whitman walked out of Grey's and straight into them.

Wow oh wow he looked so tall and fit and perfect. The bones of his face just made her want to cup them in her palms and let her fingers trace over his taut skin that stretched over his cheekbones. She wondered how he'd feel. Warm? Would his skin be smooth? And his hair, so thick and the way it swept up and back from his forehead had always been a marvel to her. She wondered if he let lovers mess it up. He must. What would that be like, to touch the silk of his hair, see him smile, relax a little? Touch her? Need her back?

Miranda practically jumped out of her skin at the visuals and the want that coursed through her. She swallowed hard. Willed herself to stop staring and start breathing.

"I can't decide if that's an elevation or a demotion," Witt said, oblivious to the tension and want and ideas that churned deep inside her.

Of course he wasn't thinking of her like that. He hadn't even remembered her from high school while she had swallowed him with her eyes, and hid behind lockers, books, and the bleachers during his practices just wishing so hard he'd notice her. And when she'd work up her nerve to approach him with a question like joining a club—Amnesty International, yearbook, anything, he would just look through her, over her head, always on the move, moving so fast and fluidly away with a distant "No thank you. Good luck with your plans though."

"I see someone made it to Sage's Copper Mountain Chocolate Shop." He smiled at Petal who had a smear of chocolate on her lips and improbably high on her cheekbone. "Did you eat it or try it out as a new kind of blush?" Witt used the end of his dark gray and navy scarf to wipe at Petal's cheek and mouth even as her tongue speared out to try to catch the last taste of salted caramel. "Nice lizard move, but too late."

Heat speared through Miranda. He was less tense than he'd been this morning. Teasing Petal. She hoped he was warming a little to his cousin. Maybe he'd been especially tense with his new job and then unexpectedly taking over Petal's care. And he had to be worried about his dad. Excuses pinged around her brain, but she was charmed that he was a bit more relaxed now. Witt unwound. She didn't know if she could handle that. But she'd find a way. Like always.

"I'll mention the chocolate blush concept to Sage," Miranda said.

"Chocolate lip gloss too. I want fifty percent of the royalties."

"I'll let her know."

"No one would buy chocolate lip gloss," Petal chimed in, her tongue still searched her lips for any hiding chocolate. "People would eat it off as soon as they put it on."

"That would be the point," Witt said looking at Miranda—sharing the laugh—and Miranda's tummy did another dance as she couldn't help the dip of her gaze to his mouth.

Her mouth went dry. Her lips wouldn't work. To say something, anything to do with not begging him to kiss her or let her kiss him.

"Where are you two off to next?" he asked, and Miranda was so charmed that he was clearly making an effort she nearly broke into a dance involving fist pumps.

"We're going to the shop with some merchandise for Miranda's shop. We've walked all around the town doing the pickups from local stores and from a lot of local artists. Did you know a lot of people make arts and crafts out of their homes? And we went to a distillery tasting room that's in a tiny house on wheels that a guy you went to high school with builds and people buy them from all over the country. He puts them on wheels. People can live in them or have a business there. And then we walked along Bramble Lane and I saw some mansions and one..."

Petal's voice chattered on excitedly as she pulled the wagon a little ahead of them and Miranda and Witt fell in step together slightly behind. Miranda wanted to roll her eyes at how happy it made her to walk down the street with all the masculine perfection that was Witt.

"She's in a good mood," he said. "Thank you, Miranda."

Her name on his lips made her hurt inside. "I was going to say the same thing about you."

He paused, clearly thinking. Then his deep blue eyes met hers.

"I am feeling...reassured," he said. "My father's surgery went well so the immediate danger is passed for the most part. The surgery is scheduled on his femur in a couple of days and I saw the break on an X-ray, and it could have been a lot worse, and the first two days of work have gone well. Better than I expected."

"Why?" Miranda was astonished. She couldn't imagine Witt not thinking he was going to do anything less than stellar.

"I wasn't anticipating practicing here—ever—so being sent here for a month before I join a hospital in Santa Monica was…" he paused, his beautiful face shadowed "…not what I wanted. At. All."

She wanted to ask him why. Why didn't he love Marietta? Why had his eyes always been on the future and far away? But he wasn't hers to learn about his thoughts and desires so intimately.

"Petal seems to have blossomed." He rolled his eyes at the pun, and Miranda felt her chest expand painfully. "You really helped me out today, Miranda. Thank you."

His eyes were the bluest blue. She was drowning. And it was surreal. She was living her biggest high school fantasy twelve years too late. And that made her think of another fantasy she'd had then—that Witt Telford would kiss her.

She tried to not think of that, but that was now all she was thinking of, and then she realized when Witt smiled, that Petal was still talking, whereas she had felt in her own little world with Witt. It was like being in a snow globe.

"She talk like that all afternoon?" he asked softly, his deep voice almost bottoming out, which had a strange effect on her stomach and her heart, and though she admonished herself to get over it—this wasn't high school—old habits die hard.

"She's lovely," Miranda instantly defended. "I loved, absolutely loved having someone to talk to and do something with. She was very helpful." She spoke without thinking, and Witt's quick, quizzical stare made her realize how stupid that sounded—an adult woman without any friends, craving any human contact. What was next? Her rented bed and bath, filled with cats?

She'd let so many things slide while taking care of her grandfather. She'd always had at least one part-time job so she could help with her grandparents' finances and pay her own way and she'd tried to squeeze in classes at the community college when she could, but their small farm had been isolated, and the needs large. But now she was a business owner. Miranda squared her shoulders. She lived in town. She could rekindle friendships. Maybe even have a date. She looked at the back of Petal's sleek head and the curve of her cheek as she'd turn back to regale Witt with more details about their afternoon around the town talking to different merchants and collecting the local merchandise Miranda had ordered to carry in her store.

She'd always wanted children. A large family to love and play with and accept no matter how they turned out—quiet, bookish, academic, horse loving, daredevil, dreamy, active and messy. In her family there was one way: academic and ambitious. Miranda hadn't made the cut. She hadn't even really tried. She'd been so different. The youngest by over a decade and she'd gone her own way, but she would have liked to have still felt a part of them. A little.

The future was wide open.

She slewed a sideways glance up at the man walking so confidently beside her. He hadn't buttoned his long overcoat and his legs kicked it open with each long stride. He wore a charcoal-gray sweater. It looked like cashmere. It fit him beautifully, smoothing across his wide shoulders and tapering down to his narrow waist. Her fingers fluttered out from her sides as her hands ghosted the shape of his torso and her vision swam with a vibrant royal blue threaded through with a lighter blue—Montana sky blue—and cable knit style.

Not that Witt would necessarily wear a sweater like that. Or one that she made. She was just imagining again—that they'd become close enough friends that she could give him a gift, make him a sweater, see him wear it on the weekends when he was…?

"What do you like to do in your spare time?" Miranda asked, wanting to know him better and fill in the blanks of her fantasy.

He kept walking. They were now cutting along the side of the Graff, and her heart pinched a little. He'd probably take Petal back to the room to get settled in. Check her homework that Miranda had already supervised before she'd shown her the basics of molding a dragon out of clay. She'd be alone again, and it struck her how much she missed company. Needed it with an ache. She'd always been in a big family, even though they were critical and often scolding because she was slower and not into sports or competition and would usually be found reading or sketching or dreaming. Still something was always happening. Then she'd had her grandparents. Now no one.

"Wasn't a big long theoretical math equation I asked you to solve," she teased his silence because she really wanted to know more about the adult Witt.

"I was thinking." He sounded defensive and Miranda laughed a little.

"I don't think a little fun should take that much thought." A sudden thought struck her. Maybe it would work. A quick detour. Not the smartest idea with her shop opening tomorrow, but she had to try otherwise her window of opportunity would close. Witt would link up with old friends, form a pattern with Petal, move back to his family's ranch while he was here, and she'd probably only see him from a distance. Or at the coffee shop if she timed it right. Or stalked him. Which she would not do. Peering around lockers to catch a peek was fine when you were sixteen. Miranda had the feeling now it would be weird.

"How about ice-skating? You used to play a real mean game of pick-up hockey."

"You did?" Petal stopped in her tracks and looked up at Witt. "You?"

Witt stopped walking. They were like a triangle, Miranda thought. She and Witt were the base and Petal the point with her thin face flushed with surprise and hope as she stared at Witt.

"Do you still skate? Do you?"

Witt sucked in a deep breath and jammed his gloved hands into his pocket. "It's been a long time," he said.

"It's like riding a bike or skiing," Miranda said helpfully, her heart kicking up in excitement. "You never forget how."

He looked at Petal, standing so still, clutching the handle of the wagon. Nervously she chewed her lip and her eyes searched his as if the answers to the universe could be found there. Miranda braced herself for 'no' judging by the angle of his shoulders and head, the way his body was turned toward the hotel, not either of them. Then he almost imperceptivity relaxed.

"You want to join us, Miranda, as I put that theory to the test?"

Chapter Six

MIRANDA PAUSED IN the middle of the skaters circling around and around, like a school of fish, some swift, some staggering like newborn calves, and tilted her face to the sky. The lighter winter blue was fading to gray with the dark creeping in, but the last shafts of light had slipped away. Evergreens ringed the small alpine lake. Copper Mountain rose above it, a geological sentry.

"I haven't come to Miracle Lake in years," she said softly, looking around at the families skating around here, the bright colors of winter wear so vivid against the ice and the snow weighing down so many of the trees.

"Why not?" Witt asked her, surprising her, because he'd mostly been quiet as he'd skated slowly beside her as she'd held Petal's hands and skated behind her, legs wide and steadying Petal as she started to get the feel for the ice. Her goal was to get Petal to glide at least a little.

"My parents left Marietta my junior year of high school so I moved in with my grandparents. Then my grandfather had a stroke my last year of high school so I helped more with the farm and day-to-day things to help my grandmother out, and then he fell and broke his hip, so I took on more chores and errands to help them out. Then a few years ago he started mentally declining so I stayed, and between that and working at different retail stores and trying to take some classes at the community college sometimes…" She trailed off and smiled. "I guess the time really does slip away. I used to come here so many weekends growing up. My parents would drop me off with a lunch and money for hot chocolate and I'd just skate for hours with friends."

She focused on the positive memories and swallowed the sadness of her words and the sorrow of no longer living with her grandparents, losing the battle with his decline. She knew she'd given her best, but like so much in her life, it didn't seem to be enough.

"So I am so happy you invited me, Witt." She smiled. She couldn't help it, he just looked so tall and handsome and a little bit out of his element—not with the skating—her prediction that his ice-skating skills would come back quickly held true—but with Petal's clinging.

His hair was a little mussed, not swooping back from his forehead with such authority, and it softened the hard planes of his face. His cheeks were flushed with the exercise and cold, and the quizzical look he shot her made him look younger. Her stomach flipped and heat spread through her body insidiously. Being with him, sharing a moment with him was just as terrific as she had thought it would be in high school. Only better.

I could get used to this, she thought staring up at him, knowing she shouldn't.

Don't.

The voice of reason. Don't dream. Her family's voice not

hers. But this time, she knew she shouldn't ignore it. Witt was only here for a month at most. And he definitely wasn't the type of man who would date her. She bet he'd want a leggy blonde with a brain the size of Texas and career ambitions to match.

So look but don't touch, she reminded herself. Sounded like a sign in a high-end gift store. Somehow that had become her man mantra, and suddenly right there on Miracle Lake, where many couples had fallen in love, where an actual miracle had occurred decades ago when a child had fallen through the ice and drowned yet been revived, Miranda knew she was sick of just looking. Done with admiring everyone's happiness from the sidelines and promising herself that someday...

Maybe her someday, her happy ever after wouldn't come if she waited. Maybe she had to make it on her own. Seize the day and all that jazz.

"You are thinking so fiercely," he murmured.

"I am feeling fierce."

He looked like he was about to say something, but then changed his mind, and then he cleared his throat as if to speak again but said nothing.

Miranda finally broke eye contact. It was hard. And she felt aflame. Burning with some realization that she couldn't quite comprehend. She squeezed Petal's hands and held them above her head and slowly turned her in a circle like she was a ballerina. She was aware of time passing, of many things she had to do, but for once, she didn't want to do them. The work could wait. Not like it wasn't always there.

"I'd like to skate another couple of loops," she said feeling bold, but winced when Witt looked at his watch. Disappointment stabbed, but then she broke what had become a long-time rule and lightly placed one hand on his sternum.

She imagined she could feel his heartbeat through the collared shirt and cashmere sweater and her gloves. He'd unbuttoned his overcoat leaving one less layer between them, but still…so much more than just material separated them. What would it be like to really touch him? Her palm on his chest with just a T-shirt? Did Dr. Whitman Telford even wear 'just a T-shirt'? She felt a wave of hot longing sweep through her body and squat in her chest. Ache.

She'd waited for so long. Waited for so much. She'd never dreamed she'd have this chance—to skate with Witt or with any man really—and she felt like she was blowing it because she didn't know what to do or what to say to get him to see her as a woman he'd want to sit in a movie theater with, arm around her while they shared popcorn or take to dinner and hold her hand while waiting for the meal, trace the lines on her palm and tell her about his day.

"Pink Moon" by Nick Drake came over the speakers. Miranda closed her eyes and swallowed the lump in her throat.

"I've always loved this song," she whispered feeling like it was some kind of sign.

He covered her hand on his chest and then enclosed it in his.

"Then let's skate."

He tugged a little and took Petal's other hand, lightly swinging her around so that this time Witt was in the middle of their skating trio instead of Petal. They kicked off without a wobble. Witt was such a graceful skater, competently weaving around the kids and couples on the ice. He moved in time with the music and Miranda let the sweet melody and lonesome words wash over her.

She wished the song were ten times longer so that this moment—so much better than any dream she'd ever had—could last forever. The twinkle lights strung through the surrounding trees seemed to dance in time with the song and their skating and then everything blurred, looked under water. Miranda squeezed her eyes shut but still a few tears trickled down her cheek and she quickly dashed them away.

As the last few evocative chords spilled out from the speakers, they drew close to the skate shed and Witt slowed them down. He looked like an ad for some high-end product—cologne or an expensive watch or outdoor wear. And he seemed so unaware of it, helping Petal to remove her rented skates and find her shoes.

"We probably should get back." Witt looked at his watch again. "You must be tired," he said to Petal.

"I never get tired," Petal objected.

Witt opened his mouth, and Miranda could just imagine what the practical, science-minded doctor would say so she forestalled him.

"Probably not," Miranda interrupted, "but I do, and I'm chilly so I'd love some hot chocolate with a lot of whipped cream and sprinkles."

Miranda looked entranced. "Sprinkles."

"My treat," Miranda said, trying to look stern because Witt had paid for the skate rental.

"You treated this morning," he said. "But I won't argue with you because you are looking fierce again."

"Wise man."

They ordered, Petal carefully watching the whipped cream and sprinkles being swirled on top.

"Wait," Witt said, "you aren't looking to take the one with the biggest whipped cream pile are you?"

"Definitely." Petal was unrepentant and Miranda laughed.

The barista laughed too and squirted some whipped cream on a spoon and handed it to Petal who licked it off, her face a study in little-girl pleasure. Then the barista squirted whipped cream on another spoon and winked at Witt and handed it to him.

Such a natural thing. Flirting. She was probably a college kid just having fun with her job, but it hurt just a little to think that the young woman with her long dark hair swirled in a messy bun on top of her head and sparkling green eyes and curves that broadcast ideal woman likely had a better chance with him than she ever would.

"Are you going to fight me for this?" Witt laughed. "Since you've been feeling so fierce tonight?"

"I might."

He held the spoon above his head. "Let's see your moves."

Miranda wondered what he'd do if she hiked herself up

on the counter and jumped for it. Likely they'd both end up on their bottoms, and hers was still screamingly sore, but it might be worth it just to see his face.

She looked at him. Then at the counter.

"And now you're starting to scare me," he teased softly bringing the spoon down and holding it out to her.

And he terrified her. But she wasn't going to turn into a coward. She'd always done what she felt was right, often in the face of strong family opposition or the dismay of her friends.

She took a step in to him, almost touching his body, lightly circled his wrist with her thumb and forefinger, and brought the spoon to her mouth.

She only took a little of the sweet cream, letting it touch her lips like a sweet caress before dabbing some with her tongue.

Then she pulled away and took the spoon, holding it out for him.

God, his eyes were a deep blue. Bluer than Crater Lake in Oregon on a sunny summer day. A little shocked, curious, hesitant. She held her breath expecting him to say no. He was a doctor; he'd be all about germs or his health—whipped cream was on no one's list as remotely healthy, but instead he covered her hand with his and wrapped his lips that were so stern but sensuously full at the same time around the spoon, and Miranda had to stifle, seriously stifle her moan of longing.

Oh to be a spoon.

"Thank you, Witt, for letting me join you tonight.

Thank you so much."

She thought of the serious man suddenly being responsible for the young cousin he hadn't known he'd had, and helping out at a hospital he probably didn't want to work at, taking a girl he didn't remember from high school skating, helping her when she'd been injured trying to drag a discarded and broken Christmas tree out of the dumpster. Witt Telford was kind. He might seem aloof, but deep in his heart he was a kind man, and she fell for him just a little bit harder.

Kindness always melted her heart and inspired her. Kept her going. Large kindnesses like Colt helping out with small build projects in her store and small kindnesses like Witt trying to show his young cousin some fun in her chaotic word. This town was full of kindness such as the barista giving Petal extra whipped cream, or the high school boy who worked at the skate rental shack making a play list using requests from skaters. And the kindness of the Wilder brothers who had upgraded and re-strung all the lights around Miracle Lake this winter just because last year one of the brothers had fallen in love here, and they all wanted to pay it forward.

"Kindness," she suddenly yelped and grabbed his arm. "Random kindness. Only not totally random in the big scheme of things because we are all linked in ways that we don't even know or recognize. Kindness. That's it! That's what's been missing from my idea."

IT WOULD HAVE been a dark, quiet drive into town, heavy with dread and guilt if he'd been alone. Whitman tried to remember when was the last time he'd driven with anyone anywhere. Miranda was making notes on her iPhone, her face lit by the silver-blue light and she seemed a little mysterious in its glow as if she were a figment of his imagination.

"Witt, can we have music?" Miranda asked. "It helps me to think."

He hit the satellite radio button, not sure if he'd get much reception with the trees that densely lined the highway here. Once they wound their way a little lower they'd thin out.

"What music is that?" Petal demanded, her voice thick with outrage.

Miranda spun a little in her chair. "Listening music. Thinking music. It's jazz. Listen to the different rhythms that kick in and out. See if you can hear the change-ups and the different instruments coming in as they clash and then resolve."

"Oh." Petal settled in her seat more comfortably, her thin face pinched with concentration.

"Can you hear the upright bass thumping down at the bottom, keeping time but also countering what the horns are doing here? It's like a conversation."

Petal leaned forward in her seat, her head cocked much like a dog's, not that Witt had ever had a dog growing up even though he'd wanted one to run with and to play fetch. When he'd moved to Marietta there had been ranch dogs, but they'd been working dogs and even though they slept inside at night, they had never settled on his bed. They'd never belonged to him. They'd belonged, in his mind, to the ranch and the family who lived there.

"You like jazz?"

"All kinds of music," Miranda said softly.

"Do you play?"

She shrugged. "I had the obligatory lessons like all my siblings, but I didn't show a talent for anything in particular. I wanted to try so many instruments and see what they were like. Not conducive to mastery so the lessons stopped when I was twelve."

Witt winced a little. It sounded harsh, but it also sounded like something his mother had said the summer before she died. "Music scholarships aren't going to happen from your little stint in jazz band so after middle school you're done. Focus on your academic merit."

When he'd come to live at the ranch, he hadn't even told his biological father that he'd been in his jazz band. That he played the trombone and sax. Hadn't kept up with it. What do you do for fun? Miranda had asked him, and he'd come up blank. Maybe he could pick up trombone again once he was settled in in Santa Monica. Not that he'd have much time, but still…the idea lingered. Wasn't instantly dismissed like so many others over the years to keep his focus.

Miranda tucked her phone back in the small metallic silver pouch bag she had that looked like it was more for being a tourist and carrying the minimum than an actual purse. "I play a mean ukulele and sing with it, but very softly as my landlady seems to have giant ears. It makes me wish I were doing something really naughty just to give her something to be officially indignant about."

Witt bit back a smile. Miranda phrased things oddly, and he found himself smiling more than he had in a long time. Maybe forever. At first he thought it was because she was a bit odd or impulsive but it was something different. He couldn't quite put his finger on it.

"Witt, where are we going to eat? Miranda has a little fridge and a Crock-Pot. Maybe we could have soup and I can work on my dragon."

Dinner. Of course. He'd need to be responsible for Petal—all her meals and her homework and...

"The Crock-Pot is for seasonal warm drinks and soups sometimes," Miranda said. "But I didn't make anything today, Petal. With a Crock-Pot you need to put all the ingredients in early."

"So we all need dinner, Witt," Petal said, tapping her hands against the back of Whitman's headrest in time with the bass line. "Everyone is hungry."

"Petal, please stop," Miranda said gently, her voice soft. "You never want to distract the driver of a car, but I'm glad you're enjoying the music."

Witt had never noticed how melodic her voice was—like water in a brook flowing over stones.

And where had that imaginative image come from? He didn't think like that. It was a little unsettling.

The accompaniment tapping stopped. Petal sighed and Whitman relaxed.

"I'm sure Witt will figure out dinner. The hotel has excellent food, and your room is being upgraded to a suite so there will be a small kitchenette in there. Maybe I can teach you a few easy things to cook while you are staying at the Graff," Miranda offered casually. "Supervising all cooking of course. Or Harry's House has an afternoon cooking program a few times during the school year."

Whitman was momentarily distracted from the road. It had been a long time since he'd driven in wintery conditions and though the highway had been de-iced and plowed, he still was driving cautiously—too cautiously judging on how many people passed him.

"Seriously! That would be awesome."

"If Witt says it's okay."

"Is it, Witt, is it?"

He held back a sigh. Miranda was a girl from high school he hadn't even remembered two days ago, yet now she was becoming indispensable. It wasn't fair to Petal to let them get so close or to Miranda, who had a business to run. Yet she was perfect for Petal—effortlessly saying and doing the right thing. And he had a busy schedule. He'd be on call some nights. Clearly Sarah had been too distraught to think this through. Or she didn't understand the demands on a surgeon at a hospital.

"How about Mexican tonight?" he punted the problem. "I heard some of the medical staff talking about a place that opened this month called Rosita's."

"Tableside guac to die for," Miranda said. "According to Shane and Walker who work at the Graff."

"Well." Witt ran his hand though his hair and then

rubbed his face as if he could brush away the idea that had taken root in his brain. He shouldn't think it, much less suggest it. But he needed help. Petal needed someone. Not him. "Let's not die for it, but I think we can definitely order it. Do you have time to join us for dinner?"

Miranda worried her bottom lip even as she turned to face him. Her eyes shone, but held questions. Her teeth were so small and white cushioned in her plump bottom lip.

He felt a stab of worry that she'd say no, and he realized he'd thought she was a sure thing—for dinner and his possible business proposal because looking at her in his passenger seat, her focus back on him after ten minutes or so of typing on her phone's memo app, he knew he was going to ask her. And persuade her to say yes. And dinner was a good start.

"Say yes," he urged.

"Yes," she whispered.

"Yeah!" Petal cheered.

It was a practical solution. For all of them.

AT ROSITA'S, PETAL, who'd tucked her legs under her in the booth and leaned up and over to watch the entire proceeding of the artistry of tableside guac nearly hummed with pleasure as she dipped chip after chip into the vibrant green concoction, and then leaned back blissfully in her chair. She nibbled her way through chip and guac, eyes closed, and then she sighed before repeating the whole process.

"I think you have a budding foodie on your hands," Miranda teased.

Witt started a little then he looked at Petal as if he was seeing her for the first time.

"I guess we…I do."

We. The word was a live wire to her body, but reality hip-checked open the door. 'We' was his family. Not her. Petal was part of them.

Miranda looked down at the set of five crayons and the paper placemat. Petal had started a drawing of a dragon's egg.

"That's pretty awesome," Miranda said. "Can I borrow the back?"

Petal nodded and Miranda picked up a red crayon and flipped over the paper.

"May I?"

She quickly sketched a tree.

Witt watched. "You were making a lot of notes on your phone in the car. About your shop?"

Pleased with his interest Miranda looked up at him. Her breath caught at the deep blue of his eyes. The straight dark brows. The bones of his face always made her think of a dark, brooding hero on the cover of a historical romance—a lonely, misunderstood rebel or outlaw or soldier. So alone. And even years later, she still wanted to cup his cheeks and smile up at him and let him know that she wanted to help him with his burdens.

It was so silly.

She knew that.

But she craved a connection with him. Felt like she should have it. Like they once shared something special, but had come untethered. Or been cut.

"I was thinking at Miracle Lake about kindness, and giving." She sketched as she talked softly, her eyes meeting his and trying to gauge his interest. "Earlier, a couple of days ago, I heard two women sneering about Valentine's Day over drinks at the Graff, while I had been trying to think of how to decorate the shop and maybe a promotion. The hotel always has an event—a special dinner, and often a ball or something else—music and dancing and sometimes a fundraiser, and it's elegant and special, but these two women were so eye-rollingly bitter about the romance aspect of the day."

"It is pretty commercial." Witt paused, a chip with guac nearly to his mouth.

He had a beautiful mouth. Refined, but a little fuller, slightly pouty when he wasn't engaged in talking or concentrating on something as if when relaxed, a more sensual person could peek behind the focused, academic façade.

"And there's a lot of pressure on men to make some grand gesture. To be creative. And it's forced. Calculated."

"You too?" She shouldn't be surprised. "I would imagine you'd taken lots of women out on Valentine's Day. Dinner. Wine. Beautiful roses."

She liked thinking of him in that setting, but it also pinched a little deep inside her in the dark empty she pretended she didn't have.

"That's just it. Valentine's Day is forced. A preconceived

notion of what romance should be. So there's coercion and hypocrisy because men and women are shoved together and told to behave and to feel a certain way. Valentine's Day is a societal norm."

Witt didn't speak with heat, more like they were having a debate. She remembered he'd gone to state and regional championships in debate three out of four years and had placed first his senior year both individually and with his team. Petal had given up her avid chip-lathered-in-guac consumption and now listened to them, her gaze shifting back and forth between them.

"So they said," Miranda admitted. "Only with more venom, and I thought why? Valentine's Day is a beautiful reminder to all of us to cherish the people, the friendships and connections and love in our lives." As she'd been speaking, she'd been sketching and then she held up the drawing.

"The Days of Giving Tree," she said. "Fourteen days of random acts of kindness and giving. At my boutique, I am celebrating all kinds of love—romantic, friendship, community, humanity. In the two weeks running up to Valentine's Day, I am going to have people come in and record random acts of kindness that they've received or witnessed or done on some kind of arty bulletin board thingy so cynics can come in and be inspired to share their hearts."

"Thingy? Love that visual," Witt said, but his eyes were warm and he popped a chip in his mouth and waved his hand—king to peasant—for her to continue.

"And then they can come in and collect a glass heart

bead. I make them just for fun and have a lot just sitting in a bowl."

"Aren't you supposed to be selling things in your boutique, not giving them away? Just a thought," he added as she fake scowled.

"I need to be in on the giving as well," Miranda said with dignity.

"Dragons," Petal said. "People should get a dragon when they do something nice for someone."

"I can't make that many dragons that quickly," Miranda said, hating to disappoint Petal and shut down the idea. The clay was fairly expensive even when bought in bulk with her wholesale license. "But maybe we can incorporate dragons some way." That was the problem in speaking publicly before the idea was hashed out.

"Still. People shouldn't receive something for their random acts of kindness. It mitigates the message." Witt played devil's advocate instinctively and Miranda sighed. He was right.

"But you do want to get them in your store so how about a glass jar that people put in a glass bead every time they have witnessed a random act of kindness. A bead isn't as symbolic as a heart but it would roll." The quirk of his lips was devastatingly cute. "You could make it an experience like a Rube Goldberg machine or a marble run to get the glass ball in the jar. And then have the people record the kindness they experienced or witnessed to kick the cynics like me in the you know what."

"I know you're not wasted as a doctor, but you are wonderfully clever thinking of promotional activities."

Witt looked self-conscious. Adorable. His cheeks even flushed a little. Her heart flipped. He was even better than in high school.

"No. I just built on what you started. No doubt you'll refine the idea."

"Can I help, Miranda?" Petal asked.

"Of course. You're my assistant. We are going to need a flyer design. A graphic image that embodies our idea—I'll need your help with that—and then we need to post them around town, and I need to try to get on the radio and in the newspaper. We will run the random acts of kindness for the first two weeks of February and then I'll have an open house and celebration of all walks of love at my store. And we need to get this done because February starts in one more day."

DINNER HAD BEEN...WHAT?...HE mentally demanded. Easy. Fun even. He never would have believed it. He usually ate for fuel. Quick, healthy meals sandwiched between work or studies or working out. But tonight he'd shared a meal with a woman he technically barely knew but should have remembered from high school. The more she'd talked tonight, she'd been on the periphery of his life more than he imagined. What did that say about him that he never had looked up? Always inward. Or far away from here? Witt wasn't sure he really wanted to know.

And yet he'd enjoyed himself tonight—skating at Miracle Lake and the dinner. Miranda made him laugh. And she eased everything with Petal. He still felt awkward with Petal. She was stiff and suspicious of him. Keeping her distance. Wary but he'd seen glimpses of thawing. Had he been like that so long ago?

And he felt it wasn't fair on the young girl who had perhaps experienced some emotional turmoil to land her unannounced on her relative's door with no parental return date mentioned. He would be busy this month. Long hours. Lots of call. Petal was still a child. Not yet ten. He couldn't leave her alone, and he didn't want to wake her in the middle of the night and move her to a doctor call room or the nurse's lounge if he had a case.

"Miranda." The thought that had niggled all night, and though he wanted to dismiss it, he knew he shouldn't. He prided himself on independence, but Petal was too important and too fragile. "May I talk to you for a moment quietly?" he said low in her ear as they walked carefully up the circle stairs to the Graff after the valet had driven off with his rental.

"Of course." She smiled at him, and he noticed that quick flash of crooked that made her look impish. It was charming, he supposed. Not a beautiful Hollywood smile, but unique and he supposed a lot of cowboys had been trying to win that smile for a while. Weird that she was his age, hadn't left Marietta but hadn't yet married. This town had the kids who graduated high school and left fast—to college or the military—and those, often the ranch kids, who stayed. Worked. Married and started a family all within a year or two of high school. By that estimate Miranda should be about done having her three or four kids with her cowboy.

But she didn't seem to have anybody.

By choice or circumstance? Not his business and he was a little surprised he was even thinking like that. Maybe because she was so easy with Petal.

"Can I work on my dragon?"

"It's time for bed soon," Miranda said. "But definitely tomorrow. Why don't you try to stick some of those pink branches in the drilled holes of the trunk? They should be completely dry now."

Witt watched Petal dance happily over to the staff that stuck out of a white ceramic pot filled with stones that squatted near the entrance of her shop. The "rescued" artificial Christmas tree was now pulled apart and the different-sized branches were all a vivid, eye-lurching pink or red. It hurt his eyeballs just thinking about it, and he shuddered to look.

"I know little about retail, but aren't you supposed to lure people into your store not send them to an ophthalmologist?"

"I love the doctor humor, Witt." Miranda did not look offended. In fact, she smiled as Petal picked up a branch and, tongue poking out of her mouth in concentration, she walked around the tree looking for the perfect hole to jam the branch into. "You wanted to talk to me?" She glanced at her phone.

"Oh, you're rushed. Probably busy." He suddenly felt a

little nervous. What would he do if she said no? The plan had been forming and reforming and nudging him for most of their evening. In his mind it was perfect—a done deal. A win-win for both. But now he felt unaccountably nervous. What if she thought he was taking advantage of her?

He was.

But I'll pay her. She's got to need money.

"I do have a lot to do tonight, but I was checking the time as Colt said he'd come over and install a few shelves for me on the wall." Miranda was speaking, but he was so caught up in his concerns he hadn't really been paying attention. She'd been answering something he'd asked. What was it?

"He's going to show me how to do it properly with a level and drill and into the studs. So I can do more when I need to."

"He who?"

"Colt." She laughed. "You were a long way away."

"I could have shown you how to do that." Whitman heard the defensive note in his voice and clenched his jaw.

"Really?"

Witt was offended. True his mother and his grandparents, the little he knew of them, always paid for a handyman or contractor to do work around their homes, but at the ranch, he'd had to learn all sorts of things to pull his weight. And he was an orthopedic surgeon, not some useless ornament.

"Cancel Colt. I'll do it."

"I don't have any tools," Miranda said. "He's been working construction mostly since leaving the military. He's rebuilt a lot of barns and has been recycling the wood for other projects and now he's started a business designing and building tiny houses using a lot of reclaimed lumber. He's been one of my inspiration for the Days of Giving Tree because he's given me the wood for free and even found a couple of the cabinets that I'm using for décor and displays until I hopefully sell them too. I looked up on YouTube how to restore and antique old furniture, and it's fun. Something to do that has a purpose and I hope will be loved again in a new home. Sorry. Rambling. Again. What did you want to say?"

Witt stared into the warm caramel of her eyes. They were so dark and warm with little flecks of black and yellow in the irises. Her lashes were long and curled up making her look a little surprised and curious, and very, very open. She seemed so warm and trusting that he winced a little. Hoped no one hurt her even though he knew pain was a part of life. No one got away unscathed.

And why was he thinking something like that? He wasn't going to hurt her. This was a business transaction. He looked at Petal carefully plotting out the placement of the branches, mixing up the red and pink like it was an art display.

And maybe it was to her.

And this business was Miranda's livelihood and she was letting a lost little girl with no ties to her in to help. And looking for ways to connect to a community he was doing his best to avoid.

Out of the corner of his eye he saw Colt, tool belt low on

his hips and a metal toolbox dangling from his long fingers stop and say something to Shane, the bartender who was bringing drinks to several women chatting at a table in the bar. Shane laughed and waved him off. He was going to miss his chance. Miranda would be busy. Tomorrow his schedule was full. Petal had really balked at the idea of spending time at the after-school program at Harry's House, but he also didn't know if he'd be done before it closed and then what would he do? Wyatt could rearrange his schedule, sure, but he was here to help, not hinder.

"I was wondering if you'd move in with me," he blurted just as Colt entered the boutique and Miranda turned to greet him with her warm eyes and crooked smile.

Chapter Seven

Her rounded gaze swung back to Witt. Mouth dropped open.

"What? We haven't even kissed yet."

Kissed? Where the hell had that come from? But of course he did zero in on her mouth, slightly too big for her small pixie face. Crooked when she smiled, which gave her a wistful look that always made him feel like he had to do something. Be better.

"I meant…ummmm…" He was aware that Petal had stopped poking in the branches. Colt had stopped in the doorway of the boutique. Golden gaze burning a hole in him, even as he seemed poised to back out. Great. An audience, which was what he'd been trying to avoid by saying it quickly and quietly before Colt got here.

"I meant temporarily. Into my room. At the hotel."

Miranda blinked.

Colt took another step into the shop, shot a look at Miranda and then walked all the way inside, brushing past Witt. "Balls of steel, Romeo," he muttered.

"Wait. What? No. I didn't mean my bed, obviously."

Colt stopped mid stride and turned around. "Still as smooth as sandpaper, Telford. Want me to teach him a lesson for you?" Colt asked Miranda, his expression shuttered tightly. His voice was amused, but Witt had the uncomfortable feeling, looking at Colt's massive size and his large, battered hands, that he wasn't completely joking.

Miranda drew in a feathery breath. Witt's heart sunk. She was going to say no. And he really needed a yes.

"I'm sorry," he verbally jumped in before she could say no. "I'm not explaining this well."

"That's news," he thought he heard Colt mutter, pencil in his mouth as he measured the wall.

"So explain it," Miranda said. Her breathing had evened out but two twin splotches of pink bloomed on her cheeks.

"I'm just really out of options."

The board Colt was holding crashed to the floor and he stood up.

"You are the worst advertisement for higher education and really need to shut the F up right now." He gripped Witt by the shoulders. "Seriously. Twelve years in college lecture halls and this is what you got out of it?" Colt let go and shot a frustrated look at Miranda. "Ironic as anything that I have to be the one to break this to you…" his golden gaze burned through him "…let women do the talking. You nod. You agree."

He should have been pissed. He was embarrassed because he hated, absolutely hated to do anything poorly. And the social part had been the hardest part of life and of medicine for him. Excruciating failure. He wasn't smiling enough. His body posture hadn't been empathetic. His professor had made him take a dance class of all things to be aware more of what his body was doing. No one else had had to do that. And he'd gotten better. He should just live in the hospital. He was comfortable there. Had purpose.

"What I'm trying to say is I really need help with Petal in the evenings sometimes," he bit out.

"Nanny." Colt spit the word, released him and returned to the business of the shelves.

"Want to help?" Colt asked Petal and she ran over and squatted down beside him and he began showing her the various tools.

Whitman stared. That was more words than he'd heard out of Colt in middle school and high school unless it had been classroom related. And he was charming Petal. Witt hadn't seen her smile like that and engage with anyone except Miranda, but he couldn't help but notice that even in the middle of having fun, Petal's eyes would shadow and she'd tense up and look so serious again. He ran a hand through his hair. Sucked in a deep breath. But he still felt hot and prickly with embarrassment.

"Sorry, Miranda." He looked down at the floor then mentally kicked himself and looked into her eyes that no longer looked startled, but sympathetic and shiny. She was so luminous, he noted, like her pale skin was lit from within. "I'd like to start over with that." He waved his hand as if he could sweep away the awkwardness. "Can we step out of your store, and I can explain?"

To his surprise, Miranda slipped her small hand in his and led him out into the so-called hallway.

"It's like being in a fish bowl," he said, indicating the two solid glass walls of her small shop that peered across to the small bar and the pub restaurant beyond. "It makes me nervous."

"Sorry. I know there's no privacy, but that's what I was going for. It's supposed to be to draw people in." She smiled. "I'm hoping to feature a lot of beautiful art and crafts in here. Everything will be Montana born." She grinned up at him. "So I want people looking and touching a lot."

For some reason that made him think of them being naked. His hands touching her skin. And now that the image was there he was having trouble banishing it. Her skin was so smooth and creamy on her face and neck he imagined she would feel so silky and warm. That was one of the challenges of winter in Montana. Everyone bundled up like bison. No touch and no visuals to help with attraction.

Attraction?

Where the hell had that word come from?

He wasn't attracted to Miranda. She wasn't his type at all. He was about to hire her to take care of Petal while he was at work so a big no to any attraction. And he was blowing out of Marietta for a big-city hospital in a warm climate. So, no, he was not attracted to her. She was…she was all wrong.

"Witt." Miranda's small hand covered his cheek. "You're thinking a million miles an hour."

He looked at her startled by the touch and startled by her insight. Her eyes were the most interesting brown. They were dark brown, almost black, and yet they seemed lit from within, with the most interesting flecks of lighter brown, almost yellow in her irises.

"Okay. Sorry." He shook his head. "Let me start over."

NOW THAT HER heart had settled back into a normal rhythm and she could breathe again, Miranda could enjoy the view. And what a view it was. Witt, so tall and serious, his usual air of remoteness gone like morning mist. Instead he seemed a little off his stride, awkward, human. Like a puppy trying to do the right thing but banging into furniture, knocking things over. She could definitely get used to him like this—this human version of Witt, but the cool and controlled one had been the one she'd always dreamed about. Who was he really under all the rigid perfectionism and beautifully aloof exterior? What dreams and hopes beat in his heart?

Were medical residents all blind and dumb? Why hadn't he been snatched up?

"Miranda." He waved a hand in front of her face. "Where'd you go?"

Now it was her turn to color. She wondered what he would say if she told him that she'd been imagining what his hopes and dreams and fears were. And what if she'd told him she'd crushed on him in high school and that he had occupied more of her brain space than any class ever had.

Probably not a good idea. She pressed her lips together. "Continue," she said feeling a bit for once like the princess, not the peasant.

"I am filling in for two doctors at the hospital over this

month and it's a pretty brutal call schedule, which I'm fine with. I want to work. I need it." His voice dropped almost like a prayer and then he rubbed his palms together as if gathering his thoughts. "But I wasn't planning on having a little girl."

"Your cousin."

"Petal, my cousin, to also take care of."

"I thought that's what we agreed on. She'd come here after school and stay with me or go up to the room, and if you were late, I'd make sure she got her homework done and dinner. And if she decides to do something at Harry's House I'd pick her up if you were still working."

He nodded. "But I might get called out for a case in the middle of the night. I might have to work all night. I'm on call on weekends when there's no school. I'm on call four nights this week."

"Ahhh, a nanny," Miranda echoed Colt as she fully grasped Witt's dilemma. Sarah really had thrown him a curve ball, but Miranda could understand why. She'd been focused on her husband's injury and the unexpected medical complication, and she'd been worried about the long time Petal would be out of school when judging just by today and Petal's casually placed comments, she'd already missed a lot of school. She's missed a lot of things that Miranda wished all children could have but so many of them didn't.

"I'll pay you," Witt said. "I don't know the going rate for a nanny, but I am sure someone at the hospital knows. The money would help, wouldn't it, as you get your business off the ground? And I'll pay your rent for the month at your apartment or wherever you're living if you move into the hotel suite with me and Petal," he added quickly, his words rushing like water from a broken water pipe. "They have a two-room suite. I already booked it and had my things moved. Bob said there's a trundle bed they can move in for Petal so you can have your own room and some privacy. So you'd have room and meals for two full weeks. You could just charge hotel meals to the room and I could give you my credit card and..." Miranda placed her hand over his mouth.

A totally inappropriate thrill shot through her. She tried to shut it down, but it was there. Electricity shooting through her body making her feel alive and warm and a little dizzy. It was the best feeling in the world. Witt Telford needed her. That was what it was. That was all it was. That was all it could be. But her heart was doing a happy dance that she was afraid was not only about spending time with a bewildered girl hungry for attention and stability.

"Yes."

IT WAS STILL light when Witt left the hospital the next day.

"Get the hell out." Wyatt had good-naturedly given him a push toward the elevator. "You're on call tonight so try to grab a couple of hours of normal. Get some non-hospital food. Kiss a girl."

Witt had been in the process of finishing his last notes on his hospital tablet, but Wyatt's last words nearly had him dropping it. He fumbled it, slapped at it and managed to snag it so the tablet didn't hit the ground, which would likely have shattered the screen. Two nurses and Wyatt, with his Chris Hemsworth look-alike face, which Wyatt used to his best advantage, grinned at his clumsiness.

Witt had tried to ignore the fumble and the comment.

"I'm sure there is much more for me to do here," he'd said with dignity although he knew he should check on Petal and Miranda. Tonight Miranda would be moving into the suite. Taking up space. Talking. Witt had hated having a roommate in college. Clothes everywhere. Beer bottles not in recycling, empty pizza boxes stacked on the floor, friends coming and going. Witt liked things neat. Quiet. Miranda, he imagined, would be an explosion of color, chatter, clothes and feminine things. Everywhere.

"Get a life, Witt!"

And so now, here he was pulling his scarf around his neck and tucking it under his overcoat—although Dylan Morgan on the radio claimed they were hitting a warm spell—getting a life. He took out his phone, thinking he'd text Miranda and maybe help her gather up her things from her apartment if she hadn't already done so. Petal had been out of school for nearly an hour.

Her answer came immediately in the form of a picture of her and Petal making goofy faces outside of Sage's Copper Mountain Chocolate Shop, hot chocolates cups pressed close to their faces. Second day in a row. Witt had no idea how Miranda stayed so thin. The sun was a brilliant orange as it settled in the west, reflecting off the snow and dazzling him. He squinted a little and his eyes watered. His sunglasses were in the SUV. Poor planning on his part, but he'd left in the dark for work and had been expecting to come home in the dark.

As he walked along Main Street, he noticed many of the shops had hearts decorating the windows. Of course. Valentine's Day. Stupidest, most commercial holiday ever. He didn't even have to ask himself if tomorrow when Miranda officially opened her shop on February 1st if she'd have a few Valentine decorations. Miranda was the kind of woman who screamed cheesy traditions—screaming witch at her door for Halloween, blow-up snowman on her front yard for Christmas and pink-and-red hearts in her windows for Valentine's Day. That tree she'd been making was a garish monument to the day of love.

"Day of disappointment," he muttered rolling his eyes.

He could definitely use an espresso. Or two. Likely it would be a long night. But he headed to Sage's first, noting fliers in many of the windows announcing Fourteen Days of Love and Random Acts of Kindness. He stopped and stared. Read the artfully done text. The image of the sketched Giving Tree superimposed over what looked like a hand-painted heart with splashes of vibrant colors was visually arresting. Witt wondered how she'd had time to have someone design a flier for her so quickly.

At least she was putting the money he'd be paying her to good use advertising her shop and her Valentine's gimmick although he felt bad she'd be disappointed. That ugly pink tree was going to scare customers away.

"There you are." Miranda and Petal walked out of the

bookstore wearing twin red knit beanies with a pink heart. "What do you think?" she asked Witt and then whispered something to Petal, but Petal blushed and looked down. "I'll do it if you will?"

Petal looked up at Miranda and self-consciously touched her head.

"On three. Okay?" Miranda counted down and then she struck a pose, and Petal followed.

"What do you think of our signature hats?" Miranda asked helpfully as if he were hard of hearing.

"Nice?"

"Nice as in you'd wear one or nice as in ask me a different question?"

She really wanted to know. Witt marveled again how Miranda put herself out there.

"Nice," he said. Inadequate. He could tell by Petal's skeptical look. "You both look festive."

That worked. He was rewarded with Miranda's crooked smile that lit her eyes and she high-fived a more tentatively smiling Petal.

"I got you a hot chocolate." Miranda handed him the cup she was holding.

"Thank you. I'll need to run an extra mile each time you do this."

"Good thing you like to run."

"That's the first random act of kindness!" Petal jumped up and down. "Miranda, you did it! Our first one."

"That was more of a practice one. The official kickoff is tomorrow. Random Acts of Kindness and The Found

Objects Giving Tree."

"Do you want to see it, Witt?" Petal asked. "I've been helping decorate it, and I helped organize her store, and I went to the radio station and Miranda got interviewed, and the DJ asked me questions too. I was on the radio, and Miranda recorded me and sent it to Sarah and Riley and I helped make the flier and bring them all around to the businesses to post and Miranda gave me a hat so I'm officially helping on the random acts of kindness campaign."

Petal gulped in air. And Witt felt a little out of breath just listening to the list. "And she's going to teach me how to make glass hearts to give away to people who give…" She looked at Miranda.

"Give something of themselves to someone or something else."

"And I met her grandmother who taught Miranda to knit when she was my age and Miranda is going to teach me. And I met her grandfather but he didn't remember her. Sad, huh?"

"You've been busy," Witt said. He'd been at work all day, but didn't feel like he'd accomplished half as much as Petal, who'd only been out of school a little over an hour and a half. "Efficient. Have you had time to pack a few things to bring to the hotel?" he asked, checking his watch. "Tonight I'm on call so I was hoping you'd stay tonight and until Sarah returns, although I'll pay you for two weeks at least."

"How's your dad doing?"

"Okay. The orthopedic surgery went well, but now he's got a low-grade infection from one of his injury sites. I spoke with the doctor this morning and will again later." Again he looked at this watch. "Sarah's worried, but his white cell count's not too high. Do you need help packing up some of your things?"

"I don't have that much to pack up," Miranda said, looking across the street. "I can do it later."

"It's easier with help," Witt said. "I'm sure you still have work to do at your store this afternoon and tonight, and I'm on call so likely won't be around so it will be you and Petal," he said. "Let's knock this out. Get it done. I'll take my SUV so it's easier."

He didn't wait for confirmation. Just headed back to the hotel, Miranda and Petal in his wake. Weird. It was the first time Miranda had been quiet.

The minute the three of them stood in the small one-room apartment with the twin bed with a fairly large stuffed bear on it, a dresser and desk, Witt wanted to kick himself. No wonder she'd wanted to pick up her clothes in private. There was barely enough room for them to stand. And likely she'd wanted to avoid the introduction to her hovering landlady, Bobby Gentry. She'd launched an inquisition. She'd started off questions—who were his people, where was he from, why was the nanny job only two weeks long, why couldn't he watch his own child, where was the little girl's mother? He'd deflected her questions once they swung around to Petal.

He really should have planned this better.

'Sorry,' he mouthed feeling all kinds of awkward.

"What for?" she whispered.

He ran his hand through his hair. Petal was looking at a low bookshelf that was crammed with books. Judging by the titles and small photos on the spines they were romances. All of them.

More awkward. He felt like he'd been caught spying on Miranda. He didn't want to know what she read for enjoyment. What she dreamed about, longed for. This was all getting too complicated. People made life messy. And watching over Petal had really thrown him headfirst into the muck.

"I was trying to be helpful," he muttered looking away from the romances that were lined up like soldiers in pastels and swirling letters.

"You are, Witt." Miranda shoved her hands in her back pockets and looked around the small room. It had been, Witt thought, in its previous incarnation a one-car garage converted to a bedroom with a small bath. There was no closet. Miranda's clothes must be in the clunky oak dresser sandwiched between the doorway to the bathroom and a desk with a hutch that was filled with neatly labeled, stacked Tupperware containers—clearly art supplies and tools. She had a basket of yarn and knitting needles at the foot of her twin bed that was covered with a plush green comforter and a white quilt with a tree and several birds on it.

The space was small, and surprisingly tidy. He would have thought Miranda would have had her life exploding on her bed and across her floor.

Miranda pulled out a denim dress and a denim skirt and a long red wool skirt and few blouses and sweaters that were all still on hangers on a small garment rack. Then she pulled a leather backpack off the end of the rack and opened up one of her drawers and quickly folded a few things into it.

He was in the way. Not being helpful. It reminded him of when he'd first come to Marietta and his biological father's ranch. Everything had been so different. Alien. And he'd been expected to do chores that he had no idea how to do. He didn't ride horses. He didn't know how to hold down the calves for branding. The flailing hooves had frightened him. He didn't know anything, and his siblings, younger and suspicious, had stared at him like he'd come from another planet. He felt like he had. He hadn't fit into life in Marietta then, and he didn't now.

"Want me to carry those to the car?" he asked holding his hand out, almost blindly.

"Sorry, I'm taking too long."

"What? No. Although if I don't walk out of here soon, I think your landlady will return waving a shotgun to protect your virtue."

"That would be a sight."

Petal was sifting through a bowl of glass beads. They were swirls of color and Petal let them slide through her fingers.

"Are these what you're going to give out to everyone who reports witnessing or experiencing a random act of kindness?" Witt asked and looked into the blown-glass bowl. "Did you make these?"

"I was hoping to make more beads—you know, Valentine's theme. Some of these will work but I was hoping to have more red with swishes of pink, purple and white. I've ordered more squares of those colors, and they should arrive tomorrow. I thought I'd work on making more beads when the store's not busy or at night in the hotel room."

Miranda handed her clothes on the hangers to Witt, shrugged her backpack on and then pulled several tubs of art supplies and equipment off of the shelves.

"You'll love learning how to do this," she said to Petal who asked about what was in the tubs. Then she grabbed a toiletry bag from the tiny bathroom.

"Can you carry the basket of yarn?" Miranda asked Petal. "Ready." She smiled brightly at Witt, who felt dumbfounded that this was all she was bringing for two weeks, especially when half of it seemed to be art supplies. "Virtue intact," she muttered under her breath.

"What's virtue?" Petal asked as Miranda stacked the tubs and held them tightly to her body so she could scoop up the bowl of beads.

"Over-rated."

WITT TOOK THE stairs down to the lobby two at a time. He was already in scrubs and pulling on his parka to brave the cold for the quick jog to the hospital. He rapped on the glass of Miranda's store and poked his head in the through the door that she still had propped open. It was nearing eleven at night when he'd received the page, but Miranda was still working on her store. The change was phenomenal and for a moment he forgot his rush.

All the boxes had been broken down and recycled. The shelves had been hung, and now had a variety of items ranging from candles, lotions and soaps, to handmade jewelry and artsy accessories—a variety of whimsical hats, hand-painted silk scarves, and wraps. The whiskey and wine barrels that had been dropped off and stacked one afternoon were now arranged around the store and used to display hand-blown glasses as well as a variety of food-oriented gift baskets. He noted that some of the wine barrels had shelves inside and a few of the whiskey barrels were hand painted with a scene that looked like one out of a Yellowstone postcard.

She had a coatrack in the corner but on it were a variety of stuffed animals or puppets of Montana wildlife.

"You look ready to open," he said, feeling a little staggered at how she had accomplished so much pretty much single-handedly.

The damn lurid pink tree now had long silver hooks on it and a few beads dangled from the hooks like fiery charms. Miranda had safety glasses on and a small, hand-held blowtorch in her hand.

"Got called in for an emergency. Car accident. Open fracture." Why he was telling her the specifics, he didn't know.

"Petal's sleeping, right?" Miranda pulled off her safety glasses and tucked the blowtorch back on a table that looked like it used to be a door. "I'll go up. An early night would be good for me."

No woman other than a physician would think knocking off work slightly before eleven p.m. would be early.

"Will you be long?"

"No idea. I likely have to operate tonight with an open fracture, but if the case is too involved we'll probably fly them out to a hospital with a Level I trauma unit. I'll need to evaluate. Maybe there all night so you'll need to get Petal up, breakfast and to school."

"Mary Poppins to the rescue." Miranda reached over and turned off a lamp that was made of inlaid wood—probably for sale. The store was now only lit by the ambient light from the bar.

"See you tomorrow, Witt, if not tonight." Miranda walked toward him snagging a light pink cashmere cardigan from off of a table. He'd never noticed how quietly she moved. Or how graceful she was. A bit of a sprite, he thought rolling his eyes at how fanciful he was being, although her long, shoulder-length ash blondish-brownish bob and straight bangs looked more like a mom haircut than anything fanciful emerging from an ancient forest.

He realized he'd been standing there in the doorway, blocking her way and staring instead of getting a move on to the hospital. He needed to work, not unleash some latent imagination.

She waited for him to take a step back. He was so much taller, she had to tilt her head back and rock back on her heels to look up at him.

"Anything else, Witt?"

"Thank you, Miranda," he said and left feeling curiously bereft.

A LITTLE OVER three hours later, he slid the key into the lock and quietly opened the door. It was ridiculous to be creeping into his own room like a teenager who'd badly broken curfew. Normally he would have slept at the hospital in one of the doctor's rooms, but he'd worried about Petal. Stupid, he told himself. She didn't need him. Petal was far more comfortable with Miranda. But it was the responsible thing to do. Mr. Responsible he'd been dubbed in college—never going to parties when exams were close, never getting drunk, always the designated driver, never missing assignments or study groups, always prepared for rounds, always knowing the answer. The list had gone on. Witt had accepted the snide title, not really caring what others had thought of him because he was so set on his goals.

But now for a thirty-year-old man it seemed a little boring.

He was boring.

He couldn't even imagine himself doing something…what, outside the lines? Stupid? Careless? Risky? Hell no. Just thinking about it made him recoil.

There was a low light on because Petal hadn't liked the dark. Witt's heart lurched. Petal was not in the twin bed that had been set up for her in the suite's living room. His heartbeat had gone from his usual low fifties to thundering in his ear. He lurched all the way in the room, barely remembering to hold the door as it latched to deafen the noise, and hurried to check Miranda's room. Her door was open and he stopped on the threshold, his hands gripping the doorframe.

Moonlight filtered in through the window's open curtains revealing two lumps in the bed, and he gulped in a breath, a little dismayed at how freaked out he'd been. Of course Petal wouldn't have crept out of the room. Where else would she go in the middle of the night? He wasn't sure how Miranda was going to like sharing her bed. His mother hadn't.

The memory rose up even as he tried to shut it out. He'd been small because he remembered the slats on the stairs' banisters as he ran up the stairs terrified—the dark, the nightmare. He didn't remember what it was about. He just remembered the terror flooding him. Heart galloping out of his chest, unable to catch his breath and running to his mother, crying. But she'd locked her bedroom door. He'd banged on it, clawed at it, jiggled the handle to get inside, to get to what he'd thought of as safety.

She'd come out. Tall, angry. Took him back downstairs, her mouth tight.

"Don't be a coward, Whitman. No one likes a coward."

He blinked and dragged himself back. His pulse was going crazy again. His breathing ragged. Why was he thinking of things like that? He'd tried not to think of his mother, of his old life in California after his first year in Montana. He'd been stuck, but he'd seen the way out, and he'd never once taken his eyes off his goal.

His gaze wandered back to the bed. Petal's dark hair streamed across the creamy sheets. She was curled up on her side, her arms wrapped tightly around something dark and furry, and she was tucked against Miranda. Miranda was in a dark tank, sheets and comforter flung back and one arm flung up and wide, like she was greeting a long lost friend and about to grab them in a hug. He found himself smiling. Even though she was small, her personality was large and she seemed to embrace life, looking forward to the next moment.

And why did that make him feel small? Witt had the strangest urge to take another step into the room to…what? Straighten the bedding to ensure she was warm? He'd scare her. He just felt so cold. Alone. The words and the accompanying feelings squatted unwelcome in his gut, and he shoved them away. He let go of the doorframe and forced himself to walk away. He was employing Miranda. He didn't walk into her bedroom even when the door was wide open. There were lines in life that he wouldn't cross.

Chapter Eight

MIRANDA OPENED HER shop at eight on the dot. Red-cheeked and breathless, but she made it. No one was waiting for her. No one cared. Her banner that she'd calligraphied late last night had partially fallen down, but she re-tied the string to a small hook she'd placed in the reclaimed wood molding above the door.

She'd already started a social media blitz with Twitter, Instagram and Facebook and even had a story going on Snapchat. It seemed silly to act like her store was a person, but if it were, it already had more likes and followers than she'd ever have, and by carrying so many different artists, she was able to link up with their sites and promotions and they could cover her when she was promoting a certain artist, or event. She'd had fun designing her website. She'd done it on her own, but had then asked a high school kid in the computer science lab to help her give the site a few more options and pizzazz.

Sighing happily, Miranda climbed off the step stool and started walking back to admire her red-and-gold grand opening sign. She bumped into something tall and hard.

"Whoops!" She whirled around, hands out to steady herself, her mouth already forming an apology.

"Witt. Wow! It's you."

She could hardly breathe. Or swallow. How did he do that? He was out of his scrubs and had clearly showered. His hair was damp, but swept back from his face in perfect alignment as if a stylist were always at the ready. He wore navy trousers and a thick navy sweater with a zipper that exposed a snowy-white T-shirt underneath. And now her mouth dried. No words.

"Don't usually elicit a wow," Witt said, a hint of a smile curving his usually stern mouth.

"Not sure I believe that," she whispered under her breath, but not quietly enough, because one straight dark brow arched in inquiry like he was a damn hero in a romance novel.

Witt Telford needed to stop being so perfect—like yesterday.

"Congratulations," he finally said into the simmering silence. He looked over her shoulder into the empty shop.

"Thank you." She tried to think of something to say—to ease the awkwardness—like that more people would come in later or that Petal had been dropped off to school a little early, but that her teacher hadn't objected and even had a little job for her to help her with. Or she could ask about his plans for the day.

"I brought you a coffee," he said and handed her one of the two cups he was holding.

"Thank you."

"For good luck."

"You want to come in?" she said. "You could be my first

official random act of kindness."

Witt took a step back. And not just a little one, but a big step in keeping with those long legs of his.

"No, I...actually um need a favor, which is separate from the coffee."

"Okay."

"My dad's white cell count's really climbed. I thought I could fly out to see him and fly back tonight so I could be at work tomorrow. I'm off today since I was on call last night."

"Of course, go." Miranda practically pushed him toward the door. "Of course you must be with your family."

"They aren't really my family."

Miranda stared at him, and in one of the mosaic mirrors she had mounted on the wall, she could see her expression was an unusual mix of bewilderment, concern and curiosity.

"But I think I should go."

"Of course." She sounded like an echo of herself. "And, Witt, they are your family."

She sounded like a scold, like she was his teacher or something. Could she be any more verbally clumsy? And to think in high school Tanner McTavish who'd also been on yearbook staff had joked that Miranda Evans's secret power was 'awkward silence breaker.'

How the mighty have fallen.

"Do you think I should bring Petal?"

"She's your cousin, Witt. It's your choice."

"It's just that…" He paused. Took a sip of his coffee, and Miranda watched his throat convulse. It was so vulnerable somehow when she didn't associate that word with him at all. "I'm only flying out for the day. Flying back early tonight, and Sarah was so worried about Petal having a routine, and...and she was looking forward to coming by your store after school to help you set up the craft corner."

He looked at her a little helplessly. "Is it wrong if I don't take her?"

Whitman Telford was asking her opinion.

"No. I'm sure your family would love to see her, but they are probably worried about your dad right now and sitting all day in a hospital would be a challenge for a child, but..."

He was nodding so she trailed off.

"So do you mind? Can you..."

"Of course." Miranda was going for a record with that phrase. And didn't that just about sum up her life? Need help? Miranda to the rescue.

"I've got Petal. And you're right. Petal and I have plans today so go be with your family. I'll make dinner and leave you something in the fridge."

"You don't need to cook." He looked appalled. "Order from room service."

"I love to cook. The suite kitchen is so much better than my hot plate and toaster oven. I plan to have fun with it."

His expression changed to doubt.

"I'll be back tonight, maybe late."

"I'm sure the hospital will give you time off."

Witt winced like that was the worst idea he'd heard. Okay so he was as dedicated a physician as he'd been a student. Nothing new there.

"I got this."

A smile ghosted. "Yes, Miranda, you do. I'm sorry to miss your opening day." Then he reached in his pocket and pulled out a clip with money. A money clip? She'd never even seen one of those.

"I don't need money, Witt." She felt embarrassed both by the reminder of the money that now defined their relationship, but also by her childish disappointment that he wouldn't be here in her store today to be part of her grand opening where she would be offering mulled apple cider or tea, heart-shaped cinnamon and sugar muffins that she'd baked using her toaster oven she'd brought over from her apartment. She hoped the smell would drift out into the lobby as a tease.

"You're taking care of Petal."

"I'd be buying groceries anyway."

"You might want…" he looked around as if there would be something floating in the vicinity that would be a crucial need sometime today "…something," he said lamely.

His kindness combined with his awkwardness made him irresistible and now it was Miranda who took the step back and crossed her arms tightly around her waist so that she absolutely wouldn't reach out and pull him into a hug he so clearly didn't want. She would have to content herself with looking. And maybe dreaming just a little.

"Be off." She waved him away, but he still handed her quite a few twenties.

"I noticed that Petal has ended up with a black bear from your puppet collection."

"Super sleuth."

"Your first official sale."

"It was a gift," Miranda said, uncomfortably aware that he probably knew more than she ever wanted anyone to know what a shoestring budget she was going to be operating on for the foreseeable future.

"Good luck today. See you tonight."

And he turned and walked away.

"Wait." Miranda ran to the glass bowl of heart-shaped beads that she'd been making last night and grabbed the most colorful one that was bigger than all the others. "Take this as a thank you for the coffee. I'm wishing your dad good luck and a speedy recovery."

Witt took the bead, and slipped it in his pocket. Miranda stamped down her disappointment to see him go and pasted on a smile. "Safe travels, Witt."

"Thank you, Miranda." His low, melodic voice affected her so deeply she felt like she was a tuning fork. And the way he said her name made her want to puddle at his feet.

"Which would be awkward and inconvenient," she muttered under her breath as she watched him leave.

Miranda felt such a strange mix of sorrow and yet happiness that she couldn't begin to define it, so she pushed it aside like she had so many other feelings and took a deep sip of the flavored latte. Cinnamon Candy—the February flavor of the Java Café. Miranda savored the taste as much as the gesture and felt her whole body smile.

WITT WALKED DOWN the corridor, his steps slowing as he neared the surgical waiting room. His father's hospital room. He'd felt compelled to fly out to the hospital, but couldn't shake the feeling that he was overstepping his bounds. He was family technically—his father's oldest son, and yet... He paused before the wide mechanical door. He'd been in contact with the surgeon, who had decided to re-open the leg wound surgical site, remove the plate, drain the wound and flood it with antibiotics and try again to re-pin his father's femur in a few days, which would keep his father in the hospital that much longer. More risk of infection and complications. And Petal with him and Miranda. Should he have brought her? Insisted?

He dealt with illness and injury daily. Why the hell was he so rattled?

He punched the button to the door of the surgical center waiting room. Quite a few groups of people looked up, but it was his half-sister, Riley, an environmental studies major in college, who jumped up and raced across the room.

"Witt! You came. Thank you." She tackled him in a huge hug.

Stunned he stood there like a tree before some latent social skills kicked in and he hugged her back.

"Any...you look great, Riley," he said rocked by Riley's affectionate greeting. Her eyes were bright blue like her mother's, as was her long golden hair. "All grown up."

And he didn't know what else to say.

Riley continued to cling, exclaiming over how tall he was, how proud they all were of him for becoming a doctor, how he'd always been a role model for her.

That shut down his thought process. Riley had been a tow-headed toddler and then later a gawky tomboy bean pole who'd followed all of her brothers around the ranch during chores, singing and asking question after question. Always the questions. And he'd been the one assigned to make sure she always had her homework done, such as it was in pre-school, kindergarten and elementary school before he left the ranch.

Sarah also rose gracefully and hugged him.

"Thank you for coming, Witt. I know you are busy with your new job."

"It's temporary," he almost said to ensure that he wouldn't somehow get stuck in small-town Marietta, but that would have sounded churlish so he bit back the reply and instead said nothing.

His youngest half-brother, Boone, stood up and man hugged him. Slapped him on the back so hard he coughed.

"Getting soft, old man, now that you've hit the big three oh."

Witt wasn't sure how to reply to that. It was weird. They felt like strangers, but they weren't, not really. Boone had texted him when he'd been injured saddleless-bronc riding in rodeo last year. He'd wanted him to look at his X-rays. Riley always harassed him to get on Twitter or Snapchat or Instagram, and he hadn't but it didn't stop her from texting him regularly.

He looked to Sarah, who'd always smoothed the way. Like Miranda.

"Any updates?" he asked. Medical questions and facts he could handle. People, unless they were patients, were not his shining skill set.

"We just got an update from the OR," Sarah said in her soft voice. "The plate is out, and they are cleaning out the infection. It's not spread too far into the bone so that's good."

She spoke each word deliberately as if she had memorized the OR update.

Witt nodded. He'd heard as much. He was relieved. So was Sarah. The tightness was gone around her eyes and around her mouth that he'd seen a few days ago when she'd accosted him at the hospital.

Riley and Boone headed down to the cafeteria to get something to drink and to bring Sarah a tea. Witt declined their invitation to join them or bring him anything.

"Witt," Sarah said after they sat side by side on a hard light blue vinyl couch. "Where's Petal? Reese didn't come back did he?" Her hands twisted together tightly.

"No," he said quickly, not realizing how much she disliked his uncle whom he only remembered stopping by the ranch a handful of times, and not for very long when he'd swagger off again, tipping his hat and winking, not a care in the world. "I've hired Miranda Evans to look after Petal when I'm on call so she's covering today and will pick Petal up from school and help her with homework and get her to bed. She's opened a gift store at the Graff. Petal loves going there and helping out and doing some arts and crafts."

"Of course I know Miranda. She's so lovely. She'll be

perfect for Petal. Brilliant idea, Witt—so like you. Miranda probably jumped at the chance. She loves kids. She was in your year at school."

Witt felt a dart of caution. Miranda hadn't jumped at anything. She'd accepted. Maybe he was uncomfortable because it was strange to see Sarah through the eyes of an adult, without his anger that Sarah was alive and his mother was dead. The bitterness that his biological father had not married his mother or wanted his son in his life but he'd had so much time and love for three children with a woman who was not his mother no longer thrashed and burned in his chest and gut.

"Thank you for coming," she said, not looking at him. Her hand reached out, probably to touch him. Sarah had always been so physically affectionate. He had always ducked out of range not wanting her kindness or her sympathy or her friendship. She checked herself, pressed her palm against her thigh. "Thank you, Witt," she repeated turning to meet his questioning eyes. He'd not thought him coming would mean that much to her. He'd been a sullen and aloof inconvenience—a reminder of a life before her. And the mistake that had come back to haunt his father. He still wasn't convinced his father would be glad to see him or embarrassed or indifferent. Definitely he'd be surprised, if he were cognizant enough to know and remember his visit.

Witt scrubbed his hand over his face. He was catching the last flight out tonight. He had some time, but it was weird to take it. To do nothing but sit. Think. Remember. Normally Sarah made small talk, soothed everyone. But now she sat on the edge of her seat, hands gripping the edge of the couch, knuckles white.

"The infection's not so out of control," he finally said. "They got it fast. I've spoken to the doctor every day. I'm pleased with his care."

"Then why are you here?" Sarah whispered.

"I don't know," Witt said, surprising himself with his honesty. "I felt like I should come, but you probably don't want…"

"We want you here." Sarah pulled him into an embrace, her wiry arms hard, strong from years of ranch work. "We always wanted you with us. Always. I wish you'd never ever doubted that for one second."

IT WAS STRANGE driving down the mountain pass and into Marietta several hours later. He felt like he was coming home. Marietta had never felt like that before. He'd always been full of resentment—pushing anything that was Marietta away especially his family. He'd felt like his mother's death had thrust him into an alternate and strange universe. He'd never felt like he'd belonged. So he'd made himself not fit. As if by pushing Marietta and his family away, he'd be the person he was supposed to be if his mom had lived. Had he somehow in his twelve-year-old mind thought that would bring her back to life? Had he thought he'd been loyal by rejecting his father and stepmother and half-brothers and sister?

As a thirty-year-old man that sounded ludicrous.

He'd been anxious about seeing his dad in the hospital. He always thought of him as the cowboy. Not in the sneering and accusing tone his grandparents had used, or his mother's dismissive tone—like a shrug. But as a cowboy, almost with a question mark like he couldn't quite believe a cowboy was in his life. But when he pictured his dad—he was always in ranch action, almost like a trailer for a western—up on a horse. Branding calves. Standing in the bed of his truck, tossing a bale of hay as easily as if it were a bag of trash sailing into a dumpster, stringing pasture fence, hefting up fence posts or two by fours and a hammer, nails sticking out of his mouth as he prepared to repair something. Even downtimes with family had been active—riding horses, archery, kayaking in the late spring or summer or cross-country skiing or skating or snowshoeing in the winter. He'd braced himself to look at his dad flat on his back in bed, in pain and disoriented.

Instead Taryn had been sitting up shooting shit with Boone about the bull that had managed to swing around away from its handlers and pin him, gore him and broken his femur. Said Sarah would think the scar was sexy, earning groans from Riley and Boone, and then he'd compared the bull to one he'd bought nearly a decade ago as a stud that had tossed Boone off its back and he'd tucked and rolled so far he'd hit the fence.

"Naaah." Boone had laughed at his father, eyes full of affection. "Demon was ranker than the pansy that pinned you from all I hcard."

"Bullshit." Taryn had laughed. "And I still bought that beast before I bled out," he had said, pleased.

He must have tried to adjust himself to sit further up because Witt had heard Boone's voice fast and strained. "Hey, Dad, let me do that for you."

"He's going to be a great stud bull, good as Demon I hope."

"He better be after this," Riley said. "Or Mom'll skin him, tan his hide and wear him as a coat."

"Bloodthirsty." Boone had laughed.

Witt had hesitated outside the door, hearing the banter he'd never been a part of.

"Go in." Sarah had nudged him in the back, and hadn't been gentle about it. "I didn't tell him you were working in town so he's going to be so surprised and over-the-moon happy." She gave him a final shove.

"Witt! Holy shit!" His dad looked like he was going to try to get up. "You didn't have to come. Riley just told me you got a new job at Marietta Regional."

Witt winced. So much for secrets in this family.

This family.

The words brought himself up short. It wasn't his, was it?

"It will be great to have you close again. The hospital is lucky to have someone with your skills." His father had actually looked happy to see him. His smile had reached his eyes and he remembered how people had always said that Taryn Telford had a smile that rivaled the sun. It was still bright, teeth white and straight, only the creases that feathered out from his eyes were deeper, longer. Despite the injury and infection and surgery, he still looked strong. Handsome. His dad was turning fifty this year.

Witt hadn't tried to correct him. He'd opened his mouth to say the job was temporary, and then looking at his dad—noticing the small changes in him—threaded gray in his hair, deeper lines bracketing his mouth and furrowed into his forehead and seeing how Sarah had quickly perched on the bed, and threaded her fingers through her husband's, her eyes full of warmth Witt was pretty sure he'd never inspired in anyone, he'd shut his mouth. Then asked his dad how he felt.

He'd spent over an hour with his dad and Sarah and Boone and Riley, and the conversation had never once flagged. As he started preparing to leave, he'd remembered some pictures he'd taken. He held out his phone and swiped to show them Petal at Miranda's shop making a dragon, and another one of Miranda showing Petal how to make the glass beads. She had one kit that could work with the microwave, but with careful supervision, she was letting Petal use the tiny hand blowtorch. He even had a picture of the garish tree. Of course his family loved the idea of the random acts of kindness.

"That's so like Miranda," Sarah had said fondly.

"I remember that gal." His father leaned back against the pillows now, clearly fighting his tiredness. Witt felt like they should all let him rest. He was paler under his tan and his energy now flagged, but considering he'd been nearly crushed by a bull and had had three surgeries in one week, he was doing damn good. He even looked pretty fit. "Nicest girl. Bit of an outcast in her family. A free spirit and the rest of the Evanses were so convinced of their own intellectual importance and Nordic beauty. Her mother used to call her a changeling. Couldn't abide that woman after that and told her so. Couldn't believe she'd reject her own child like that."

Witt had found it hard to swallow after his dad's recollection. His dad must have felt that about him—this sullen, cold, dark-haired kid—head always in a book instead of outside playing with his siblings and never seeming to take any joy in the animals on the ranch. But he'd kept trying to find something that would engage Witt. Kept trying to build a bridge for Witt to cross instead of knock down.

And why had he remembered that now?

It was like he'd started thinking of his childhood differently. Of all of them differently.

He had wanted to say something. Apologize, realizing for the first time the effort it must have taken for Taryn Telford to take in an oops from a quick and casual encounter years before into his home with his family. And for his wife to have daily faced her husband's past. It had been like he'd been seeing strangers in that hospital room, and that he'd been the person coming up short.

"Miranda was sweet. Helpful," Sarah had recalled. "Her parents always seemed like Marietta was too small for them. I was surprised they stayed as long as they did, but Miranda's a true hometown girl. Family-oriented and always volunteering at the school and church and in town."

Witt had felt like maybe it was a dig at him because he

hadn't been able to wait to get away from his family, but instead his father had smiled at him. "I'm glad you thought of her to help you out with Petal. She was always the first to help out in the Sunday school. Always holding the little ones and playing with them and doing little craft projects. Figured she'd have a passel of kids by now but..." He'd sunk a little further back against his pillow, trying to hide his wince, and they had all tried to ignore it too. "She was barely sixteen when she moved in to help her grandparents. Single-handedly tried to keep the ranch running and them in their own home. Not much help and not many dating or schooling opportunities out on their small farm."

Witt had shifted uncomfortably in his chair. It seemed as if Miranda had missed out on a lot during her twenties. He had too, but he'd been building something—his education, his career, his future life. He'd been in the driver seat of his destiny. Miranda, it seemed, had been merely staving off the inevitable.

But she was happy, wasn't she?

"I always thought she had such a crush on you, Witt. She just thought you walked on water." Sarah had smiled fondly. "She'd watch you at the church youth group or at the basketball games, other school events, but you always had your head in a book when you weren't excelling athletically or intensely engaged. Poor girl never had a chance."

Witt had been startled by Sarah's memory. Surely Sarah was exaggerating or making it up. And she wasn't thinking Miranda had a chance now, was she?

"She's focused on opening her gift boutique in the

Graff."

Not me.

The memory of that conversation still niggled. But that had been years ago. They'd been kids. The adult Miranda didn't have girlish fantasies. He swallowed hard. He was leaving in less than a month. She knew that. And even though she didn't have a lot of higher education, she was definitely smart. And savvy. And sweet and giving. She could see what a black hole he was.

Witt slowly drove through town. It was completely dark although only just coming up on six o'clock. He self-parked his SUV. Turned off the engine and stared through the windshield at the back of the hotel. People were expecting him in there. And he liked the feeling. He wouldn't have to go straight to his room alone with his own thoughts.

He climbed out and, automatically, his hand went to his pocket but it was empty. He'd given the red heart-shaped bead to his father. He'd told them about Miranda's Valentine's Day—her plan about the random acts of kindness, which would culminate in a community celebration at her store and the Graff bar and lobby.

They'd been charmed—everyone had marveled over the glass bead.

"It's for good luck with your recovery." Witt had suddenly felt stupid giving his father so little when his father had given him so much, and that had burned a hole in him he couldn't fully explain. "And to remind you of home."

"You be sure to thank that girl," his dad had said after Witt had gone to awkwardly hug him and then, afraid of hurting him, he'd pulled away and shaken his hand. He'd felt like an idiot, everyone staring, trying not to look judgmental or disappointed or whatever it was that he sensed that had always made him feel like his skin was too tight.

He had a lot to thank Miranda for, but had no idea where to start. Dinner probably. And words—words that were so easy for her, and always so painfully hard for him. But he'd lived his life in pursuit of becoming better—smarter, faster, more skilled and knowledgeable as a surgeon. He could learn to be a better person. More connected. Less aloof. No longer so driven to prove himself. He could be friendlier. He just had to try. And learn. And he couldn't think of anyone friendlier to teach him than Miranda.

Poor girl never had a chance.

He wondered, as the bitter cold motivated his near jog to the back entrance by habit now, how much of Sarah's words were actually true—not about him. He didn't believe Miranda had thought about him for a moment—but in other ways.

Chapter Nine

WITT STOPPED STOMPED the snow off his Romeos he'd been forced to buy since coming back to Marietta. They looked enough like regular shoes poking out beneath the hem of his trousers while still allowing him to walk between the hotel and the hospital quickly. His dad and Sarah had urged him to move back into the house until he found a place to stay but accepted his excuse that it was easier for Miranda to nanny Petal if he stayed at the hotel.

Why hadn't he told them his job in Marietta was so temporary? That he was only in town through the end of the month?

Head down he strode down the hallway, wondering at his reticence. Witt stopped short when he heard a warm laugh. He looked up, feeling as if he were waking from a dream. The glass wall that ran along the hallway was lit with red-and-gold twinkle lights that cast a warm, welcoming glow in Miranda's shop that spilled out into the hallway. Miranda was talking to two customers, a man and a woman, holding hands, probably about his own age.

Miranda was smiling, her dark eyes sparkling with enthusiasm as she showed off various food products on the big round table that he'd seen her lovingly restoring over the past couple of days. Petal held a basket filled with what looked like straw and as the couple made their decisions, Petal would put it in the basket, arranging and rearranging as things were added or substituted. Witt noticed that Petal's hair was braided in a complicated style and a plaid red, silver and gold ribbon was woven through the long pigtail braids.

Her little face was pinched in concentration, but every once in a while, she would look up and smile at Miranda, a little tentatively, but still her face shone with pride and even her posture seemed straighter, not so closed off.

Like I'd been.

He felt struck dumb. He wanted to go into the store. Be a part of it, but he didn't want to interrupt. And as he hesitated—stay or go, Miranda, as if sensing him, looked up. Her entire face lit up. She gently touched the woman's arm and said something and then rushed out of the store. He took a step toward her, a little surprised, but pleased by her enthusiasm.

"You're back!" she said and then hugged him.

The side of her face fit perfectly against his chest, right where his heart was, and Witt dragged his hands out of his pockets to hug her back after his initial surprise.

"Welcome home," she said. "Sorry for mauling you." She blushed and stepped back as if embarrassed, but even as she stepped away, he missed her, felt her absence. Perverse as he hadn't returned the hug.

Miranda tucked her hair behind one ear.

"How's your dad?" she whispered. Then she took his hand. "Come in. I'm closing up soon," she said.

"Better than I thought," Witt said, meaning it. "He looked like he'd pop out of bed at any moment. Not sure how he's going to take to his leg being immobile for any length of time."

"He's a cowboy." Miranda didn't let go of his hand as she led him back into the cheery shop. The scents of pine, apples and cinnamon assailed him. He breathed in deeply taking in all the changes that she'd somehow managed over the past couple of days and then today. "Nobody can keep a cowboy down for long."

"Hey Witt! How do you like my hair?"

"Love it."

He introduced himself to the couple. Angela and Guillermo Garcia.

"Your wife is going to need to get bigger gift baskets," the woman, whose name was Angela said. "She's a natural salesperson, and what a beautiful eye. We always come through Marietta on our way skiing in December and February and I can tell that next year, I'll be doing most of my Christmas shopping here. What a wonderful idea to focus on all local products and artists. And your idea of the random acts of kindness is just so sweet and needed in today's political and social climate," Angela sighed. "That's what brought us in here," she said.

"Baby, you're going to talk the poor man's ear off and all he wants to do is be with his family after a long day. Miranda needs to close her shop so we need to make our final decisions and meet our friends for dinner at Rocco's."

"Sorry," Angela said and smiled at Witt. "Your daughter's been such a help. Adorable."

"Oh," he said looking at Miranda and then Petal. Miranda was super busy putting cellophane around the basket. Petal measured out the ribbon against a yardstick, her pink tongue poking out in concentration. He felt a little bit like laughing at the sweetness of the moment, and correcting the assumption didn't seem to matter. Wife. Daughter. It should sound so alien, and he was always so quick to correct mistakes.

But he let it go. Pretended it hadn't happened. Didn't matter.

Why? He'd always been such a stickler for facts. Statistics. Now that made him seem old and priggish.

"Petal, do you want to tie the bow on the basket this time like I showed you?"

Witt noticed Petal had a dragon curled around her finger. It looked a little like Miranda's dragons, only more misshapen, but it was cherry red with a red bead for a heart and the wings matched the ribbon in her hair.

"Petal, smile for Aunt Sarah and Uncle Taryn," he said softly instead.

He snapped her picture and texted it to Sarah before he could think too much about why he didn't feel the need to correct anyone today or to create distance.

Angela added a few more items, and Miranda never seemed fazed or rushed. She never checked her watch. She discussed the merits of each product and often she listened. Witt was gaining a new respect for retail. He had imagined Miranda would just scan things or ring them up using her

Square and iPad, but she was creating an experience. An environment.

"Hot apple cider, Witt, or coffee or chai?" Petal asked him.

"Cider," he decided. He hadn't had hot apple cider since he was a kid, but tonight, here, it just sounded right.

Petal skipped off, one hand held high as if her dragon were flying above her. Angela whispered something to her husband and he wrapped his arms around her and kissed the top of her head.

"You are truly blessed," she said to Miranda, as Miranda scanned each item. Miranda paused and looked up at her. Her lopsided smile looked so charming that Witt felt as if the cold that had seemed to grip him even in his short walk from the car to the hotel and the worry about his father fell away a little more.

Miranda looked around her shop, her eyes lit on him and she winked and then she looked at Petal. "I am," she said. "I truly am."

He sipped his cider as the couple paid. He noticed quite a few white and hot pink tags hanging from the tree, tied on with red ribbon.

"Isn't that just the most amazing thing?" Angela asked as he stood there reading first one, then another and then another. "We were in Sage's buying some chocolate for my mother. And we saw the flyer and thought it so quaint, but then I saw a man buy two hot chocolates for two teens who looked like they might have been on a date, and they were deliberating between some chocolate and the hot chocolate, and it was clear that money might be an issue and while they stood around the boy and girl both nervous but not able to talk about the real problem, the man just slid a ten over the counter to the sales assistant, who made the hot chocolate. It was random and anonymous, and I just wanted to come by this shop to say what I saw, and Miranda had me write it down and add it to the tree. I feel like a little piece of us will be here for the month of February."

※

"Good day?" Witt asked after the couple had left and Miranda had closed the store.

"Amazing. It really was like a dream."

He looked skeptical, and she felt herself color. "I suppose your dreams are quite different from mine."

He didn't say anything. And what could he say, Miranda wondered. "My life must seem so small compared to yours," she mused as she wrote down a few notes for herself for tomorrow.

"Why would you say that?" he asked, pausing in the act of blowing on the fragrant, steaming cup of cider.

"You've gone away to school. Earned your degree. Went to medical school. Completed your residency. You are poised to start a whole career so far from where you started—like you've always wanted." Her voice broke on the last word, which was just stupid. She hadn't wanted to do those things. They'd been expected of her, but she'd loved living in Marietta, and hadn't had the drive to leave.

"Not so far." His mouth twisted a little wryly.

"I thought you said Marietta was only temporary."

"Oh it is," he said decisively. Very decisively.

And she'd known that so it was stupid to let her heart sink.

"But my grandparents are in Los Angeles. They both are doctors but are in research. My grandmother was a top researcher in Parkinson's disease as well as an adjunct professor in a medical school, and my grandfather was a researcher as well with a biotech firm. They still live in Los Angeles."

"So you are in a way going home," she said. "That makes more sense now. I always forget that Sarah is your stepmom. She was always so involved with the high school booster club because of all your sports that I saw her at every game, and she was always taking pictures of you. She was so proud and at every game. She just seemed like, you know, the perfect mom. I was always a little envious because by the time I burst into the world my parents were tired of parenting and didn't participate at the school or in much of anything really."

She noticed Witt staring at her, a funny expression on his face.

She touched his hand. "Sorry. I talk too much. You must be tired."

"No, I don't mind. I'm getting used to your talking."

Miranda laughed. "High praise from the doctor. Your grandparents will be pleased to have you back and so close."

He looked at her, and his face was briefly bleak, but she

must have imagined it.

"I think excited is an overstatement," he said. "They...well, we're not close. They didn't approve of my dad, and well, I didn't see that much of them when I was growing up before my mom died. I think..." He broke off and looked at Petal, straightening off the long farmhouse table where she had her clay out, and he could see some coloring supplies as well as some tools and a large handful of the glass beads.

"You still making beads?"

"We gave out ten today, Witt," Petal said coming to his side. "Miranda let me make some. The ones she had were multicolored. She wants to only hand out Valentine-themed ones." Petal spoke carefully as if she'd memorized a speech or had been practicing the same phrase over and over. A shy smile stole across her lips—fleeting, but Witt noticed. "I made some after school, and got to give a few out when people came in and told a story of an act of kindness they saw or experienced. Do you see my dragon?"

"I have been admiring your dragon." His eyebrows quirked. "Girl or boy?"

"Girl." She lifted it up and down and did a few twirls in mid-air.

"Does it have a super power?"

Petal stared. Miranda nearly hugged herself. Witt and Petal were forming a bond. She was so happy for Petal. She needed a man who would be kind and accepting. Even in the few days she'd known Petal, Miranda was amazed at how smart she was, but unique. And unique was not always easy for a child. She needed a family who would… She broke off. Witt wasn't staying in town. He wasn't close to his parents. He might head off to his new job and new life in LA and barely give Petal a passing thought.

Miranda felt a little sick. How could he do that? She'd only been watching out for Petal for three days and already she couldn't imagine her days without her.

"Always an open, wounded bleeding heart," she heard her mother's voice as if it were in the store.

"I didn't think of a super power," Petal said.

"What's wrong?" Witt asked.

Miranda stared at him feeling like she was already accusing him of abandoning Petal, which she knew wasn't fair. It wasn't as if Petal were his child. And he certainly hadn't agreed to her care beyond when Sarah and Taryn returned to their ranch. But Sarah would have her hands full. Miranda swallowed her worry audibly.

"S'mores." She latched on to the first word to enter her head. "I promised Petal urban Valentine s'mores. We were going to taste test a new recipe."

"Urban s'mores," Witt repeated. "Is fire involved?"

"I have a hot plate that I brought up to the room. It's better with gas, but the hot plate will work in a pinch."

"Am I invited?"

For some reason, the light in his eyes, almost teasing, and the way his face seemed more relaxed than the first few days she'd spent around him, Miranda found her heart kicking into high gear and her stomach flipping over.

"Always," she whispered without thinking of the ramifications of that.

She felt like she was holding her breath. Holding herself back so that she didn't step into his arms. She was technically working for him, she reminded herself, much as she had throughout today when she'd kept checking the time and wondering when she might expect him back.

"So let me clean up a little for tomorrow and we'll head up to our room. Your room." She flushed at the implication.

Miranda checked her records on the iPad against the notes she'd jotted down with each purchase and replaced some stock, straightening as she went. She smiled, encouraged when Petal approached Witt and pointed at the cork bulletin board that Miranda had cut out in the shape of a heart and used 3M sticky pads to stick it to the side of an ancient armoire.

"A lot of people came in today and they filled out the little slips of paper Miranda had me cut with special heart paper. Come see." She slipped her little hand into his and led him toward the front of the store where the tree, now pink and red, had dozens of red glass beads hung from white ribbons. "This morning there was one slip of paper and now there are…thirteen. That's good luck isn't it?" She touched each one reverently. "I wrote this one up."

Petal plucked the heart-printed paper off the corkboard and held it in one hand and the pink push pin in another.

I was shopping at Big Z's and was distracted when my two-year-old ran out the door. A teenage boy caught him in the parking lot and did a few magic tricks and then helped me load my car and kept my son entertained with magic tricks.

"There are more," Petal said softly. "My favorite is at the Java Café. Someone paid for their latte and the latte for the person behind them and it went all morning with people paying for the person behind them. Two hours. The barista came in after her shift and told Miranda all about it. And she said her tips were the biggest ever."

"Sounds like your Valentine plan is a success."

Miranda looked up and realized he was talking to her.

"I hope so. It's day one. Thirteen more days to go. People have liked the red hearts. I saw a couple hanging from car rearview mirrors so I thought I'd cut longer ribbons. On Valentine's afternoon I'm going to have a Valentine party for everyone with a red heart bead so you should hang on to yours." She tried to sound teasing, and not too obviously longing for him to come.

"Looks like I'll have to do another good deed," he said. "I gave my bead to my dad for good luck when they go back in to stabilize his femur. He'll have to come to your party via Skype."

"That was sweet, Witt."

He laughed and ran a hand through his hair, and suddenly it was hard to breathe. He looked so sexy when he did that. Younger. Happier.

"Don't think that word has ever been used in a sentence about me before," Witt said. "I won't tell if you won't."

She could really fall for him, she thought. Who was she kidding? She'd already fallen hard. Years ago. Only that was the Witt in her imagination. This one was all too real.

"I'm ready," she said softly thinking how lovely it was to

have him in her store, to have someone to go home with even if it were just for a few days. "We can go on up."

URBAN S'MORES. WITT couldn't believe he was actually doing this. The three of them sat around the larger table in the suite warming big fat marshmallows speared on fir tree twigs. Miranda already had the graham crackers and chocolate prepared. And a shaker of red-and-pink sugar crystals. She'd also ground some pink Himalayan salt in a pestle and mortar. Miranda sat cross-legged, elbows on the table as her two marshmallows began to brown and get gooey and started to droop off her stick. Petal had already lost one marshmallow to the hot plate, which had had to be turned off and cleaned and fired up again.

"Don't want to set any smoke alarms off," Miranda said. "Or get the fire marshal out of bed."

"You could claim it was training practice for him to keep it sharp and give yourself a heart," Witt said. "Or perhaps if you give him one of your s'mores he might consider that a random act of kindness and I could inform Petal and earn another heart."

"You will have to work harder than that," Miranda said. "It is not that easy to earn a heart," she said, her words light, but Witt's mind had already gone where it probably shouldn't.

"Nor should it be," he said softly.

Miranda smoothed the marshmallow on a graham cracker and sprinkled the sugar and then a pinch of salt on the marshmallow and closed it with another graham cracker. She handed it to Petal.

"This one and the marshmallow you are cooking and then it's brush teeth and off to bed."

She handed the other s'more to Witt. He took a cautious bite. And chewed slowly letting the salt and sugar and chocolate melt over his tongue followed by the warmth of the marshmallow and the crunch of the cracker. Petal gulped hers and licked her fingers. Then she yawned.

"And wash your hands and face," Miranda added. "You can sleep in the trundle or with me. Your book is on the nightstand."

"Night, Witt," Petal said shyly scooping up her black bear puppet. "Night, Miranda." She hugged Miranda quickly then like a flash disappeared into Miranda's bedroom.

Miranda turned to him. "What is the verdict? You look like you are studying for a test."

"These are surprisingly good," he said.

"And you had to think about it that hard."

"No. I was thinking about if I ever had a s'more before."

"Seriously? Did you go to camp or…?"

"No. Never. Well, science-oriented camps, when I was young because my mother worked full time. She was very goal-oriented. Everything had to have a purpose. Life was black and white. Everything was about achieving. School and homework were king."

"Sounds like my mom," Miranda said. "She hated it

when I'd climb trees with my sketch pad or a fantasy book and just lose myself. 'Artists don't make money,' she'd say. 'There's no jobs reading books. No job security without college,' and it went on, and she wasn't wrong, really. It was her view of the world, and she wanted to prepare me, but…" Miranda speared one more marshmallow and prepared the crackers with the chocolate for two more. "I always felt like she wanted me to be someone I wasn't."

Witt nodded. "I think it was similar for me, only my mom and my grandparents to some extent wanted to mold me into them. And I think they were so afraid that I would turn out to be a bad seed because of my dad."

"Seriously? They said that?"

Witt felt disloyal. He'd never discussed his mother or grandparents or his feelings about his father with anyone. Ever. But somehow, with Miranda, it just seemed natural. She opened something inside of him. A door he didn't know he had.

"The cowboy. That's what they called him. I didn't even know his name or what he looked like until I was brought to the ranch."

He could see her thinking, her mouth forming words that then she'd discard. And why now? Now that the words hung there, out in the open, his lack of information about his father sounded awful. Miranda swallowed. He heard it. She touched his hand, running her finger down one of his. "Witt, I'm sorry," she said. "It just sounds so…so…cruel."

"It was so strange today," he admitted. "I spent my whole time in Marietta wanting to get away, get back to where I belonged, where I'd started with my mother and my grandparents, but that wasn't really a home either. The things you do in your shop—the spiced cider, making the shop reflect your personality, thinking of other people and their comfort and happiness, I never had that before. Never. I don't think I ever knew it existed. And then when my mother died, I hated going to my father's ranch because…because…" He sucked in a deep breath aware that he'd been on a precipice—about to step off into a void he had no way of navigating.

Miranda didn't push him. Instead she roasted the marshmallows until they were golden and gooey and captured in the chocolate and graham cracker. She sprinkled on the red crystalized sugar and the cocoa nibs and handed him one and took one for herself. Then she scooted her chair closer to his and laid her head on his shoulder.

"This is pretty damn magical," he said, not sure if he were limiting himself to the taste of the s'mores.

"I think so too," Miranda said.

They finished their treats, not talking, and for Witt, for once his mind felt still and his body calm.

"I don't think I've ever done anything like this. So simple but so enjoyable. You make the everyday a little magical, Miranda."

He saw her eyes get a sheen. "That's definitely the nicest thing anyone has ever said to me."

He felt pleased. And a little embarrassed. He wanted to say something else—something to make her smile, but he didn't want to make it awkward. He didn't want her to think he would try to take advantage of her. She was so sweet and kind and deserved so much more than a man who had trouble showing emotion. It had been so discouraged by his mother and his grandparents, and at his father's house he felt like he was intruding, and he was the oldest kid so he should set a good example, but he was never sure what that example should be. They were so different from him. Loud and laughing and busy and always talking and teasing.

He found himself looking at her—really looking. She was petite. Boyishly slim, but her face was so sweet, heart-shaped, huge brown eyes that showed every thought and every emotion and shone with warmth and enthusiasm. And her mouth. It was small and sweet like a little rose bud. She didn't seem to wear makeup, but her lips were a dark pink, almost red as if she were wearing a tint, but he didn't think she was.

He wondered how many men she'd kissed. Why she was single when she clearly had so much love to give.

"You can live life the way you want, Witt. What happened before is in the past. How you felt in the past doesn't have to be how you feel in the future. People are capable of great change."

"You really believe that?"

"Absolutely. Every day is a different day. Every day you can choose how you want to be."

He sighed. "That's just it," he said, and then didn't speak for the moment it took him to gather his thoughts. "I don't know how."

Her eyes searched his, and he felt like she was seeing

him—really seeing him, not the doctor, not the academic, not the perfectionist who knew how to study and out-work everyone but know so little about how to communicate. There was no judgment there. None. And that felt so freeing.

He told her something he'd never told anyone ever.

"My mom always made it seem like my dad wasn't interested in me. She told me he lived in Montana and had his own family. When I had to go live with them, I was so nervous and angry that he'd treated my mom like that—treated us like that. I felt like he'd had his chance to be my dad and he'd blown it."

He expected Miranda to say something, but she didn't. She just leaned forward, her small hand resting on his arm. It was the gesture of a friend—and he hadn't really allowed himself the luxury of many of those—and it warmed him through. Miranda always listened with her head, her heart and her body.

"And then when I arrived, everyone came out to greet me. It was so strange because I was the only kid who looked like him. The others—Boone and Rohan and Riley—looked like Sarah. And then when I came into the house there were all these pictures on the wall of all of the kids, but I was there too. School pictures only. And some baby pictures, and I thought maybe it was a trick like they'd gotten the pictures from my mother somehow after she died, but my mom never put pictures in frames. Just art."

"She must have sent him pictures each year," Miranda said quietly.

"But she never told me that," he said, and even after so

many years, he still felt the frustration and the anger run through his veins. She'd kept something from him. But why?

"That night I crept down into the living room with a flashlight and took the pictures off the wall to see if he'd just put them up after he got the news that she'd died, but there was some discoloration. I could see a faint shadow in the shape of the frame. And I looked behind all of them." He ran a hand through his hair, shamed. "I never asked about the pictures," he finally said. "I never gave him the chance to explain."

"So if you get bored of doctoring you could try detective work." She knocked against his shoulder, and Witt found himself smiling.

His guilt over his lack of trust and his lifetime of coolness toward his father eased a little. Miranda had lightened his mood as he began to take himself once again too seriously. She was right: each day was new and he could try to reach out more to his father, to his family. They'd never slammed the door on him. He just had to open it from his side.

"Your shop," he said, letting his curiosity about another person for once loose. "Is that what you really want?"

"Yes. I love having my own space and being able to turn it into whatever I want and changing it when I want. It's mine. I know it's small, and I know I'll at best just be able to keep it open and live a simple, frugal life, but I really, really like having my own business and connecting with people—not just customers but other merchants and artists too. I feel like I'm a conduit for people's visions and people's wants, and that I can be a part of their lives and bring pleasure and happiness even if it's just in one interaction or one sale. If someone buys a quilt at my store, the artist and I make money, but the customer has a memory."

"So it's enough?"

"What do you mean?"

"Is that all you want?"

"You mean in life? Do I only want to own a store?"

"Yes."

"No. I want more. Of course I want more. I would love someone to fall in love with me." Her voice caught and she looked down at her hands twisted together. "And I want to have a child—more than one if I'm honest. And I want to be part of the town not just by being a business owner, but by being of use, being integral. Volunteering at my church and in the schools or with one of the many fundraisers around town. I love knitting and taking pictures, and lately I've even started making some frames out of recycled wood and weird random things I collect at flea markets or in old barn sales that I've started going to to buy vintage items to decorate the store so I like to challenge myself with creating things to give away as presents or maybe sell. My own store allows me to try new things, be creative yet also create traditions. So to answer your question, yes, it is enough, but Witt I want so much more."

He stared at her eyes sparkling with enthusiasm. They seemed liquid. Her breath came quickly. She was so full of life and plans and vibrancy. In comparison he was empty.

"Like dancing," she said.

"Dancing?"

"I was running my idea about having an open house celebration the afternoon of Valentine's Day to celebrate the random acts of kindness by the hotel manager and the events coordinator to make sure my plans wouldn't interfere with the Valentine's Ball." Her mouth curved up in the crooked smile, and Witt, knowing Miranda's stories always built on themselves, found himself leaning forward to hear more.

"Walker Wilder is planning the ball. It's a dinner and dancing and each year it's a different theme, and I realized as he was talking about the theme, *Love through the Ages* and how there are going to be dance instructors there to teach couples several historical dances like the waltz and the jitterbug and the samba, that I had never been to a dance."

He felt a bit startled. She looked forlorn. This was a cowboy town with a slightly upscale saloon, a bar and a brewery—FlintWorks—that he knew had music on the weekends at least. There must be plenty of opportunities for young women to dance. He knew men were supposed to hate dancing, at least most men he'd gone to medical school with unless they were drunk did, but Witt knew how to dance. Sarah had made sure of that. She and Taryn had often country danced at the many events they attended, and even would turn music on in the house, shove the furniture aside and make sure all of the kids danced with them. It was one of the few things he remembered doing with them where he hadn't felt awkward.

"So your last dance was prom?"

"Actually I never quite made prom," she said, ducking her head, not meeting his eyes.

But he'd seen it. The hurt. Not going to prom. Twelve years later it still stung.

"There's dancing at Grey's," he said wanting to make her feel better, but going to a bar sounded so totally unMiranda like that he immediately felt stupid, but she'd said that each day held the potential for a reboot. Maybe she could do a little reinventing herself. "I went in for one beer with Wyatt and his brothers and even in the early afternoon there were some cowboys two-stepping their way into getting lucky."

"Um maybe," Miranda said. "Not sure I'll be too successful in that arena. I think cowboys and other men at Grey's are looking for something more…more…something." She flushed. He stared at her, trying to decipher what she meant.

"I'm more of an acquired taste, or not." She whispered the last part, bit her lip, and then smiled a little tremulously.

It was the first time he'd seen her look unsure of herself. And he didn't like it. Not. At. All. But what did a man say to the truth? Miranda wasn't a quick and easy pretty. She didn't shout out sex appeal. The gaze of most men entering a room would pass over her without note. Hell, he'd attended middle school and high school with her and hadn't remembered her. He'd blocked out most of his childhood, but so many of the memories were coming back hard—his past was starting to feel like a tsunami—it had been sucked far out to sea, but the wave was forming and racing toward him.

And the touch of sorrow in her eyes was undoing him.

"Like a fine wine," he said without thinking how the words would sound out in the open. Sexual. The *sipped, savored*, not said hung between them.

She looked up at him, doubt edging her expression. A tingle of hope.

She looked so ethereal sitting on the chair, her legs all tucked up under her, her pixie face so pale and earnest and her eyes drinking him in. He felt such a tug toward her that he couldn't quite explain, but he was starting to wonder what it was and why now. And also if he weren't planning to pull up his stakes and head to California at the end of the month if he'd want to explore this pull.

She wasn't his type, but even as he thought that, he brushed it aside impatiently. What was his type? Tall, athletic professionals who were busy and focused on their lives and careers and only made time for him for brief and sweaty sexual encounters that ended with him or them leaving before the sheets got cold with a vague promise to text and get together again.

Sitting here having had a cup of lentil and vegetable soup along with the s'mores made those encounters seem soulless and faintly disturbing. She said anyone could change, be different. He wondered if that were really true, at least for him. For the first time, he hoped so.

Witt, who always planned every move, in advance after much analysis before he acted on anything, didn't.

Instead, he leaned forward, cupping her face in his hands, his eyes brooding over her pixie features, wide cheeks, faintly freckled, pointed chin, red lips that always looked poised to speak or laugh and then those damn expressive eyes that just saw through to his soul. She was undoing him like he had been wrapped in icy gauze and she'd pinched one edge and was slowly unraveling him one layer at a time, and he wanted her to stop as much as he wanted her to continue.

"You," he said, not even aware he'd spoken. So much crashed around in his head, he couldn't sort it fast enough. The intellect he'd been so famed for in school and residency utterly failed. "Something about you."

Her lips parted a little shocked, and his thumbs, grazing her neck, could feel the race of her pulse. "Something I can't explain."

Or define, and it fascinated him. Normally his brakes would have jerked him to a stop long ago, but Witt plowed forward, tilting Miranda's face up to his, like he owned it, his eyes searching her liquid brown ones with their pinpoints of gold and darker brown that heated him until he caught aflame. He lowered his head, catching her quick, shocked exhalation as it mixed with his breath, and he kissed her.

What started out as sweet, exploratory, quickly spun out of control. Miranda tasted delicious. Warm, willing woman mixed with chocolate and the peppermint flavor of the sugar crystals. He folded her into his body and her hands were in his hair, down his back, and his were under her sweater, touching the warm, taut skin of her abdomen. Her hair teased his skin sending delicious shivers through him.

Her mouth opened, warm heated honey, and he found himself pressing in closer, fingers spearing through her hair.

"Witt," she whispered. "More."

The heated words had the opposite effect. More? He couldn't give her more. It wasn't right. He was temporarily employing her. Petal was sleeping in the adjacent room. He was only here for the month. Miranda wasn't fling material. She was precious. She deserved to be cherished and taken care of, not discarded when convenient. What the hell was happening to him? He didn't… He couldn't… His mind grasped at reasons to have him break the kiss, but somehow his motor cortex had been ignoring the flashing red lights and warning sirens.

Her whispered 'more,' was the dash of cold water that woke him from the dream. Miranda deserved so much more—more of everything—time, affection, emotion—than he could ever give her. She deserved a man comfortable in his own skin, who would build a life with her and take her dancing, not this awkward man who never fit anywhere but in the OR.

"Sorry," he whispered, meaning it, and yet when he leaned his forehead against her to get a grip on his libido and her lips chased his, biting down lightly, a new arrow of heat speared him. "Sorry," he tried again.

She cupped the back of his head to keep him in place and he felt like he was drowning in the melted chocolate of her gaze.

"I'm not. I'm not ever going to be sorry I kissed you," she said fiercely. "Not now. Not ever."

Chapter Ten

THE NEXT FEW days passed in a blur. Miranda couldn't get the kiss out of her mind, yet she was so busy, she didn't have time to dwell.

Her random acts of kindness promotional campaign seemed to have a life of its own. People came into her store to tell her about kindness they'd experienced or had seen, but others had suggestions for her—have a link on your website so people can participate that way. So she figured out how to do that. Sky Wilder, Colt's sister in-law, came into the store one morning, her beautiful little girl in tow and her belly sweetly rounded with another pregnancy, and looked around for a "future gift."

Miranda thanked her for making her the door handle for the store out of scrap metal, and was surprised by Sky's vagueness. She didn't know why she would need to be mysterious. She didn't really know her, but she'd grown up with Sky's two sisters-in-law who were twins, Tanner and Tucker McTavish, who'd been only a couple of years behind her in school. She'd also gone to school with Colt.

"Actually, I do want to buy something, but I'm not sure what," Sky said after her daughter, Montana, had slipped her finger into one of the dragons Miranda and Petal had made together. Miranda could tell Petal had natural artistic talent and was improving to the point where she wouldn't have to help her anymore either with making the dragons or the heart-shaped beads, although because of the small hand-held blowtorch she would always be near and insist Petal wore protective gear.

"And I'm sorry, but what I really wanted to ask you about is your tree."

"My tree?" The heart beads hung from the tree. She'd started with twenty, but in the five days she'd been open, she'd had to make twenty more, and yesterday she was down to a few so last night, she and Petal had stayed in the store after closing to make ten more beads before heading up to their room to make dinner and hang out and chat and paint each other's toenails a brilliant scarlet.

"I know my brother-in-law, Colt, told you I was a metals artist and you so kindly let me experiment with the handle for your boutique's door," Sky had said sounding a bit shy as if Miranda hadn't heard of her or didn't know that the Copper Mountain Rodeo Association had already asked Sky to create a sculpture for them to celebrate the grand re-opening of the fair and rodeo grounds late next summer in time for the rodeo. The town had been devastated when a fire had swept through and destroyed the grandstands and most of the arena and damaged several outbuildings.

She also knew Sky was married to Colt's brother, Kane, who was one of the top bull riders in the world so she didn't exactly fly under many people's radars in a western ranch town where so many people raised or trained bulls to compete on the various rodeo or professional circuits.

"I have a commission where I need to create an outdoor sculpture that incorporates LED lights that can be programed to turn off and blink and change colors and do a different pattern to music, but I'm still playing around with the concept," she said. "How to make it work, and usually I make several small to-scale models so I can see how all the pieces are going to go together and figure out the balance I'll need and if I can make a mold or weld."

Miranda listened fascinated. She hadn't approached Sky about her work other than taking the handle Colt had offered rather off-handedly because she was getting commissions from all over the world for hotels and office complexes and wealthy collectors who owned companies. Not many in Marietta could afford her work unless they were related to her.

"That sounds like it would be beautiful. I saw a light system in the Apple store that can be programed to change color. It sounds a little like that."

"Exactly," Sky said. "And, well, here's the tricky part. It's a tree."

"Oh." Miranda felt more was needed from her but what?

"So I'm going to have several tree sculptures in different sizes and different artistic approaches left over, and I'll also need to experiment with the lighting, and well, I wondered since you have a very seasonal tree in here if you'd want one of them when I'm done, and you could change the lighting to match the season if you wanted."

Miranda stared. Not quite sure she was hearing correctly.

"You are offering me one of your samples to buy?"

"Oh." Sky colored. "No. Of course not. As a donation if you wanted. You could use it as a permanent fixture—you know at Christmas or if you do the Valentine's random acts of kindness again next year. Colt said he could put a bolt in the floor to anchor it outside in that little niche so it wouldn't block the passageway, and I think..." Sky swished her arms up and out in one direction a little like a high dab "...that since it's supposed to be a tree in the wind the lines might be kinda cool because the branches would point up to the lettering of your store and the lights of the tree would provide a visual cue to draw people in."

"You're offering to give me a metal sculpture tree with lights?"

"A copper tree with lights. If you want. I thought it might work better with the historic look of the hotel lobby and the entrance Colt made."

"You're giving me a sculpture?"

"Is that so hard to believe?" Sky laughed.

"Giving." She'd clutched Sky's arm. "That's perfect. That's the little piece I've been missing."

Miranda was practically jumping up and down with excitement, and by the time she had helped Sky pick out a leather woven bracelet that had turquoise-and-silver beads through a few of the leather strands and an ornate but masculine clasp for her husband who had had to head back out on the bull rider's tour without her and their little girl for the first few weeks, the idea was forming in her head, and as Sky paid for the purchase and her daughter, Montana, had chosen a dragon that Sky had insisted on paying for even though Miranda had tried to comp it, she was writing the radio copy for the announcement in her head.

And as Sky walked out, Miranda was already booting up her computer to make yet another link to her website for people to list some needs or wishes during the month of February so that she could try to match up a need with someone who was willing and able to give.

A kiss.

The word filtered in and out of her consciousness during the day as she worked on her website, helped customers, recorded random acts of kindness and even entered her first need on the website. She also physically wrote it down and tied it to the tree, thinking that people could come in and choose the need off the tree like how people or families would "adopt" a child or a family during Christmas.

She blew at her thick bangs. It had been nearly two years since she'd had a haircut or a hairstyle. One more thing on her list. She called the radio station, and to her surprise, Dylan put her on air so she could thank all the people who'd been participating in the random acts of kindness as well as announce the extension into a tree of giving. Dylan had asked so many questions including those about the Valentine's afternoon celebration that she was forced to make a few hasty decisions on the spot about the celebration and hope she remembered them long enough to write them down and make them happen.

"You're really enjoying yourself." Miranda leaned against the wine barrel where they'd had dinner last week. Had it really only been a week ago? "This is quite an engineering feat."

Witt leaned back on his heels and looked at the extensive marble run he and Petal had been working on since last night. It was part of her random acts of kindness and giving campaign. Anyone participating got to put a marble through the marble run and watch the collection of marbles in the jar at the end of the marble maze grow. It was in the front window of her store near the pink-and-red tree that was, in a way that still made him itch, growing on him. Sort of. It was still ugly. But it was sweet in an offbeat way and defiantly cheerful. A testament to second chances and who was he to scoff at that?

"I never did do anything by half measures," he admitted although in this case, maybe he was getting carried away. "I always wanted one of these kits when I was a kid."

"So you ordered five wooden marble run kits and overnighted them." Miranda laughed.

He'd been surprised that she hadn't helped with the marble run. It seemed like something she would enjoy especially as Petal had jumped in early and enthusiastically. But that was probably why Miranda had stepped back. It wasn't necessary, he told himself as he watched Petal, her tongue poking out of her mouth like it always did when she was concentrating, which seemed to be most of the time although he was seeing far more quicksilver flashes of a smile.

"Shall we test it?" he'd asked.

Petal scrambled to her feet and stepped back, hands clasped as if in prayer. It had been hard for him to give up control of the marble run. It looked a little lopsided in parts and less elegant than he'd envisioned, but Petal had been pleased, and the crazy vibe fit Miranda's store. It was fun and colorful. He would have preferred a wood marble run, but Miranda had commented that kids were often in her store so a wood one would get knocked apart unless she glued it.

"And then you'd be stuck with just one version of your marble run," she'd said practically, but somehow the words had stuck with him throughout the day.

It was strange. He'd been dreading his month here, and yet he was well into his second week, and he looked forward to each day. The patients were friendly, compliant, so grateful for his care, and they followed medical advice for the most part, which was not how his residency or rotations had gone. And the staff was professional—friendly, which he'd been worried about—but totally professional. They'd welcomed him like he was a permanent surgeon, not just a fill-in. He'd even been invited to a family dinner, which he'd declined because of Petal, and usually he would just say no thank you, but he'd felt compelled to give a reason, and then Petal had been immediately invited along with Miranda.

The 'no' that was always so readily on his tongue hadn't emerged, and instead he'd agreed. And then had texted Miranda to ask. Her immediate yes hadn't shocked him, but the rush of warmth when he saw the word had taken him by surprise. So tonight they were going to dinner at a colleague's house. Another orthopedic surgeon.

Miranda was wearing dark skinny jeans and a long white sweater that had glittery silver strands running through it. Her hair was tied back in a low stubby ponytail. She looked simple, yet elegant in a way he hadn't imagined, and he found himself staring. She glanced at him, her gaze soft and warm, enveloping him with a sense of belonging.

"I'm almost ready," she'd said. "Are you going to do the honors this time or Petal?"

Witt handed Petal the marble, and she took it gravely and looked up at him as if waiting for some magic word of permission.

"We should get going after this last test," he said, checking his watch.

"Just tying the bow on the box of Sage's chocolates and the frame as a hostess gift," Miranda added quickly as he'd looked up, probably looking as startled as he felt because he hadn't thought of getting them anything except a bottle of wine, and even that he hadn't planned other than stopping at the liquor or grocery store on their way out of town. "And I got a new shipment of wine dropped off this afternoon and you can choose something from there. The tasting notes sound yummy."

"Miranda, you can't give your inventory away."

"I'm not." She grinned. "You're paying so pick an expensive one."

WITT WASN'T LATE for work, but he rushed anyway, knowing he was going to hit the wall of bone-chilling cold even if it was only to walk a block and cross the railroad tracks to get to the hospital now that he'd wised up and made coffee in the room instead of walking to the Java Café. The past few mornings Miranda had taken to making him either avocado toast or a bagel with almond butter and an apple for breakfast. He knew he should object but what exactly was he supposed to say?

He'd tried once. "You don't need to take care of me," he'd said, when his breakfast and coffee had been waiting when he came out of his bedroom, his hair slicked back and his tie half knotted as he finished it easily without a mirror from long practice.

"I know," she'd said and had returned to braiding Petal's hair while Petal read to her.

He'd realized Petal had a bit of a lisp on some words and he'd debated whether he should email the teacher or text Sarah when his dad was home to check into it and as Miranda mildly told her to slow down and try the word again, he stopped short.

Miranda had noticed and was helping Petal to practice without making a big deal of it.

"Late tonight." He'd said the words before he'd thought them and then had frozen. He hadn't told his schedule to anyone since Sarah—since she'd be the one picking him up or he'd often had to coordinate using the car to pick up one or more of his half-siblings.

It had felt weird because it didn't. It had felt normal, like Miranda and Petal were part of his life.

Both Miranda and Petal had looked up at him and smiled.

"I'll make something in the Crock-Pot," Miranda had said. "So no matter when you come back you can eat."

"Bye, Witt. If you come back in time can you test me on my math facts flash cards?"

He'd heard the shy hope in her voice and tried to push the guilt away, but it edged back. "I'd like to," he'd said, meaning it. "But I can't control my schedule, Petal. It depends on if patients need surgery or not. I'm the last orthopedist working tonight. I'll try, but not likely."

"Okay," and instead of shutting down like she'd done last week, she'd slid off her chair. "I'm going to start making my Valentine's cards tonight."

"After you study," he couldn't help saying, and he'd seen Miranda smirk.

"After I study," Petal had repeated and looked at Miranda, a shy smile playing on her lips. "You were right. He did say that first thing."

They both laughed and he stared at them. Shocked but a bit pleased. They'd been teasing him. Teasing. When had he last been teased to his face: true, friendly teasing, not mean-spirited? He hadn't been able to remember.

"Both of you have a good day," he'd said mock serious, but as he closed the door behind him, he smiled.

He slowed as he walked past Miranda's store. The red lights that framed the door and the edges of the glass window glowed, giving the store a warm, homey, slightly romantic feel. It seemed like every day he'd notice changes in the store—new merchandise or the marble run had been slightly reconfigured. But also he'd noticed the tree. It now had large red hearts hanging from it—those were the asks—someone needed help with a project or to borrow something or an item they couldn't afford but needed for a family member, and then there were the pink hearts, which were attached when the ask had been answered.

It was so sweet and clever and yet simple. It made him feel a little strange inside. A bit like an ache. Or…? He wasn't used to thinking about how he felt. And he wasn't sure if he liked it or not.

He pushed open the door. The sky was a brilliant black, stars spangling. He hadn't seen the sun in two or three days since it rose so late and fell so early. Another black sky start to his day, but instead of internally complaining, he found himself looking for certain constellations as he made the quick trek to work.

The day sped by, and he'd been right. Today would be a late day. Normally he gloried in that. But he felt a little pang that he wouldn't be able to help Petal with her flash cards or see her start on her Valentine's cards. Her enthusiasm was infectious.

After the first of three back-to-back surgeries, he briefly let his mind wander to Miranda and Petal, wondering what they were doing. It was such a foreign thing to happen to him it brought him up short. He normally never let his focus drift, nor did he participate in the OR banter that was common. Today everyone was talking about the Valentine's Ball at the Graff.

"It's a fundraiser for the schools this year," his scrub tech informed all of them. "So anyone with kids better get their dancing shoes on and get their ass on the floor and be prepared to participate in the paddle raise as well."

There were a few grumbles and a couple of the younger guys said that left them out as they weren't even married.

"You're fertile," she'd said. "Expect to see you there building the future."

There were a few good-natured protests. Witt didn't say anything, but an idea popped in his head. Initially he dismissed it. But as the day wore on, and more cases were added, the idea persisted. Miranda had done so much for so many people—moving in to help her grandparents. Setting up a store that showcased local business and artists. And now she was organizing to teach a knitting class at Harry's House in the spring. She also, according to Petal, was making recycled frames to sell, which had photographs in them that Miranda had taken. Miranda was so modest that he hadn't even known she took photographs until this morning when she'd given him a frame with a picture of him and Petal making the marble run.

Miranda had blushed and been casual. "For you to remember your time here," she'd said softly. "Or you could give it to your father and Sarah."

"Do you love it?" Petal had demanded hopping from foot to foot as Miranda braided her hair. "It's good huh? Miranda's so good she's going to do a photography summer camp at Harry's House. Can I take the camp, Witt, can I?"

Such a simple question. And the 'yes' had been on the tip

of his tongue until he realized he'd be long gone by summer.

Witt let the conversation wash over him before the next patient was wheeled in sedated, and he and his team ran through their final checklist with the anesthesiologist.

"I've never been to a dance." He remembered Miranda's wistful tone.

She was trying to make so many others happy, banishing the cynicism surrounding Valentine's Day by engaging so much of the town in her random acts of kindness and Valentine tree of giving. But who was making her happy?

He could.

Just one evening out. One Valentine dinner and dance between two friends.

Not a date.

That's what he'd tell her. They'd done a lot of things together. None of them had been a date—ice-skating twice on Miracle Lake, sledding on her favorite hill with Petal, dinners out, dinners in. None of them had been dates. So the Valentine dinner and dance would just be one more activity between friends.

Chapter Eleven

"THIS IS DUMB," Miranda said, looking glumly in the mirror at Copper Mountain Chic. "It's not even a date."

"It's a date," Shane insisted. "Whenever men say it's not a date, it's a date. And if you wear that dress, it will most definitely be a date."

"You're just making that rule up."

"Hard and fast one. Men like to think they're all casual, but when they do, that means they're falling and hard."

"I'm pretty sure Witt is firmly on his feet," Miranda said. She'd even had a glimpse of his email inbox as he'd been working late last night while she'd been finalizing plans for her afternoon open house Valentine celebration at her store. He'd had several exchanges with a University Hospital. So he was still leaving and this was not a date, and she had to keep reminding herself of that even though it was too late. She was in love with him. Her crush from high school was a pathetic, flabby weak thing compared to her feelings now. And it was going to gut her when he left.

Not a date.

So why was she going?

"It's so...so..." Miranda could hardly tear her eyes away

from her reflection and the gorgeous dress she was trying on.

"You," Shane said firmly.

Miranda plucked at the scooped neckline that fell in soft folds framing her small pert breasts and making them a little more interesting because the soft fabric teased a view of her small, but rounded mounds as she moved. The color was gorgeous—vibrant and unapologetic red. But the dress was very fitted, as the fabric not only had a sheen, but was also stretchy. And it was backless, and low, very low, and the fabric draped in a few thin folds over her booty giving her a little bit more flare there.

Her thinness was suddenly elegant and feminine. She wasn't used to that. She was used to being told she was scrawny, that she should eat more, that she had the body of a boy or a prepubescent girl or that she was lucky she could eat and eat and fat would never stick.

Miranda frowned. Shane's tall, blonde, Nordic, model looks should not appear in the same mirror as any other woman. The contrast proved God played favorites.

"I'll look like I'm trying too hard."

"It's perfect," Shane said. "And it's time you try."

Miranda had fussed over the deeply discounted price, which her former boss, Sandra Reynolds, now married to retired Judge Kingsley, had blithely ignored and then pointedly reminded her that it was the month of giving and random acts of kindness.

"Yeah," said Shane, who had dragged Miranda shopping because she hadn't gone and the ball was tomorrow night. "Stop harshing her giving gig."

Sandra laughed.

"What?" Miranda looked up.

"And yes to the shoes and yes to the pantsuit," Shane said to Sandra, who'd smiled like she'd just won a grand prize.

"I can't buy all that." Miranda had been scandalized. "I'm on a budget."

A really tight budget.

"Live a little, girl. You showed me your closet, and you can't wear the same thing to your open house that you wear to the ball, both of which are tomorrow, girlfriend, so get with the program."

Even Miranda knew she had to wear different things, but more because she'd get the dress dirty before Witt even finished with work. But the pantsuit was so elegant, and the little beige leather pointy-toed ankle boots so stylish that Miranda barely knew herself. She felt like it was false advertising, not that Witt would see her. He wouldn't make it to her open house. And even though she knew it shouldn't, his absence was going to hurt. A little shine was off the day. She knew it wasn't his fault. He'd had his schedule made out for the month before he'd even arrived in Marietta. But still. She'd pictured him coming in with Petal. Celebrating a little. Seeing all that she'd accomplished with their help and support.

Boy, oh boy did she have it bad. She bit her bottom lip.

"The pantsuit makes you look elegant and retro, and I'm wearing a black one when I play my upright bass at your store so we'll look thematic."

No, she'd pale in comparison to Shane even though secretly Miranda loved the pantsuit. It had a wrap top that Shane insisted could be sweet and sexy as long as she ditched her beige bras. Miranda had a feeling if she let Shane alone in her closet for fifteen minutes she'd have very few clothes left and no bras or underwear.

"Seriously." Shane had waved a holey pair of navy blue panties at her. "The color's faded, the shape is gone and…so are they." She'd tossed the lot of them in the trash and had insisted on taking Miranda shopping.

She shouldn't have admitted to Shane that she had nothing to wear. But she couldn't have shown up to the ball in jeans. And Witt was so handsome. And always so well turned out. She took one last look at herself in the dress. It was beautiful. But she'd never wear it again. She'd have to donate it. She touched her too thick hair that hung around her face like someone had upended a taupe flowerpot.

"Oh, and the hair's going too," Shane had said as they'd left the store. "I already booked an appointment. Facial, hairstyle, mani-pedi. It will be fun."

THE NEXT DAY was so frantically busy, Miranda thought she wouldn't have time to miss Witt, even though she kept checking the wide door to see if he'd arrived though he'd told her he'd be cutting it tight to make it by the start of the dinner. He had coverage on his call starting at six.

She'd thought she'd have most the morning to prepare

for the open house random acts of kindness celebration, yet her gift store remained busy all day. Sales were brisk. Almost all of the gift chocolates had sold as soon as she'd opened. The hand-painted silk scarfs were now gone as well as the last three recycled wood picture frames she'd made. She'd also sold the handmade carved wooden jewelry boxes a local woodworker had consigned with her store. He'd inlaid them with stones and crystals, and since Miranda had only made the display for the boxes last night when he'd sheepishly dropped them off, she knew he'd been thrilled.

"You're not ready!" Shane said as she breezed in lugging her large bass.

She looked beautiful in the black pantsuit that emphasized her slim height and pale beauty.

"I brought makeup and hair gel. Good thing."

"Shane, I don't…" She trailed off a little intimidated by Shane's scowl, which wasn't really fair since she'd never seen Shane wear more than a lick of lip gloss until today.

"Tough. Deal. I'll freshen it up for you tonight and then leave you alone, but you didn't fix your hair like the stylist told you to."

Miranda touched her layered, asymmetrical and jagged bob a little self-consciously. She loved it, but she felt like someone else, a little exotic, and she'd been too embarrassed to face Witt last night and shove her makeover in his face. So, she'd scrubbed her face and jammed a beanie on her head while she and Petal had snuck off to the Graff's kitchen to make cupcakes and cookies for the party with the help and permission of the hotel's pastry chef.

Shane squirted a dime size of pomade and rubbed it around her fingers and then started pulling at chunks of Miranda's hair.

"I love the few highlights. So subtle," Shane approved. "You are a true ash and with all the layers and thinning out your bangs and changing your part line, it really highlights your gorgeous, sky-high cheekbones and eyes. The new brow shaping is perfect too."

"I'll never be able to keep it up," Miranda worried.

Shane paused in her ministrations. "You will if you want to, Miranda. It's up to you."

Miranda pouted her lips as Shane drew in her lip line.

"I'm not really used to doing things for myself," Miranda confessed.

"Not breaking news," Shane said. "But sometimes, you should celebrate yourself too."

"Like tonight," Miranda said, trying not to think that Witt would only be in town less than two weeks more.

His father would come home from the hospital in another day or two. Witt would likely move to his family's ranch taking Petal with him. Of course he would. Their arrangement had always been temporary. A temporary family. A glimpse of an ideal. Of perfect.

"Don't bite your lip." Shane smiled, her eyes were so beautiful and kind, Miranda thought trying to stave off the unhappiness and loneliness that she knew lurked around the corner ready to rush her. "You'll ruin your lipstick."

"I wish it were real," she whispered. Tears pricked her eyes.

Shane dapped at them with a cotton ball. Her eyes were kind. Sad.

"Believe in maybe. Not never, Miranda."

Miranda needn't have worried if people would attend the Valentine celebration. Quite a few people and families stopped throughout the afternoon. She had refreshments, arts and crafts for the kids, and Petal and Parker had designated themselves in charge even though a couple of teenagers from Harry's House helped out and offered face painting. A couple of local vintners took turns offering wine tasting and then the tastings spilled out to the bar where several local boutique brewers offered samples of their beer.

Miranda made sure she greeted everyone—most people she knew, and she was thrilled with their support. She'd made a collection of all the random acts of kindness notes and the Valentine giving hearts so that her guests could read the notes.

"This was such a beautiful, beautiful idea," she heard on more than one occasion.

She'd done this. Miranda hugged the knowledge to herself. With the help of the town, they had all pulled together to create something beautiful and to share their time and kindness.

The afternoon progressed almost like a dream. The best part was when her grandparents and quite a few of their new friends from the May Bell Center arrived to enjoy the celebration. Her grandfather hugged her. Then her grandmother.

"You've created something so beautiful here, Miranda

Panda," she whispered, kissing her cheek. "We are so proud of you. I never doubted for a moment you'd be a success."

"Grandma, it's only been two weeks." She'd brushed aside the compliment out of habit. Her gran had shaken her head, smile warm, blue eyes twinkling like they used to, and Miranda realized the move had been good for her gran and grandpa too.

"It's just the beginning, Miranda. Just the beginning. Your second act."

The Wilder family all showed up to see what Colt had been up to with the reclaimed wood and to meet Parker's new friend, Petal. Sky had sent pictures of her tree sculpture prototypes, and Miranda had been so blown away, she hadn't been able to choose and had shifted the choice back to Sky. They delivered the tree during the Valentine celebration, and Sky showed her how it worked. Shane played her bass for about an hour and Miranda even joined her on a couple of songs with a borrowed hand-made ukulele that was for sale and after two songs, she sold it.

"Your store's going to be empty by the end of the day, congratulations," Shane said as she prepared to head back to the bar to start her shift and rounds and rounds of specialty cocktails.

"Thanks for everything," Miranda said.

Shane smiled, but it didn't reach her eyes. "Have fun tonight."

"You too, and I promise I'll change into the dress. I'll even take a selfie to prove it."

"Only change your clothes. Not yourself." Shane looked

around the store. "This is something, Miranda. You've created your own place. Your own reality. Your own home and your own family."

Shane's words filled her with pride, but also a tinge of sadness. It sounded like an end as much as it sounded like a beginning.

As the afternoon wound down, she had a lot of help cleaning up and closing up her store. She ducked into the bathroom and changed into her red dress, touched up her makeup and her hair. Petal charged in and hit her with a couple of pumps of a spray that smelled like honeysuckle.

"Shane's idea." Petal smiled and hugged the bottle close. "It has glitter in it."

"Sparkles do make everything better," Miranda said, but her stomach clenched with nerves.

She barely recognized herself. Her eyes looked huge, smoky and dramatic. Her lips were plump and sultry. The hint of blush highlighted her cheekbones, the white highlights in her ash-brown hair added life, and the new cut, wispy around her face and cupping her head like a cap, lent her a sophisticated, glamorous appeal that Miranda had never had before.

"Not a date," she reminded herself in the mirror although her heart didn't seem to want to believe her.

She walked out of the bathroom and stopped short. Witt looked devastating in a dark suit. He'd obviously snuck back to the hotel and showered and changed and then made it down to her store before she'd even begun to worry that he'd gotten caught up at the hospital. He was standing with Petal and Parker who were showing him some Valentine's Day cards they'd made.

"I had to make a lot," Parker had bragged. I have a dad, a mom and three uncles and aunts and twin baby cousins, and Montana and Sky has a bun in the oven."

"I have a lot too." Petal shoved her hair out of her face. "I have Witt and Miranda and Aunt Sarah and Uncle Taryn and then Boone and Riley and Rohan, but I haven't met him yet."

Parker nodded in sympathy, and Miranda held back her laugh. It was so touching.

"We'll get out of your hair," Colt said.

He and his wife were taking Petal and Parker out to dinner at the Main Street Diner and then a movie. Miranda watched the four of them depart. She felt like her heart jumped in her throat and was afraid she'd choke if she didn't dispel all these uncomfortable feelings.

"You look fantastic," she said quickly, wanting to get this awkwardness over, but she continued to smooth her hands down her dress nervously even though she reminded herself to stop.

And when he said nothing, just stared at her, it was really hard to breathe.

Say something.

Only she was suddenly afraid he was going to say that this was a mistake. That they should turn back now.

"You look amazing," Witt said. "Just amazing." Witt finally gathered his thoughts enough to speak. "And not in the casual way bandied about, but in your own truly breath-stealing Miranda way."

"Really?"

Witt's eyes took her in. He saw her swallow. He'd never noticed how long and elegant her neck was but now her thick hair had been cut to frame her cheekbones, and it swung and curled in layers rather than the thick, angular bob. Her bone structure was so refined. Her skin and eyes glowed and her hair seemed to have more depth as it framed her elf-like features.

His eyes dipped lower, traced along her delicate collarbone. Miranda could look so fragile, but she was so strong, vibrant, full of life. And she was in a dress. A beautiful, long, brilliant red dress that clung to her body, and had an elegant split up one side. And she'd done something to her hair. It was totally different, highlighting her cheekbones and eyes. He sucked in a breath. She'd really made an effort. And it had paid off, but what if…

Don't be stupid.

Women liked to dress up. What did he expect—that she'd wear her gray slacks and a blouse or her worn-out Wranglers? It didn't mean anything. She was just entering into the spirit of fun, of a night out. She knew he was leaving, that they were friends—sort of—and in a working relationships—sort of.

"I ah…I hope this isn't too forward," he said. "I haven't seen you wear jewelry but…" He broke off. "I saw this and thought of you."

He pulled out a narrow box from an inner pocket of his suit jacket.

"Witt."

"It's symbolic for me at least, but if you don't like it, I can…" She laid her hand over his forearm and took the box from him.

"Thank you. I love it."

"You haven't opened it yet."

"If you chose it for me, and it had meaning to you then of course I will love it."

She sounded like she meant it. Miranda slid off the ribbon and opened the box. The chain was delicate. Tiny platinum hearts linked together with a tiny diamond in the one slightly larger heart that should rest in the hollow of her throat.

"Oh," she breathed and stared.

He couldn't tell. Was that good? Bad? Did she hate it? Had he overstepped his bounds? Would she have preferred gold? He thought platinum suited her more—rare, less obvious, more precious. And the hearts. He'd done it because her whole store was hearts. Not because…oh. No. She didn't think… Damn. The necklace was a bad idea. Tonight was a bad idea.

"Can you put it on me, please, Witt?"

He placed the delicate chain around her neck. She held herself so still, almost holding her breath. It fastened easily, yet he kept his fingers lightly skimming her bare shoulders.

"Beautiful," he whispered even though he kept telling

himself to step away and keep his distance. "Perfect."

She turned around.

"Exquisite."

None of the words seemed to do her justice. They faced each other. He had an urge to drop a kiss on the sweet, beckoning spot where her shoulder and neck met. He breathed in deeply through his nose and stilled his hands, light on her shoulders, trying to keep control. A kiss would definitely send the wrong message. Witt had planned out the evening—a cocktail in the bar, dinner, some dancing, and then picking up Petal and cooking s'mores in the room. But he hadn't counted on Miranda acting so differently, looking so differently. It felt like a date.

Really felt like a date. But it wasn't. They were…friends, he guessed, and he didn't have too many of those.

And he'd never had one who made him feel this uncertain. Or this sense of belonging.

"Not a date, huh," Shane whispered as she slid a cocktail toward Miranda and then one toward him.

He saw the delicate blush stain Miranda's cheeks. "One of your famous themed concoctions?" Miranda asked, clearly changing the subject. "What's in it?"

Shane smirked. "See if you can discern the ingredients," she challenged.

"At least it's not pink," he said, before he realized that Miranda's drink was indeed pink. Or at least the ice cubes were.

"I've found men avoid pink. Perhaps too emasculating. Cheers." She winked at Miranda then added in a not too low voice, "I dare you. Walk on the wild side."

Her chin tilt indicated the drink, but Witt felt Shane was exhorting Miranda to take some kind of a risk. Not good. Not. Good. At. All.

"Cheers," Miranda lifted her drink up.

He set her enigmatic gaze and touched her glass with his.

"To friends," he said stating the obvious.

Miranda echoed his toast, her gaze unwavering and Witt found himself relaxing just a little.

"Oh, it's sweet," Miranda said. "And it has a little kick at the end."

"Really? Mine's savory, rich, dark, some herbs and spices in an unusual combination."

"May I?"

Witt had never shared a drink or food with a lover…no not a lover; he mentally shook his head. He'd never shared food or drink with another person, but somehow with Miranda the ask didn't seem obtrusive.

"Do your worst, but I need to warn you, I like it so don't drink it all."

Miranda laughed, and pushed her drink toward him. Then she held up his drink, her expression curious and expectant.

"To joy," Miranda said.

"Joy," he repeated, surprised. They clinked glasses, and he braced himself for a wash of cloying sweet. But no. The drink had a honeyed flavor, but then there was a burst of lavender blended with currant and anise. "Shane has some serious bartending skills."

"I know right? Do I need to worry you won't give mine back?" she teased.

"Tempting. But I love mine. It's like together they make the perfect cocktail."

Miranda's smile widened as did her pupils. He could see her pulse flutter in her vulnerable neck. He needed to be careful of what he said so she wouldn't read too much into it. He hated this, Witt realized. Being uncomfortable with her. These past two weeks had been some of the best, easiest, most enjoyable times of his life. He hadn't censored himself. He'd felt accepted and hadn't worried that he was too stiff or awkward or boring or superior-sounding. He'd been relaxed. He and Miranda and Petal had had fun. And conversations that weren't so fraught.

Maybe he was making too big of a deal with this. Miranda knew the score. She'd probably gone on a lot of dates that hadn't ended up becoming anything more. This town was packed with fun-loving cowboys. Witt just wanted to get back to where they'd been. Comfortable. Happy. Enjoying each other. He wanted her to be happy. He wanted to put a smile on her face.

And now he felt helpless. A socially awkward mess all over again—trying to read cues that may or may not exist.

"Have you had a hard time with all the pink?" she asked tilting her head toward her store.

"Ahhhh," he drawled, and then smiled in relief when she laughed.

"No worries. March first that wall will be Kelly green. And I'll have some clovers and gold and sparkly dark green accents. Much more soothing."

Witt deliberately moved her drink back to her and slid his back to him.

"I hope you text me a picture of it," he said. "You know my contract is only for a month," he added. And then felt like he was holding his breath.

Miranda paused. Her eyes lowered and she picked up her drink, but when she held it to her lips, her eyes were clear, even as her hand shook a little.

"You can be my West Coast color consultant," she said her voice light and even, warm and melodic like it always was. "And if I am thinking of carrying a certain type of wine, perhaps if you have time you could text me a few tasting notes to dazzle customers with." Her smile reached her eyes, and Witt felt like the sun just rose in his chest.

"Count on it," he said. And meant it.

※

THE NIGHT UNFOLDED like a fairy tale. They finished the cocktails and then went into the sumptuously decorated ballroom.

"Perhaps you should wear sunglasses," Miranda teased.

"I was actually expecting a lot worse," he said as he held her chair out for her.

The food had been delicious. Not too heavy and the courses had been spaced between raffles so that they could walk around, chat with others if they wanted, but Witt found himself sliding his arm around Miranda's side. Social interactions en masse made him uncomfortable, and Miranda knew a lot of people here. And as the new doctor, he too was attracting a lot of attention.

"I think I take joy in the mundane," Miranda answered a question he didn't remember asking. He was so caught up in a crème brûlée. Definitely extra gym time tomorrow. Maybe he'd even attack Colt's punching bag.

"Perhaps it's my super skill, but I just love people and being alive and living each day whether it's fun or hard or sad. I've had a lot of sad lately with seeing my grandfather decline and see how hard it is for my grandmother to cope with him, and I am sad that I'm not closer to my family, but if there's one thing opening my own store has taught me these past few weeks, it's that there is joy out there. We just have to decide to seize it. My family is convinced my store will fail, and if I listen to that, it will fail. And I'll fail. But if I believe in myself and push myself I have a really good chance of success."

"Miranda, of all the professors I've had, you outshine them all with your wisdom. I came home to Marietta thinking it had never really been my home. Spending these two weeks with you and seeing Sarah and my dad." He laughed. "Weird. I'm calling Taryn my dad. I always thought of him as my biological father to keep him at arm's length, but I'm starting to see my years here so differently. My family so differently. And that's you," he said. "That's you."

"I'm happy," she said. "So happy for you."

WITT CHOSE COFFEE over a glass of port. He loved port but didn't often indulge, and he'd promised Miranda dancing and he wanted to be alert and nimble. Several dance instructors were getting on the floor preparing to do demonstrations before calling the crowd up, and the musicians did their final tune-ups.

He'd moved his chair closer to Miranda to share the dessert and the coffee. He could smell her delicate beachy fragrance and feel the warmth of her small body pressed to his. For most of the evening, he'd had his arm casually draped around her shoulders, but every now and then, his palm would brush her bare back and he could feel arrows of heat shoot to his groin.

The first dance was a waltz.

"Easy," he murmured as he helped her up.

Only it wasn't. He held her close, felt her body move with his and the pale skin of her back teased him to touch and to linger and her scent was like a whispered promise that drew him in. It was all he could do to let her go when the tango was introduced. The tango. Not a dance to calm a rising libido.

He hesitated, but Miranda's look of excitement did him in. He'd wanted to give her a night to remember, only he was starting to worry that he wouldn't be able to forget even a thousand miles away from her.

Witt knew he was in too deep after the dance class ended and the band played a variety of music, but much of it tilted toward jazz. He hadn't expected to enjoy the evening so much. Miranda was a fun companion. She was chatty, but she was also an extraordinary listener, and he found himself talking about medical school, residency, what he remembered of his mother and grandmother—far more than he'd ever talked about his past. With anyone.

Miranda was kind and funny and a keen observer. She made him laugh. And she made him think. And she loved to dance—usually during the slower or jazzier songs. As the last strains of an Alison Krauss song faded away, Miranda laid her head against his chest, murmuring that the song was one of her favorites. Then she stopped dancing, and on the middle of the dance floor she looked up at him, her pixie features luminous with joy and her eyes shining with emotion.

"Witt," she said.

"Tired? Had enough? Ready to go?" He could feel panic clog his throat and jump-start his heart like he'd been connected to a high-amped defibrillator. Miranda stopped dancing and gazed up at Witt.

"Thank you for tonight," she said. "It's been so beautiful, Witt. Beyond my wildest hopes or expectations. You've made my life so beautiful."

"Miranda?" His voice carried disbelief. He had to stop her before she said anything more.

"I know, I know," she whispered. "Play it safe. Don't be stupid. Keep my heart locked up tight so I don't embarrass myself or get hurt, but I can't, Witt. I can't live like that. I can't hide, and I can't pretend. I don't want to."

Another song started. More upbeat and she was jostled against him.

He steered her off the floor and toward their table. Maybe they'd get a nightcap at the bar or…suddenly he realized there was no escape. Not really. They were sharing a suite. But Colt would be bringing Petal back soon. That would put a damper on any true confessions. She knew he was leaving. He'd been clear from the beginning.

He didn't want to hurt her. He didn't want to hurt anyone. He just wanted to do his job. He just wanted to stay uninvolved.

Safe.

The word filtered through his consciousness.

"Witt." She stopped and grabbed hold of his sleeve on the edge of the dance floor. "I want you to know. I want to tell you so you can carry it with you." She touched where his heart was, and he knew he was lost. Defeated. "Every day of the past two plus weeks has been so beautiful and special because you've been in it."

Witt shook his head a little, stroked his thumb along her cheekbone. There was no escape, and he wasn't sure that he really wanted to anymore. "That's you Miranda. You've done that all on your own. You are the one providing the light. I came here angry. Resentful. You've made me see my life differently. You've made me see what I missed so many years ago. You hold the light. I hold the dark."

"Don't think like that. It's not true. You have your own light, Witt. You do. You just have to see it. Believe in it. Share it. I want that for you. I do."

He felt the doubt, but with it, a little hope bleeding in.

"Miranda, there's something about you. I can't begin to

calculate what," he began, and Miranda bit back a laugh.

"Witt, that's so you. I'm throwing myself in the deep end and you are going to calculate. That is why you are so precious to me. So special."

She cupped his cheeks with her hands. Laughed. Cried a little, flung herself into his arms.

"What is it, what?" he asked as she did an impression of a burrowing animal except her fingers speared through his hair.

"You are so lovely, so so lovely," she whispered, her eyes tearing up. "And so, so very lost, and I wish I could hold on to you forever. Show you where your home is."

The rest hung in the silence between them. With her. In Marietta. And Witt had no idea what to say. What to feel. What to think. He was a giant blank.

And that shamed him to his soul.

Miranda lifted her head. Tears leaked from her eyes. Surprising from a woman so strong, so fearless. He wiped them carefully off her cheeks with his thumbs.

"I'm sorry," he whispered, stricken to his toes. "I wanted to make you happy. Tonight was about making you happy."

"I am happy," she breathed. "Happier than I've ever been."

Something in her voice, her expression, the lilt in her body warned him, and he wanted to stop her before she jumped. She looked up at him, eyes and face shining like the sun.

"You've made me realize I need to reach out and grab my happy. I don't want any regrets. I don't want to wish I'd tried harder. But you have to know Witt. I love you. I've fallen totally in love with you. With everything you are. And I'll always love you."

He felt the words like a lance skewering clean through his heart. Damn. He'd wanted to give her a fun night. A special memory. Not this. Anything but this.

>>><<<

"No, no, no, no," he said his thumbs pressed on her lower pouty lip as if to stem the flow of her words, as if he could save her by silencing her. "You can't. It's impossible."

I'm unlovable.

That was it, he realized. He'd felt unlovable always. His mother had always been distant. He couldn't quite get close enough. And his grandparents had been cool. Exact. Not really interested. And then his father, well, he'd been the cowboy in love with another woman with whom he'd build a ranch and a family all without him. And then he'd been friendless in school—pushing everyone away so he could achieve. Be the best. Prove himself in another way, a way he understood and could win at.

"You can't," he repeated, dead certain.

"I can. I love you." Her hand smoothed down his chest. "I love you. I always have." She smiled sadly. "I know I sound ridiculous, but even in high school I loved you. I felt like your soul was crying out to mine and I tried, Witt; I tried so hard to reach you. And now here for these two weeks, I felt like I did. Like I was here." She touched his chest again, her palm over his heart. "And even if you don't love me, I love you. And even if you don't want me, I want you." She took his hand and placed it over her heart. He could feel it slam into his palm. "You are here. Always here, safe and loved by me."

The music stopped.

Did time stop?

Witt stared at her, his face worried, tortured a little.

"I'm sorry, Miranda. I'm sorry."

Sorry didn't begin to cover it.

Chapter Twelve

MIRANDA STARED AT the dark ceiling. Five a.m. February fifteenth. The first day of the next part of her life. Her eyes were gritty. Her body cold. Sore. Empty. Witt was gone. She'd heard him leave his room half an hour ago. Doubted he'd be back. He'd work out. Shower in the hotel gym or at the hospital after his workout.

She turned on her side and stared blankly at the alarm clock.

Petal was still nestled next to her. Miranda closed her eyes. That too would end. Sarah was bringing Taryn home tomorrow. They'd want Petal to be home with them. Adjusting to her new life. The Graff had been a detour.

But that's what made life interesting.

Right?

Bullshit Miranda mouthed the word. Wondered if she'd be the kind of woman who started swearing after a breakup. Drinking fruity cocktails at Grey's and smearing mascara on cowboy's shirtsleeves while she moped about the one who got away.

Breakup. Right. They hadn't even been a thing to break.

And the pink fruity drinks at Grey's always looked like they'd be cloying.

Maybe she'd start tossing back whiskey and two-stepping.

Doubtful.

Miranda closed her eyes and wished she could sleep. Or cry. Or scream. Tell a girlfriend who'd hug her and somehow make her believe that really, really it would all be all right.

Even when it wasn't.

Sunday was supposedly a day of rest. But today it would provide too much time to think. Witt was working so it would be her and Petal pretending that everything was all right, when Miranda knew that it wasn't, at least not for her. But she'd known the risk, and she'd taken it.

Time to suck it up.

AN HOUR ON the treadmill didn't begin to silence the crap that rolled around his head and his gut. Last night had been perfect until it had lurched into the disaster zone. He never should have taken Miranda out. How stupid could a man be? But how could he have guessed that she would have declared love in a ballroom? Shouted about love above the music just as it stopped.

Shit. He couldn't even have privacy when he screwed up.

And Miranda was going to have to live with it. He was blowing out of town in a couple of weeks. And he definitely couldn't stay at the Graff with her another night. He'd have to help her move back to her apartment. He'd pay her for an extra week. But he'd have to take Petal to the ranch. Stay there with her. Prepare for his father's arrival home. Only today he was on call so his grand, dickish distance gesture would have to wait.

He ran another half hour full out. Then careened mindlessly through weights. He looked at the long cylindrical punching bag Colt had hung. God, had that only been two weeks ago? Smug bastard. Everything worked out for Colt. He got his happy every after and then stood back and pointed out everyone else's shortcomings.

Witt stalked up to the bag. He eyed the bag and then the gloves. Screw it. He'd give it a try. Pretend it was his own ego. His own hubris that he knew best. He tied on the gloves and gave a few experimental punches. Harder. But he was worried. He was on call today. He couldn't afford even a strained finger although that probably made him sound like the biggest pansy in Montana. Especially in Montana.

He stepped back and kicked the bag. Harder. And again. More for force. He was getting into a rhythm when he heard the door open and the bag swung back and hit him, knocking him off balance. He fell to the floor and put up his hand before the bag swung back crazily for his face. Only the bag stopped in mid-flight. Colt peered down at him.

"Told you," Colt said. "Feels good to hit it."

Witt popped to his feet. "Out of my way."

Colt swung the bag back hard. Witt kicked but staggered.

"That's almost as smooth as your moves on the dance floor."

Of course Colt would hear that Miranda had basically

declared undying love and he'd all but left her standing there alone.

"I hate small towns."

He kicked the bag and Colt punched it back at him. Shit Colt was strong. He could get that strong, Witt thought. Definitely. In fact he was going to buy one of these punching bags. The biggest and heaviest he could get. Install it in his apartment. Kick like he was a black belt in savate.

"There are assholes in big towns," Colt drawled. "As I'm sure you'll soon attest."

Point taken.

But Witt wasn't going to give him the satisfaction of knowing he'd drawn blood. He tried a combination kick just because he didn't know when to stop and he was a fierce competitor and Colt had always wound him up with the fewest words possible. Predictable and stupid and it was like high school all over again.

And of course he fell on his ass.

Colt caught the bag one-handed like it weighed nothing and held out a hand to help him up.

"Told you you'd get knocked on your ass coming home."

"But I always get up," Witt popped to his feet barely recognizing himself in this man clearly spoiling for a fight. "Another round," he jerked his head toward the bag. "Hit it. Hard."

THE MINUTE HE hit the hospital, his life swung into focus.

He had pre-ops to see. Post-ops to check on. Appointments. A meeting. A phone call with his father's surgeon. Taryn was being released tomorrow. Witt was on call Sunday. Usually that meant a day off the next day, but since the department was lightly staffed, he'd be working past noon so he could meet them at the airport. His thumb ghosted over Miranda's contact information automatically. Petal would be in school. Maybe he should take her out early. Bring her to the airport. Not rely on Miranda.

I love you, Witt.

Impossible. No one fell in love in a week or two. She'd been caught up in the moment. They had nothing in common. They were two different people with different goals. They were going to live hundreds of miles apart in a matter of days. He was her complete opposite. She didn't love him. She didn't. And he shoved the conflicting feelings that churned in his gut far, far away.

But he had to make a decision. He had a week plus a few days of work. He could stay at the Graff. Miranda could move back to her apartment. Or he could stay at the ranch. Try to build on the relationship with his parents. He hesitated. But knew the answer.

He didn't want to be the same man he'd been when he'd arrived in Marietta.

He spent the day and night at the hospital and texted Miranda that he was slammed at work. It was true, but he could have gotten away. Grabbed a meal with them. He'd been doing that the past two weeks no problems. Hell, he'd had fun, and it had been an enjoyable break from work.

Now he was looking for things to do.

Coward.

By Monday before lunch, Wyatt threw him out. "Get some rest. Go pick up your dad at the airport. Go get some lovin' from your girl. Get out of here."

The last part burned. He hadn't wanted to lead Miranda on. But she'd known he was leaving. She'd even admitted it, but she'd still made her big pronouncement. It was weird not to see her. Not to stop by the gift shop and see her sparkling eyes and lopsided smile that always made his heart feel funny in his chest. She always made him laugh and took him out of his head.

Now he went through the Graff's front entrance. Took the stairs two at a time. He'd have to talk to her. He knew he did, but... He glanced at his watch. If he rushed, he could pick up some basics at Monroe's Groceries and drop them off at the ranch before heading to the airport. No, he'd bring Petal with him. Pick her up early. He'd text Miranda to let her know. He slid the key in the lock, his mind making and discarding plans. It would only take him a few minutes to pack up and check out. He'd pay for the room through tomorrow, he told himself so that Miranda would have a chance to pack up and move back to her apartment.

He'd just zipped his garment bag shut when he heard the key slide in the lock and the click.

Shit.

"Miranda."

"Witt." She looked around the room. Looked at his three pieces of luggage. Her mouth opened. Then closed. She took in everything. Spotless. Except for her old suitcase.

"You were at least going to say goodbye to Petal, weren't you?"

"Yes. I'm not leaving. Exactly."

She waited.

He was so bad at this. She looked pale. Her eyes looked dull and a little red and swollen. He'd done that.

"I'm picking up my dad and Sarah at the airport. I'm bringing them back to the ranch. And I thought I'd bring Petal with me to greet them. Get her settled back into the ranch. I'll stay there to help Sarah with my dad." His words came out like automatic fire.

"That's good news then. I'm happy for all of you."

She sounded sincere except she was a stranger. Her voice lacked animation. He'd done that.

"So…?"

He roused himself. "I ah wrote you a check and left it on the desk in your room."

She jerked like he'd shot her.

"I'll pay for the room through tomorrow so you have time to move out."

"No need."

"There's a need. Miranda." He took an aggressive step toward her and his voice was a growl. Who the hell was he?

Again she jerked like he'd pulled on her strings.

"I didn't mean for this to happen," he said feeling helpless. "That wasn't the plan."

She rubbed her hands up and down her arms. "Love doesn't work like that, Witt. If you learn nothing else, I hope you learn that. I hope you fall in love someday. I want that for you more than anything," she said, her voice sincere even though it broke, but there was a spark of warmth in her eyes before it flickered out and left the normally beautiful, rich caramel brown a little flat.

"I just wanted to do something nice for you. You were doing all these nice things for people in the town, and I wanted you to have something nice." He tried to explain himself, but knew he sounded lame.

She cocked her head and looked at him for a long time. He wondered what she was seeing. Nothing good. She was probably feeling like she dodged a bullet.

"So I'm going to stay at the ranch with my parents. Try to get to know them a bit before I leave next week. I'll pick up Petal from school. I packed up her things."

Miranda just stood there. She breathed in. Then out. Then she smiled, and it was the saddest thing he'd ever seen.

"Thank you for the dance then," she said softly. She stepped forward, reached into her pocket and handed him one of the red heart-shaped beads. It had veins of orange and glittering black and purple running through it and it dangled on a silky black ribbon. "You got the last one."

And then she walked back out, the door clicking softly behind her.

"I'm glad you don't want me to make leprechauns for March," Petal said, her hands pulling off a chuck of green sculpty clay, but instead of immediately diving in and starting to form a dragon, she just held the clay in her hand. Miranda thought she might be warming it, but there was something in her stillness that warned Miranda that something was wrong. Something had been wrong for her since she'd opened her big mouth and declared her love to Witt, and he'd started to avoid her. And now he was gone. Back to the life he wanted.

Everything felt wrong, but she knew she needed to push that defeatist thinking aside. She still had her store, and even though she didn't have the foot traffic that she'd had during her random acts of kindness promotion, she still had customers. Business at the hotel was picking up—not just with bookings but also people coming in for dinner or even to sample Shane's specialty cocktails. A few artists had contacted her about featuring their work, and David Reyes, the Graff's manager, and Walker Wilder, the Graff's events coordinator, were even working with her on having some of her rebuilt frames and photos displayed in the lobby and offered for sale.

So she needed to think of all the positives—her business looked poised to grow, she loved teaching a knitting class at Harry's House, Petal came by a couple days after school to help her, she took her grandmother out once a week for coffee and to do errands and had dinner with them twice a week, and with customers coming into her store throughout the day she shouldn't feel so lonely. She had plans. She had her craft projects—she still couldn't think of them as art even though Witt had pushed her on that front. A fresh stab of hurt rocked her. And she closed her eyes. Absorbed it, and then knew she had to self-talk it away. She wouldn't spend her days moping and crying for what would never be.

Her life was good. She was healthy. Independent. She was making friends again in town with the merchants and hotel employees. Her life would not be empty and without purpose just because Witt was gone. She might never marry or have children because she couldn't imagine loving anyone as fiercely as Witt, but... She bit down hard on her lip to center herself in the present. The word 'fierce' reminded her of skating with Witt and Petal, and how he had laughed a little at her and called her fierce.

She wasn't feeling very fierce now.

"I miss Witt." Petal's small voice floated across the room from her work station where Miranda did craft projects when the store was quiet or kids came in and wanted something to do.

"Me too."

Petal turned around, her eyes flooded with tears. "I really, really miss him."

"Me too," Miranda admitted. Petal ran across the room and flung herself into Miranda's arms. "Oh, sweetie." Miranda held her tightly and rocked a little as if Petal were a toddler and not a nine-year-old, who fancied herself so much older on too many days. "I really, really miss him too and think about him all the time." Miranda let her loss wash over them both.

Petal peered up at her through tear-soaked eyes. "You love him. I knew it. If you love him why doesn't he come back? Why wouldn't he stay?" Her voice rang with all the anguish Miranda was trying to keep under wraps. "Why doesn't he love you back?"

That was like a javelin hurled by an Olympian with deadly aim through her heart.

There were so many reasons why Witt probably didn't love her, but to think of even one would be too depressing and defeatist and would hardly pull her or Petal back from the brink. She sighed and kissed Petal's sleek, dark head.

"Sometimes it's just like that," she said softly. "You love someone, and they like you, but they don't love you in the same way. It doesn't mean you're unlovable," she said staunchly. "Or that they can't love. You are just not the exact right person for them. And you can still be friends."

Not that Witt had left the friendship door open. If he came back to visit his family, she doubted he'd make a stop at her gift shop to say hi. He wouldn't want to chance the awkward reunion or to give her hope when there was none. She wiped Petal's tears from her cheeks with her thumbs, and feeling Petal needed more, she forced herself to say the sunny-side up words. The words she'd said to so many friends over the years who'd been nursing a heartache. They were words that she wasn't sure she truly believed anymore, but she said them anyway. "And sometimes it's like magic. You meet someone and they feel so special right away. And you feel special to them. And you just know. You love so strongly and they love you back like that."

"Like Uncle Taryn and Aunt Sarah?"

"Exactly."

"But..."

"And Witt will find that person who calls to his heart and soul," she said firmly.

"And you will too?" Petal looked up at her again, her gaze full of all the doubt that Miranda felt.

She felt like her heart seized in her chest. She opened her mouth determined to say the lie. Even though she hated to lie to anyone, especially someone she cared about. But was a lie to comfort really a lie—a black check on her soul? She wanted to make Petal believe in second, third and fourth chances. She wanted her to believe in herself and in the universe. Miranda needed that for herself too yet her mouth felt too dry to speak. She moistened her lips, swallowed hard and then smiled, determined to make it so. Even if she didn't believe it now, when the chasm of hurt gaped less, she could believe it later. Hope was hope and should never be cast aside.

"Yes," she said. "Fingers crossed."

THE VIEW FROM the sprawling Frank Lloyd Wright-style house off Mulholland Drive was spectacular. Floor to ceiling windows looked out over the Los Angeles sprawl. If the view from inside the glass box of the massive living room were not enough, two of the glass panes were sliders leading out to a deck that spilled in several layers down the canyon. The top layer featured an outdoor kitchen, fire pit and several round planters with cushioned seating and palm trees wrapped in

LED lights that switched colors and a "natural" waterfall feature that spilled down to the lower deck that featured a partially indoor and outdoor gym, yoga studio and salt water lap pool and hot tub.

Everything about the house—the size, amenities, furnishings, technology and original artwork—trumpeted the owner's success. And everything about the catered party was meant to impress—gourmet exotic appetizers on silver plates handed out by circulating wait-staff, hired jazz trio on the deck, and men in custom-fitted designer suits or tuxes and women in glittering jewels and similar frozen expressions—probably Botoxed or nipped and tucked by the same sought-after plastic surgeon.

Witt accepted a glass of Champagne Salon he didn't want and stepped out on the deck to escape the twitter of meaningless conversation and to suck in some air that wasn't fragrant with the clash of different perfumes and cologne. He was comfortable with his Zegna suit. He'd always loved to wear ties and suits, and spent more of his residency stipend on higher end, tailored suits than he should have, but as for the rest of this evening, he hated it.

The conversations were all questions or statements geared to gauge or prove social standing—where they'd gone to college or med school or what private school their kindergartener had been accepted to. Or it was about their ride or other toys or vacation house or latest getaway. Or professional one-upmanship—who their parents were or spouse or... It was like fencing with words instead of rapiers, and Witt found he didn't want to engage. He'd never enjoyed small talk, but was an excellent listener, except tonight he felt the urge to…he wasn't really sure. The word *escape* kept burbling up to his consciousness.

But this was what he wanted; he frowned at his antipathy. This was what he'd strived for for so long yet as he stared out at the lights coming on in the seething metropolis below, he felt hollow. Thousands of hours of study—all of his twenties really out-studying and out-working so many of his classmates. Utter focus. No vacations. No hobbies. Working his mind and his body all for this end. And now here he stood on the brink, but instead of feeling like celebrating…

I love you, Witt. I've always loved you. The memory of Miranda's voice plunged into the dark thoughts clogging his mind.

He'd been startled Valentine's night by her declaration. Stunned. Pulled completely out of his body. No one, he'd realized as she'd gazed up at him so intensely, had said those words to him. Ever. Maybe his mother, when he'd been a baby or a toddler, but he had no memory of her telling him that. Certainly never his grandparents, who had never once visited him in Montana. Nor could he ever remember anyone ever looking at him with the warmth Miranda always had. No one's face ever lit just because he walked in the door. No. He'd been more of an obligation. Something his mother had taken seriously, but had found little joy in.

Watching Miranda interact with Petal and the way she included him had almost been like watching an anthropological documentary on another culture. And spending time with Miranda and Petal had started reminding him how his dad and Sarah had always attended his high school games or track meets and cheered him on, and how he'd been dragged to his brother and sister's rodeo events and how Sunday brunch had been sacred until he'd gone away to college. So why had he felt so apart from them? Why had he deliberately separated himself?

And by taking the fellowship in Santa Monica, wasn't he doing it all over again?

"But this is what you want," he whispered.

Only the words were as empty as he felt.

And he was alone on the deck. He bit back a bark of laughter. Typical. When was he not alone? In the OR. And when briefly Miranda had been part of his life. Happy to see him. Including him. Giving him a life outside of work. No other woman had done that. Not even close. Not once. They'd always been colleagues or just sex, so casual that they'd almost been benefits without even the friends part.

And while he'd been trying to fathom Miranda's declaration, he'd made the mistake of looking into her beautiful rich caramel eyes—so warm and liquid with hope and emotion and courage. He'd known she'd been utterly sincere, and he'd known he was completely unworthy to be her friend, much less her lover. And she'd known by his silence, his physical withdrawal—something he hadn't been able to help because he always froze up when he was emotionally blindsided—that he hadn't returned her feelings.

Only she'd been wrong. In a way.

He hadn't felt too little. He'd felt too much. He hadn't

understood everything clashing around in his head the month he'd been in Marietta. So many memories. People. Events. He'd kept crashing into his past over and over, but seeing it through adult eyes. Seeing the lies he'd been told by his mother and his grandparents about his father. Swallowing their fears and disappointment, about who he might become if he didn't work hard. And he'd repeated those lies to himself, had run from what he thought of as his dark beginnings into the light.

Or here. Above the light that marched toward the shore of the vast, black, and restless Pacific Ocean. The last sliver of sun slipped below the waves. Witt smiled cynically, knowing the sunset was an illusion. It never touched the water. But each day the illusion repeated. Beautiful and false. Much like the people at the party, who were so jaded by the daily fiery display they didn't even bother to pause in their verbal sports to view it.

Would that be him? Was that him?

He had left Marietta because he was scheduled to leave. He had left Miranda because she scared the hell out of him and made him realize how different his life could be. And he'd felt unprepared, unworthy. But people weren't static. Or they didn't have to be. They could choose another way. His mother had felt her "time with the cowboy" had been a mistake that had defined her life and she'd tried to "get back to base" every day, but what if her time with the cowboy had been an opportunity missed?

The cowboy. Never her cowboy.

Another choice.

He rocked back on his heels and watched the last orange-and-pink slivers slip to gray on the horizon before it turned an inky black.

"What's this?" he'd asked his dad on his last day in Marietta when he'd been handed a leather notebook that had been hand-bound by Sarah, who had also embossed 'me to you,' just like that. No capitals.

"When your mom refused to marry me after probably the tenth time I begged her, and refused financial support and didn't want to give me any visitations until you were old enough to understand, I started writing letters." His dad hadn't broken eye contact. "I didn't want to fight her legally and cause conflict in your life, but I wasn't ready to cut all ties and pretend that I was happy with her decision or pretend that you didn't exist. So I wrote letters—usually one a week—mostly when I'd pull into town to compete and then later on Sundays after I retired and Sarah and I started building up the ranch. I just wrote about my life, my thoughts, the family Sarah and I were making and that you weren't a part of even though you were always there in our thoughts. I thought when you were older—eighteen I guess I had in my mind—I was going to find you, get to know you. And I figured there'd be some resistance on your part—massively underestimated that." His dad had smiled tightly, and Witt had figured he was in pain from his surgeries and pissed that he couldn't do everything around the ranch he was used to doing, but maybe it was more the missed opportunities. The choices he hadn't gotten to make.

"I kept writing the letters even after you came to live

with us. Not as many, but it was better than putting my fist through walls because I was so pissed that I hadn't found you sooner, that I hadn't fought harder to have you in my life from the time you were a baby. I thought I was doing right by you especially when I was still riding, but I married Sarah when you were three. I should have insisted then. Still chaps my ass that I didn't."

Witt had held the book of letters; his stomach had churned with dread. He'd wanted to apologize but lacked the vocabulary to begin to express what was banging inside his head, his heart. Just like he hadn't had the right words the night Miranda had held her beating heart out to him, and he'd been unable to take it, to cherish it—not because he lacked the desire, but because he lacked the skills. He didn't deserve her. Never would.

"Why look back?" he'd asked his father helplessly. "You didn't do anything wrong."

"Why look forward so much?" his dad had countered.

And Witt had realized his dad was right. He'd spent his teens focused on how to get out of Marietta. He'd come "home" for the month focused on getting back on the road to his fellowship at one of the premier hospitals in Southern California. So that afternoon, the unopened book of letters on his lap, Witt had realized that he wanted to be different.

How? He had no idea.

But he'd always been good at making plans.

He spent his last day in Marietta with his family. Petal stayed home from school and he and Boone played hide-and-seek with her for a bit, and he and Boone hung a tire swing in the barn for her. And he'd done all the chores with Boone and actually enjoyed himself. Petal and Sarah had baked a coffee cake and they all ate it during the mid-morning break. Later that afternoon he'd helped Boone check the cows to estimate if any were due to give birth in the next week or so and, if so, corral them in the birthing pens. Just as they'd decided to call it a night and head back for dinner, Petal had slipped her hand in his and all three of them watched a cow birth the first calf of the season. A beautiful bull that had had Taryn and Sarah high-fiving.

"You'll be sore tomorrow." Boone had laughed at him when he'd gone for a shower before dinner. "Ranch work isn't like any gym."

And Witt's muscles had ached and protested in a way they hadn't for over a decade.

Witt had been in Southern California two days. He hadn't read the letters. He also hadn't contacted his grandparents. He'd intended to visit. Tell them about his fellowship. But why? To prove himself to them?

He found he no longer gave a shit.

He took a sip of the cuvee champagne made from chardonnay grapes that he'd coveted and had planned to order a case of once he signed his contract and then stared at the bubbles in the glass while the fruit danced on his tongue.

His phone vibrated and he pulled it out of his pocket. Riley. A short video. He turned the sound down and pressed play. Petal was at Miranda's gift shop. She was strumming the ukulele while Colt's son banged on a drum with his hand that was in a lighter cast. They both looked so full of joy. Shane played a large upright bass, and the kids accompanied her. Riley had panned the camera around the store. Miranda was pouring tastes of wine and the store was packed with people. He saw his dad on crutches, Sarah next to him.

The cork bulletin board tree was filled with the notes people had written about random acts of kindness they'd seen or experienced. He wondered how many red heart beads were now hanging from rearview mirrors or pinned up somewhere as a reminder around Marietta homes. He found himself smiling and his thumb caressed Miranda's sparkling smile as the camera panned over her again as she squirted whipped cream on what looked like hot chocolate. Then Riley switched the camera to herself.

"Last day of February. Last day of the month-long celebration of love and giving. We miss you, Witt, and wish you were here. Hey." Riley held up the phone so he got a wider angle of the room and people. "Everybody say hi to my oldest brother, Witt. He's in California starting his dream job and we miss him and wish him the best."

People waved and shouted out. He even saw Wyatt glowing with happiness shouting out something indiscernible over the noise.

"Be happy, Witt," Miranda shouted out, and the video stopped. Returned to the frozen first image of Petal, the play arrow over her face.

Be happy.

Was it really that easy?

A choice?

Witt tossed out his champagne into a planter, put the Waterford crystal flute down and left the party without saying goodbye to anyone.

Chapter Thirteen

MIRANDA PUT THE last swipe of Kelly green on her wall and, roller still in hand, stepped back to survey her efforts. It was long past midnight, so March 1st, and the thought of bundling up and walking the seven blocks to her apartment sucked. She closed her eyes. It was the one place she shouldn't miss Witt so much. He'd only been there for a few moments after insisting that he should help her pack her things and move in with him, for two glorious weeks. She'd felt like a character in a fairy tale—whisked out of her everyday life in her very own fantasy life complete with a tall, dark and handsome prince, who'd had a spell cast upon her.

Well, the ball was over. And the dress might not have poofed back into rags—in fact it hung on her garment rack like an exclamation mark of all she'd never had and never would.

No. Stop.

She couldn't go there. Despair. Witt had always been wrong for her. More like the members of her family—ambitious, unemotional and driven far, so far away from her and Marietta—but yet the few times he'd been hers, she'd sensed a spark in him, a longing, something warm and beautiful just wanting to get out but not knowing how to be unlocked. And yet she, ever the optimist, thought she'd held the key to his locked-up emotions and needs and wants.

"You and your imagination," she muttered.

"That's some green."

Miranda whirled around. She stared. Blinked. Shifted the green-soaked roller and pinched herself.

"Still here." The Witt apparition that looked so real and beautiful, right down to the rigid control, spoke.

Miranda tried to swallow. Witt was here. In her store. At midnight. Looking more frozen and foreboding than ever, but she could see the pulse pound madly in his neck. It matched hers, and that gave her hope where she'd had none. And hope was hope. It should never be rejected, but this was really going to drop her to her knees when he walked out that door again.

"I..." She had to say something. It was clear he wasn't going to be able to squeeze anything out of his granite-hewn lips. "I don't understand," she whispered.

Anything. Was this really happening? She'd fallen asleep in her store before. This could be a dream. She pinched herself again.

Witt looked more pained than ever. "It's real," he said. "I'm real."

They stared at each other.

"And stupid. I should have written it all down."

"All what?" Curiosity started to edge out shock.

He made a helpless gesture. "Everything."

She sucked in a breath. Still dizzy.

"Everything being...?" She was starting to have this crazy

hope, and she wanted to embrace it, go for it, but it didn't make sense to her—Witt in her store. Witt back in Marietta. Witt was starting a new job—his dream job, in the sun, near the beach, back to where he felt he'd always belonged.

"Me. You. This." His hand moved again indicating them. "I can't even explain it. I don't have the vocabulary. But I had a long time to think about it over the sixteen plus hour drive."

Her breath snagged and she had to remind herself to breathe.

"You drove here from LA?"

"Had to."

"Witt, what are you saying?" she asked, the words fracturing on the way out.

He just kept staring at her and Miranda couldn't hold back anymore. She hurtled through the distance between them feeling like she was at the end of a very long race, and he was the finish line. She crashed into him and held on hard. It was like their first meeting, her falling into his arms only this time he held her back and his arms were like steel cables and didn't feel like they'd ever let her go. Miranda closed her eyes and breathed him in. If this were a fantasy or a dream, she didn't ever want to wake up.

He kissed the top of her head. Miranda sighed and snuggled closer. Then she felt his chest rumble against her cheek.

"Are you laughing or hungry?" She tried to pull away but one hand cupped the back of her head while the other was at the small of her back. He pressed her closer to him, and Miranda let him.

"A little of both," he admitted. "This is like the first time we met except now you have green specks in your hair instead of red. And they're probably transferring to my clothes, much to the chagrin of the dry cleaner, who shook his head darkly when I brought in the red-specked sweater officially last month now."

Miranda giggled a little. So did Witt. All full sentences and lovely adjectives whereas she felt completely crazy and inarticulate inside.

"Sorry," Miranda said softly, not sure if that was completely true. More words burbled up, but she squashed them. Miranda had no idea why he was here or for how long, but she didn't want to break the moment like she had on Valentine's Day. She'd jumped to the finish line before he'd even gotten on the starting blocks.

"I wonder what color I'll find in your hair and likely on my shirt in April?"

"Witt." She pulled back to look up at him and this time he let her.

He was so beautiful and so deadly serious. April. That was a month away. Thirty-one beautiful, perfect days if he were in them, and if she dared to hope.

"I'm sorry, Miranda." He let her go, and his large hands smoothed down her arms. "For all my drive and education, I'm really, really slow."

"You're perfect," she disagreed, and this time he did smile. It was brief and lit the sadness in his eyes and the sorrow stamped on his face.

"A million miles away from that aspiration, but…" he

caught her hand and traced the lines on it much as he'd done during their first dance together "...I'm hoping since you are so much more enlightened than I am, that you might also be forgiving of my many faults."

Her fingers tightened on his. She searched his face for clues. He looked raw. Nervous, and she wanted so much to make this better for him. Easier. But she'd been so very wrong before, or maybe she hadn't. Hope soared. She let it fly.

"You, on the other hand, are pretty damn close." He tightened his fingers around hers and then brought her hands to his mouth. Kissed one and then the other, his dark blue eyes steady on hers. "I want to be a better man, Miranda. For you. And for me. And for Petal. And my family. My patients. Hell even this damn town. And I don't have a clue how to do that without you."

"Witt?"

He closed his eyes as if in pain and then opened them again, and Miranda thought they seemed extra shiny. She stepped closer in to his body, wanting to comfort, wanting to be held.

"See, even my name. Witt. I like it so much better hearing it on your lips. Whitman sounds like a prick, and I don't want to be that guy. I want to be the man you see. The man you thought you'd fallen in love with."

"But you are. I am in love with you. I don't think it. I know it."

He shook his head. Sucked in a breath and breathed it out like it was his last. "I am the luckiest idiot alive. I thought about what I was going to say the whole drive over here. The whole ride back home."

"Seriously?" She still couldn't believe that crazy impulse. "You drove from LA? In winter? Today?"

"Don't even remember most of it. Just stopped for gas, and I think some water. Just these thoughts, these..." he put a fist on his chest "...these feelings churning around in me that I can't explain or define, but I want to. I walked out of a party welcoming me and several others to the surgical fellowship, sat most of the night on the beach in the dark reading letters from my...from my..." His voice broke and he leaned down his forehead, resting it on her head. "This is so damn hard," he whispered. "My father—a far, far better man than I could ever hope to be. And I knew I couldn't stay in LA, away from you and my family. I knew Marietta is my home. You are my home. I left before dawn. Not sure of the time. Declined the fellowship in an email, broke my lease, woke Wyatt up to ask for a job and headed north."

Miranda stared up at him. For once in her life she had no idea what to say. But clearly he didn't either.

"I love you, Witt—that hasn't changed. That won't ever change. But it just seems so...so impulsive."

"Yeah?" A smile kissed the corners of his lips, and he ran a shaking hand through his hair that nearly caused her to swoon. "I hope you'll have to get used to that," he said sounding a little embarrassed. "Can we go somewhere to talk?"

Miranda looked around her shop. She'd been closed for hours. The lobby was dimly lit with only Cathi at the front desk drinking some tea. The bar and restaurant had closed down a couple of hours ago.

"Do you have a room?" she asked, heart thudding hard. "Or you want to go to my place?" Her landlady would freak, but Miranda didn't care.

"I was thinking somewhere else." His voice sounded strained. "Do you have a coat?"

※

MIRANDA CLUNG TO Witt's waist and pressed her face—still numb even with her infinity scarf wrapped around her head—against his back. She was still completely bewildered that Witt's idea of a place to talk had involved a twenty-minute silent ride to his parents' ranch and then he'd driven past the dark house down a recently plowed ranch road to an equipment shed where he'd fired up a snowmobile. He'd stuffed a thick fleecy blanket under the seat compartment and tucked her into a Carhartt farm jacket that had a thick fleece inside.

"I thought you hated the cold," she said as he pushed the snowmobile outside and helped her to mount it.

"Relearning to deal."

Then he fired up the engine and took off. Miranda hadn't been on a snowmobile since high school. She'd forgotten the thrill of the speed and the beauty of a white world whizzing by. Miranda lost track of time. She was exhausted and everything had taken on a dreamlike quality, and she didn't want to miss a moment of it. Witt cleared pastureland and headed into some evergreens as the ranch started climbing into the rolling, lower foothills of the Absaroka Mountain Range.

He cut the engine. Sat there. Then he turned sideways on the seat.

"I've always prided myself on my education," he said, his voice hinting at bitterness. "But from the start I got so many things wrong." He took one of her gloved hands in his. "I came to live with my dad and Sarah when I was twelve," he said. "My mom died in a stupid accident. Totally random. I was stunned. And in shock and angry. I was a little shit. I didn't want to be here. I didn't want to get to know my dad. What I didn't know then was that I had been prejudiced against him by design. What I don't know now is why. But my actions as a teen—those are on me. Those are mine. I had plenty of opportunity to open my eyes, and I chose to be blind."

Witt made a sound. "My mom never had a good word to say about my dad. She didn't talk about him much. She'd roll her eyes, and if I did something she didn't like, she'd say she hoped I didn't turn out like my biological father. My grandparents called him 'the cowboy—that no good lazy cowboy who never amounted to anything.'"

Miranda couldn't stop the shocked squeak from emerging. She'd known Taryn Telford from his years as a rodeo star but also how much he helped out local youth organizations teaching kids to rope and ride saddleless broncs and bulls. He was the first to help out other ranchers, volunteer on projects in town. Help kids with their 4-H projects, and he'd been her advisor when she'd been in FFA in high school. No one had a bad word to say about him ever. And he ran a successful, though small ranch breeding and training bucking broncs for the rodeo and was now starting to breed bucking bulls with Tanner McTavish, whose ranch shared a boundary with his.

How had Witt's family gotten his father so wrong?

"My mom had met him while on a break between graduating college and entering grad school. In her words she wanted to cut loose, live a little. Have some fun. She'd been an only child of academics and she'd studied all her life. Maybe she wanted a little wild before hitting the books again. She met my dad at a rodeo, where he'd received the all-around cowboy buckle at the event. His third even though he'd yet to hit twenty years old. She said it was such an alien world and he'd been so different from any man she'd met, and she'd wanted new experiences so she'd just gone with it for a couple of months before returning to her real life. He didn't want anything to do with me or her or so I'd been led to believe."

Witt stood up and walked away a little restlessly. His voice was quiet in the stillness of the waning night and the snowy landscape. Miranda pulled out the blanket and joined him looking out at the snow-wrapped foothills glimmering white in the eerie light of the nearly full moon. She wrapped the blanket around Witt and herself. It was the most he'd talked about himself in one sitting without her constant prompting and if she died of hypothermia it would be worth it.

"Spending my last week in Marietta at the ranch was so wonderful and strange. It wasn't the way I remembered it at all. And my dad, Sarah, Boone, Riley. I'd always felt like an alien. On the outside. Different. They were this tight-knit family, and I wasn't part of them, but when I was at the ranch..." Witt broke off and then gulped in a deep breath "...I realized that I'd done that—separated myself, convinced I was different, that my aspirations were more worthy. Still not sure why they all didn't kick me in my pretentious ass years ago."

Miranda laid her gloved palm on his sternum and laid her head on his shoulder.

"I'd bought into my mom and grandparents' sense of superiority and lorded it over them. I was a selfish little shit."

"Witt, you'd lived with your mother and loved her. You were grieving her sudden loss. I'm sure Taryn and Sarah understood. I don't think they ever thought you were selfish."

"Because they're nicer than I ever was. They both talked to me before I left. I'd ended up helping Boone with chores and checking on the pregnant cows. Even watched one give birth. Before I left they said they'd always have space for me at every family dinner or celebration or to stay for as long as I wanted. I didn't think I'd take them up on it, and yet I couldn't quite let go of the idea."

"What changed your mind?"

"You." He finally looked at her. He gently smoothed her spiky tufts away from her face. "You're so loving and accepting and you make me see things—my life and my goals and people—differently. I always felt so apart from everyone. So driven toward this unachievable perfection, always pushing, moving the goal posts until I no longer knew what my goals were and why. You connect me."

Miranda felt her heart swell. It was all she ever wanted for him. For her.

"I want that for you. Happiness. Love. I feel like you didn't have that early on and then when you did, you didn't know how to accept it—but, Witt, you are so lovable. You deserve love."

"We both do." His face was as stark as his facts. "Only I spent my life running away from it, and you were running toward it. I want to stop. I want to be a better man," he repeated the words. "One who would truly deserve your love and know how to return it. I didn't know I was missing anything until I met you."

"You have me, Witt. You have me."

He closed his eyes. "To be given another chance…" He shook his head. "I learned more at the ranch even though I still drove away, thinking I had to keep going or else my whole life would have been wasted. All the years of studying. All the years of shutting myself down and away and my emotions off. My dad did want me," Witt said finally. He sucked in another deep breath. "He contacted my mom to see if she was okay because there'd been a couple issues with the condoms, and when he found out she was pregnant he wanted to marry her. She was, in his words, horrified at the idea of marriage. She was twenty-three and in a graduate program doing genetic research and he was a barely twenty-year-old rodeo cowboy."

"Oh, Witt." She felt awful for Taryn. To be dismissed like that. And awful for Witt. Taryn had missed out on so much of his son's life. "My mom was so big on responsibility. So hard-driving about making your best effort and besting it. Perfection was always the goal. Being independent, not needing anyone else was her mantra. She was a geneticist like her mother and she would always talk about the importance of genetics and how genes determined our lives and our abilities and our potential."

He laughed hollowly and ran a shaky gloved hand through his wind-mussed hair. "God, it must have killed her to have gotten knocked up by a cowboy. I used to think about that all the time when I got older. How much she must have resented me. I know my grandparents could never fully connect with me. It was like everyone was holding their breath waiting for my genetic destiny to manifest and for me to screw up in epic proportions."

Miranda made a strangled sound and she grabbed his shoulders. "I know she was your mother, Witt, and I know you lost her so young, but I really want to dig her up and yell at her. She of all people should have been aware that genetics can be a crap shoot. People may think they can play God, but ultimately they can't. Besides, what about genetic diversity?" she demanded.

"Miranda, I love you. God, I can't even begin to explain how much you mean to me. How much you take me out of my head and connect me to the world. I love the way you think. I love the way you are so kind and warm. But I love most how you make me feel. Alive. Loved. A part of…everything. I love you so much." He pulled her in to his body and held her so tightly that she could barely breathe, and she didn't care. He needed this, and he needed her.

Wow. It was an epiphany of sorts. Witt Telford had so much going for him—smart, handsome, driven, good career. But he'd never been truly, deeply loved. And he craved that as much as she did.

"I love you." His voice shook, and she could feel him trembling beneath his parka, or maybe that was her. "I love your sweetness, and I love your fierceness and I love how you hold on to the people you love so tightly. When I think of what I nearly tossed away…" He broke off. "Because of what? Pride? Arrogance? Stupidity? I am literally the luckiest bastard on the planet to be given a true second chance with you. And with my family. When I told my dad I was taking the fellowship offer in Santa Monica he didn't object or try to change my mind. No. Not the cowboy with more integrity than my mother or grandparents combined. Instead he gave me back the glass heart that you'd given to me, and I'd given to him at the hospital, and told me to hang on to it for luck and for love. He also gave me a book of letters he wrote to me during my entire childhood even after I arrived at the ranch in the back of a social worker's car. I didn't even have the balls to read them before driving out of town."

"But you did read them," Miranda pointed out. "And you came back. And the door to your father, to your whole family is wide open. You just have to walk through it."

"Always the optimist," he said, gently cupping the side of

her face with his hand. "And I need that. I want that. Walking through the door to make a relationship with my family isn't the only door that I want open. I came back for you. I know it's too soon, and we only…" He couldn't get the rest out because Miranda closed the small distance between them, pressing her chilly lips to his.

Warmth flooded through her. Witt whispered her name, his gloved palms cupped her cheeks and his lips kissed hers over and over—tiny, flirty kisses easing her lips apart so his tongue could play. She whimpered and felt like the world fell away leaving only this man for her to love and hold on to.

"Before we freeze to death," he said, "what do you think about the view?"

"Amazing," she breathed running her fingers through his hair now that she'd plucked off one glove so that she could once again feel his silky strands fall through her fingers. Seemed like she'd wanted to do this her entire life. "Absolutely amazing."

She stood on tiptoe and kissed him again, loving his immediate response, and the way he moaned low in his throat and pulled her in to his body more tightly.

"You're supposed to be looking behind you." He smiled, breaking the kiss after several passion-filled moments.

"Why?" Miranda chased his mouth with hers.

"I'm thinking of buying this land."

"What?" Miranda spun around and stared at the vast expanse of white speared through with evergreens and framed by the black of the sky pierced by stars.

"Witt, it's beautiful, but I don't understand." Wasn't he

the quintessential city guy or at least a townie?

"It's tiny by Montana standards, but it joins up with my family's ranch on the southern tip, and also with the Wilder spread on the western border. It's got great pastures in spring and plenty of water sources. Besides it's got a peekaboo view of Miracle Lake. I thought it would be a fresh start for both of us if you want it."

Before she could respond, Witt dropped to his knee and took her hands in his.

"I know this is crazy timing and neither of us has likely slept or eaten tonight, but I don't want to waste another moment trying to be someone I was never meant to be. I don't want to waste any more time being alone or focusing only on my career. I want us to build a home right here, on this ridge with this view. I want to come home to this and home to you. I want us to be a family. And if I really lay my cards on the table I'm hoping we can petition the court to revoke the parental rights to Petal so that we could adopt her so she would always have a home and Sarah and Taryn can finally have some time again to enjoy each other without kids and parental responsibilities."

"Really? Really and truly, Witt? For real?" Miranda gripped his arms. Tears rolled down her face and she didn't wipe them away. "Witt, that would be the most perfect life ever."

"I love you, Miranda. Even when I didn't know what love was or what it felt like or looked like, it walked in and knocked my lonely heart sideways and made itself at home. I want you... I hope with all of my once-frozen heart that you would do me the immense honor of…"

"Yes." Miranda flung herself into his arms. "A million times yes."

Epilogue

IT WASN'T JUST one pop of a champagne cork. It was ten or more. A cheer erupted and foaming champagne was quickly poured into glasses and held high in the air.

"Speech!" Wyatt called out.

"Speech, speech, speech." The words echoed around the small gathering in the red barn that had been tirelessly repaired by Colt and a small crew of Army veterans who were now learning new skills and trades in construction and working for a local company.

Witt pulled Miranda into his arms. "Are you ready?"

She smiled at her husband. Even after five months it still sounded so new and gorgeous.

"Aren't you going to make a speech?" she teased.

"Hell no. It's move-in day to our new home, not an award ceremony." He swung her into his arms.

"What are you doing?" Miranda looked into his deep, deep blue eyes. That never got old. She brushed her fingertips across his lips.

"Carrying you across the threshold because the house wasn't done before we got married and you put up with living in a barely renovated bunkhouse for five months practically on top of my family."

"Yeah, that was hard," Miranda teased and speared her fingers through his hair, loving the way the silk felt falling through her fingers. "Living so close to the best in-laws I could have imagined and being invited to dinner practically every night and sharing recipes and being accepted as a part of your family and having them help us with the application process and interviews to start the adoption process for Petal. And helping out around the ranch when you were working late."

"But we never got much alone time," Witt said ruefully. "Or a honeymoon, and now I'm going to remedy at least the first problem. The second will have to wait until I can get some vacation time and we can find someone you trust to run your store for at least a week."

"But we're having a party."

"It's a work party to move our things into our house."

"And maybe we should be working? Notice the pronouns—our house, our things. We are an us."

"Today, the theys have it. The most important room is done, and we've fed everyone and celebrated so they have no excuse. They can move in the furniture we've had in storage and our packed boxes while I carry you upstairs to the master bedroom and slam the door so we can be alone."

Miranda looked around at everyone gathered in the barn, the one building on the property that had been salvageable. His family was here, even his younger brother Rohan, who was on leave, as well as so many doctors and nurses and medical staff, employees from the Graff. Colt Wilder and his brothers had all had a hand helping to restore the barn and

Miranda had become good friends with Colt's sister-in-law, Sky, the artist who had donated a beautiful copper metal tree that had become a permanent fixture in Found Objects just waiting for the second annual month of giving and random acts of kindness to roll around, and it would next week. The fliers were done. She and Petal and Parker and a few other classmates had already made the glass heart-shaped beads during an after-school art class series she'd taught at Harry's House. Each heart-shaped bead was unique and beautiful and in Miranda's mind told a story about love and community.

"I think you're forgetting something," she said nipping his ear with her teeth.

"I have an excellent memory."

"We have at least forty guests."

"They'll be busy."

"And there's no point in going to the master bedroom. We haven't found a bed yet."

"About that."

Miranda's eyes widened. Witt, she had discovered, could keep secrets like nobody she'd ever met. He surprised her often. A smile lit up his face.

"Prepare to be wowed."

"I already am," she whispered tangling her fingers in his hair.

WITT MADE QUICK work of the distance between the barn

and the house. Miranda was tiny, but when he was off work he helped out at the ranch, and he'd also been working out with Colt in his personalized gym with bags and a rope climbing system that still kicked his butt. Funny that their old rivalry still held fast. Witt would never be as sculpted as Colt, nor did he really want to be, but Colt pushed him to get stronger and faster. He also learned more about communication from watching his former academic rival interact with his son and his wife Talon when she was home from school on weekends and breaks. Yeah, he still got caught up with his job, and he still planned to stay on top of every technical innovation, but his career was no longer his life. He had a new focus now—the woman in his arms and the family and friends outside who waited for him to show Miranda her surprise before they started moving in the furniture they'd slowly been buying and storing in the barn while their house was built.

"Close your eyes," he ordered softly as he entered their new home. Technically it wasn't finished, just the entry, great room and kitchen and then the master bedroom and another en-suite bedroom for Petal. But it was perfect for them now. The rest would come.

He nudged open the master with his hip.

"You can open them."

Miranda caught her breath and gripped his shoulders. "Witt," she breathed.

Anxious now he searched her face for clues.

"Too much? I should have waited for you to help with the design?"

She arched and he let her down. It had seemed like such a brilliant idea. Colt had been game and it had taken him a couple of months to build the wooden bed, and Sky had made the copper dragon sculptures that perched at the foot of the bed, each one with a brilliant swirling glass heart in reds and purples. Sky had also designed the leaf carvings that twisted up each foot of the bed.

"Too much?" he asked again as Miranda turned in a circle taking it all in. "Colt built the bed and dresser and he's going to make us a rocker for when… I know—don't jinx it." He drew in a shaky breath just thinking about how excited he would be if and when they were blessed with a pregnancy and baby of their own. "The wall was my idea. I painted it. I thought…"

She pressed her fingers against his lips.

"I love it," she said taking in the glossy red accent wall that the bed butted up against. The other walls were a soft dove gray. She wandered around the room, touched the bedpost, with the hand-carved leaves, then she traced the tree silhouette that spread out on the red wall behind the bed. It was made of cork, and he'd already pinned a message to it.

"Being sent back to Marietta, walking in and seeing you painting a wall a vivid red and building the world's ugliest tree for the most beautiful concept was the best thing that ever happened to me," he told her. "I wanted to re-create a little of that moment…the first glance of us so that we would never forget how lucky we are."

She came to him then, her ash-brown hair cut to frame her pixie face, her brown eyes shining with love and happiness. "I'll never forget." She stood on tiptoe and cupped the back of his head to draw his mouth close to hers. "We'll always remember, and we'll always do our best to share and to pass love on in all its messy but beautiful incarnations. And about that other project you wanted to get started on…" Miranda laughed and hopped up on the bed. "Should we give Colt's work a test drive?"

Witt didn't bother to answer. He preferred action to words.

The End

Holiday at the Graff Series

Book 1: *Halloween at the Graff* by Sincliar Jayne

Book 2: *Christmas at the Graff* by Kaylie Newell

Book 3: *New Years at the Graff* by Marin Thomas

Book 4: *Valentine's Day at the Graff* by Sinclair Jayne

Book 5: *Love at the Graff* by Jeannie Watt

Available now at your favorite online retailer!

About the Author

Sinclair Jayne has loved reading romance novels since she discovered Barbara Cartland historical romances when she was in sixth grade. By seventh grade, she was haunting the library shelves looking to fall in love over and over again with the heroes born from the imaginations of her favorite authors. After teaching writing classes and workshops to adults and teens for many years in Seattle and Portland, she returned to her first love of reading romances and became an editor for Tule Publishing last year.

Sinclair lives in Oregon's wine country where she and her family own a small vineyard of Pinot Noir and where she dreams of being able to write at a desk like Jane Austen instead of in parking lots waiting for her kids to finish one of their 12,000 extracurricular activities. ...

Thank you for reading

Valentine's Day at the Graff

If you enjoyed this book, you can find more from all our great authors at TulePublishing.com, or from your favorite online retailer.

Made in United States
Troutdale, OR
09/16/2024